"Who are you and what do you want?"

"If you'll give me a chance," Samantha said, her voice rising, "I'll be happy to explain."

He sat on the edge of the chair opposite her, leaning forward. He had the upper hand, and he knew it. "I'm waiting."

She took a deep breath. No more games. All she had to do now was give him the facts, and leave the rest to him. *Oh. And one more thing.*

She moistened her lips, wondering why she felt so nervous. He certainly didn't look as scary as his photograph. He was taller than she'd expected, and filled out more.

His eyes caught hers and she realized he knew she'd been checking him out.

"Confirming I'm the right man?"

His tone was not amused. Neither was the glint in his eye.

Dear Reader,

Any author will tell you that story ideas are generated from a variety of experiences, questions and revelations. Knowing identical twins in my workplace raised a few questions of my own. Such as what would it be like to look at another person and see your mirror image, and how difficult would it be to establish your own identity when people are constantly mistaking you for your identical twin?

These are some of the questions I asked myself after I decided to make the heroine of *A Father for Danny* an identical twin. The bond between twins—that almost mystical link of thought and emotion—has been the subject of innumerable scientific studies and texts. But the question that captured my interest most of all was what happens when that connection is stretched almost to the breaking point? When identical twins who shared everything as children and teenagers suddenly become distrustful of each other?

Tackling the novel from that vantage point, I then had to figure out how these sisters could regain that unique rapport. What better way to accomplish this than through a frightened boy and a lonely man— both in need of love and a family?

Families coming together is a common theme in many of my novels, and the various intricate and delicate relationships between family members can provide many plotlines. In the end, isn't the whole idea of family the ultimate goal of all romance?

Janice Carter

A FATHER FOR DANNY
Janice Carter

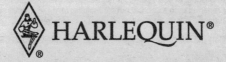

TORONTO • NEW YORK • LONDON
AMSTERDAM • PARIS • SYDNEY • HAMBURG
STOCKHOLM • ATHENS • TOKYO • MILAN • MADRID
PRAGUE • WARSAW • BUDAPEST • AUCKLAND

ISBN-13: 978-0-373-71515-2
ISBN-10:   0-373-71515-3

A FATHER FOR DANNY

www.eHarlequin.com

Printed in U.S.A.

ABOUT THE AUTHOR

Janice Carter is a Toronto-based author and teacher. Her hobbies—besides writing—include cooking and reading. She is married with two grown daughters and looks forward to retirement and "grandmothering" in the near future. This is her eleventh novel, and she hopes to write many more family sagas.

Books by Janice Carter

HARLEQUIN SUPERROMANCE

Don't miss any of our special offers. Write to us at the following address for information on our newest releases.

Harlequin Reader Service
U.S.: 3010 Walden Ave., P.O. Box 1325, Buffalo, NY 14269
Canadian: P.O. Box 609, Fort Erie, Ont. L2A 5X3

Dedicated with love to my mother,
Lois Gene Carter
1920–2007
And to the best father in the world,
William Henry Carter

CHAPTER ONE

"I FIND THINGS, NOT people," Samantha Sorrenti repeated. "Things like rare books or antique coins. Art objects. Once I even had to search for an original Winnie the Pooh Teddy Bear." She grinned, hoping to lighten the mood. His brown eyes didn't flicker. Sam sighed. "What you want is a private investigator. Did you check the Yellow Pages?"

"Your Web site says you find anything."

"Any*thing*. Not any*one*."

"It didn't say you just look for stuff like old books."

"I'm sorry, but I really can't help you. My advice is to check out an agency."

He stared at her for a long, painful moment. Then he pushed his chair back and got to his feet so abruptly that it toppled over. The clatter echoed in the small room. When he reached the doorway, he turned around.

"I can't afford a private detective. Your ad says you don't charge anything unless you find it."

It! she felt like shouting. "Why the urgency? I mean, you could probably find him through the Internet yourself."

His face darkened. "I don't have time for that."

"But it might take only a few weeks and it's free. How can you lose?"

He took a step toward the desk. "How could I *lose?*" His voice cracked.

He was going to cry!

"You just don't get it. I need to find him because…
because my mother is going to be dead in six weeks.
Maybe less." He wheeled around.

Sam swallowed. "Wait," she said.

He stopped, turning slowly back to her. His eyes and
nose were red.

"Maybe I can do something," she murmured.

He stared as if he hadn't heard right.

Sam pointed to the toppled-over chair. "Sit," she said
quietly, trying not to sound as exasperated as she felt. After
all, he was only twelve years old.

He didn't rush back to the chair, but shuffled instead,
in that awkward walk of boys wearing ridiculously baggy
pants. He slowly righted the chair and sat on it, slouching.

Sam knew this nonchalance was an attempt at face-
saving, but it still rankled. He could at least *pretend* to be
appreciative. "Look, I'm expecting an important call, so I
can't be long, but…uh…I know someone who may be
able to help." Sam stopped. Did she really want to take that
step? She looked at the light in his eyes and her heart sank.
She had to take it now. "Someone in the FBI."

"The FBI?" It came out as a croak.

"Do you have a problem with that?"

"No, but this is going to be just between us, right?"

"Are you talking about confidentiality?"

"Yeah. That's what I mean."

"I think you've got me confused with a lawyer. As I
said, I'm not even a private investigator. I look for—"

"Yeah, you told me. Things. Not people."

Sam felt her blood pressure rise. "Do you want me to
get you some help or not?"

She saw him flinch, but didn't regret her harsh tone. He
might be only twelve, but he'd managed to barge into her
office all on his own.

"Yes, I do. It's just that you mentioning the FBI…it sounds serious."

More serious than you can imagine. "Okay," she said, reaching for her notepad. "Why don't you tell me your story and I'll make some notes? Then I'll get back to you."

"When?"

"I don't know. As soon as I can."

He chewed on his lower lip for a few seconds, then began. When he finished, less than ten minutes later, Sam didn't trust herself to look his way. She stared at her notes, the words blurred by tears. She sniffed, blinked twice and finally raised her head.

His eyes met hers, and Sam thought she caught a glimmer of satisfaction in them. *He knows I'm hooked.*

She cleared her throat. "Okay, so let me review this. Your mother has had no contact with your father since you were born."

"Since *before* I was born. She says he never knew about me."

"But she never tried to contact him, to tell him about you?"

He shrugged. "I dunno. She always told me he never knew. I think he moved to another city, anyway."

"Maybe your mother can fill in some of these gaps."

"Why do you have to see my mother? Can't this be just between us?"

"Does your mother know you came to see me?"

He looked away.

"She doesn't, does she?"

"She has enough problems."

Sam had no reply to that. He was right of course. "The thing is, you're a minor. I can't legally help you without your mother's consent."

His eyes flicked coolly back to hers. "But you're not a real private detective, anyway."

And you're no typical twelve-year-old. "I can't do anything for you without your mother's knowledge. Anyway, you told me she was the one who suggested finding your father."

"Kinda."

"What do you mean, *kinda?*" Sam's voice rose.

His gaze dropped to his hands, interlocked in his lap. "When she first found out about the cancer, she said it was too bad my father didn't know me."

Sam felt as if she'd just plunged her other foot into quicksand. "Well, I'd have to talk to her if you want me to help," she eventually said.

"Okay, okay." His eyes met hers again. "But don't upset her. Please? She already feels bad because she knows I'll have to go into foster care after…well, after."

He didn't need to clarify. "I won't upset her, Danny, I promise. But she needs to know. Can you tell me anything at all about your father?"

"His name is Danny, too. I think my mom forgot his last name."

Or never knew it. Sam was beginning to wonder if Danny was the product of a one-night stand. Which meant the task she'd taken on would be impossible. "Anything else?"

His face brightened. "He liked motorcycles. My mom said he had a real cool tattoo on his right arm and long hair, like a rock star."

"Oh," was all Sam could think to say. The picture forming in her mind wasn't exactly a poster for fatherhood. "So Benson is your mother's name?"

"Yeah. Emily Benson." He craned his neck, looking at something behind her.

The clock, Sam realized. "You have to go soon?"

"Yeah. I told Minnie I'd be back about five and I gotta take a couple of buses."

"Who's Minnie?"

"Our next-door neighbor. I've been staying with her for the last two weeks."

"Your mother—"

"She's in the hospital."

"Oh. Is she having surgery or something?"

He shook his head. "Nope. All that's finished. Now she's just waiting. In… I can't remember the name for it. A special room in the hospital."

"Palliative care?"

"Yeah. That's it. Mom calls it the Waiting Room. She jokes about it. You know, how hospitals are always making you wait for something. She says she even has to wait to die." His voice cracked again and he turned his head toward the bookshelves at his right.

Silence shrink-wrapped the room. Sam badly wanted a glass of water. No. Make that a double of any alcoholic drink available. Unfortunately none was.

Finally he said, "Minnie says I can stay with her for now but…well, she's old, you know." He looked back at Sam. His eyes were red-rimmed. "She's living on a small pension and can't take care of me for too long."

Sam cleared her throat. "I'll need her telephone number."

Danny complied, then said, "She's in the apartment across the hall from ours, so I can go back and forth, take care of Mom's plants and stuff." He got to his feet. "So…uh, when should I call you?"

Sam knew she was sinking fast and there was no way out. Maybe a couple of phone calls would convince him she couldn't do much more. "Like I said, I have to, uh, talk to someone who may be able to help and then I'll get back to you."

"Will that take long?"

She felt her face heat. He was persistent. Not one to be put off by lame excuses. "I'll do my best, Danny."

His eyes held hers for a long moment, then he turned abruptly and walked out the door. Sam dropped her forehead into her hands. *What have you done now, Sorrenti?*

"ARE YOU SERIOUS? What in heaven's name possessed you, Samantha?"

There had been a time in Sam's teen years when she'd answer a question like that with a flippant quip. But she and her mother had finally managed to establish what they euphemistically called a "working relationship" so Sam wasn't even tempted to play the smart-ass, as her mother used to say. She regretted, however, bringing up the afternoon visit from Danny Benson during her weekly tea and chat with her mother.

"Mom, he's twelve years old and his mother is dying. He has no other relatives and…well…he almost started to cry right there in my office. What could I do?"

Nina Sorrenti set the teapot back onto the tray and handed Sam her cup and saucer. "You could have pointed him toward the many agencies available to help children in his situation."

"I know, I know," Sam muttered. "I'm a sucker for a sob story."

"I didn't say that, darling."

"But I am, I admit it. He just looked at me with his big brown eyes and I remembered—" She broke off.

"How you felt when you were his age? When your father walked out on us?"

Sam took a long sip of tea before replying. "Mother, I'm

not in one of your therapy sessions. Maybe we should just drop the subject and talk about what I really came here for—your upcoming sixtieth. "

Nina waved an index finger at Sam. "Darling, you're not going to persuade me to have a big party. I refuse to acknowledge this particular birthday."

Sam stared at her mother ensconced in the easychair across from her, one sleek leg gracefully draped over the other. She was wearing a knee-length straight skirt and tailored shirt, which highlighted her slender but shapely figure. In spite of the streaks of gray in her short hair, Nina had the face and skin of a much younger woman.

Nina went on, smiling, "Besides, you're not getting out of this so easily. I'm just pointing out something that must be obvious to you."

Sam knew the subject wasn't going to be dropped. She sighed. "What I think is that you're purposely overlooking the blatant differences between Danny's situation and mine. You're doing the psychologist thing with me and I don't like it."

"And you're still evading my question."

"Not evading so much as putting it into perspective. Of course I can relate to his problem, because I understand what it is not to have a father-figure in my life. But he never knew his father, whereas Skye and I were—"

"Abandoned."

Sam shrugged. "If you want to use that word, go ahead." She put her cup and saucer back on the table and sneaked a peak at her watch.

"*Now* who's playing therapist?"

"For heaven's sake, Mother!"

Nina laughed. "Okay, I'll give it a rest. But—"

Sam held up a palm. "Say no more. Session ended. So, tell me what's new in your life?"

Nina leaned forward to set her cup and saucer down, then smoothed her skirt as she sat back in the chair. She seemed to be taking her time to answer, Sam thought.

"Mmm, not too much, dear. I've been asked to speak at a conference next month."

"Great. Where's the conference? Anyplace exciting?"

Nina smiled. "Just here in good old Seattle. That's why I accepted. I'm not up to traveling all over the country anymore for these things. Same old, same old, as the expression goes."

"You used to love to travel."

"I know, but I don't feel the urge now. I'm all for curling up in front of a fire with a good book."

Sam laughed. "Yeah, right, Mom. Funny how I can't picture you doing that." She studied her mother for a moment, trying to see her objectively. An attractive woman, an accomplished clinical psychologist and still working at it daily.

"You're not really that upset about turning sixty, are you?"

"No, dear, not really. Though I admit it's given me much more pause than turning fifty did. But I'm hoping to make some time for myself now. I've decided to whittle down the size of my practice—I'm not taking any new patients."

Sam mulled that over. Nina had always been driven by her love for her career and her love for her children. She couldn't imagine her slowing down. But then, she also couldn't imagine her getting any older. For a long moment Sam couldn't speak.

"Well, Mom, don't think that this means we won't be celebrating your birthday," she tried again.

Nina raised an eyebrow. "I wonder where you get that stubbornness from?"

"It's genetic, I believe." Sam stood up. "What do I owe you for the consultation?"

"How about a kiss?"

Their eyes locked and they both smiled. Sam leaned down to kiss her mother.

"Will you come for dinner next Monday, rather than tea, and tell me more about Danny?"

"I'd love to come for dinner. I'm sure by then Danny will have realized I can't help him."

"Maybe your sister can be of assistance."

"How?" she asked, though Skye had automatically came to mind when she'd been talking to Danny.

"Isn't that her field? Doesn't the FBI handle missing-persons cases?"

"This man isn't really missing. I'm assuming whatever relationship he'd had with Danny's mother simply ended and he left town, not knowing he'd fathered a child."

"Skye might be able to steer you in the right direction or give you some advice."

Sam made a face.

"What's *that* for?" her mother asked.

"Nothing. I thought I might call Skye, but I'm sure she's far too busy for something like this. Besides, I have to talk to Danny's mother first. She may have a problem with him searching for his father."

"Well, of course you have to do that." Nina paused. "When was the last time you spoke to your sister?"

"Christmas." Sam leaned against one of the French doors separating the living room from the hallway and knew what was coming.

"Samantha, that was five months ago. What's happened between you two, anyway?"

"Nothing, Mother. You're reading too much into it. She lives in another part of the country."

"But you're sisters. Twins. You're supposed to be close."

"Is that what the psychology books say?"

"Don't be sarcastic, Samantha. It's not becoming and I don't deserve it."

"Sorry. But being twins doesn't mean we have to be joined at the hip."

"Don't exaggerate. You know what I mean."

"Yes, I do. It's just that whenever Skye and I are together the whole competition thing kicks in, and I'm tired of it."

"It's normal for siblings to be competitive. Especially twins, when they want to establish their own identities."

"I'm talking *perverse* competition, Mom. Obsessive. Whatever you want to call it. And Skye is always the one to initiate it."

"I've been hearing refrains like that since you both were twelve. And you're still saying it at thirty-three."

"You're right, Mother. There's no point in belaboring the point. I have to go now, anyway."

"Anywhere special?"

"Just meeting Dawn for a drink." She turned to leave, but was held back by her mother's next question.

"Any word from Todd these days?"

"Nope," she said, fighting to keep her voice level. "I told you, it's over. Finito. See you next week," she said, waved goodbye and made a quick exit before her mother could ask another question.

THE PHONE RANG just as Sam was removing the bubble-pack taped around a rare, framed Japanese print. She glanced sharply at the console but didn't recognize the number. Her client, Jean Mawhinney, pointed at the phone. "Go ahead," she said. "I can wait another five minutes."

Samantha gently set the package down on her desk and

picked up the phone. It took her a moment to recognize the high-pitched voice. Danny.

"My mother wants to meet you," he said. "Can you come to Our Lady of Mercy Hospital at ten-thirty?"

"I have a client right now, Danny. And it's already ten. Can I call you back?"

"But ten-thirty is good for Mom because she'll be finished with her bath and stuff. If you wait any longer, it'll be time for her morning nap and—"

"Aren't you supposed to be in school right now?"

There was a pause, followed by a muffled response Sam couldn't hear. She noticed Mrs. Mawhinney eyeing the package she'd been patiently awaiting for three months.

"Look, Danny, this isn't a good time. How about after lunch?"

When he finally answered, he sounded as exasperated as she did. "I wasn't going to be here after lunch."

"Do you need to be there when I talk to your mother?"

"I guess not," he muttered.

"So what time does your mother have lunch?"

"Noon."

"Okay, I can be there about one."

"She might be napping again."

Sam exhaled loudly and noticed Mrs. Mawhinney's startled expression. She smiled an apology at the petite, middle-aged woman and said to Danny, "I'll be there at twelve-thirty, Danny." Then she hung up. "Sorry for the interruption, Jean. Shall we see what we've got here?"

"Oh, yes, Samantha," Jean said as she rubbed her dainty hands together in anticipation.

hE WAS STANDING next to the information desk in the hospital lobby and wearing what Sam already identified as his trademark scowl. She felt a surge of annoyance. Wasn't *she* the one being inconvenienced by this last-minute interruption in her workday?

"She's really tired so I don't know how much time we'll have before she'll need her nap," he said as Sam drew near. "You took a long time getting here. Now I'm gonna have to miss school this afternoon, too."

"Look, Danny," she said as they moved to the bank of elevators. "Let's clarify a few things. Number one, I am not working for you in any capacity. I am here as a *favor*, got that? Second, nobody told you to skip school. I could have met your mother on my own. And last of all, you are the child and I am the adult. I don't know what your mother taught you in the way of manners, but you have no right to speak to me in that tone." Then she stopped, realizing half a dozen people around them were cued to her every word. Fortunately the elevator door opened at that very moment, and the group trooped aboard.

It was an uncomfortable ride up to the tenth floor. Samantha kept her eyes on the floor-indicator panel, wishing that she'd set Danny straight about helping him when he'd come to her office two days ago. The problem was, her resolve to say no disappeared the instant his dark brown eyes met hers.

As soon as they stepped out of the elevator and the people behind them had dispersed, Sam said in a low voice, "Listen, I'm sorry if I sounded like—"

"It's okay," he said. "You were right. Kinda." Those same dark eyes bore into hers. He wheeled around and headed into a room diagonally across from the elevators.

Sam had the unsettling feeling that the child-adult roles had been reversed, but she ceased caring about it the instant she entered Emily Benson's room.

Danny's mother lay propped against two pillows that

dwarfed her. Her hair—stringy and limp—might have been blond once upon a time but now was more the color of a mud puddle on a rainy day. Her head turned slowly toward the door as they walked in. The transparent oxygen line inserted in her nostrils moved at the same time. Sam's gaze shifted to the large red tank on the far side of the bed.

The dark-circled eyes, sunk deep in her small face, brightened when she saw Danny. Sam wondered how a simple glance could convey so much emotion. But what she knew, right then and there, was that she would not be leaving that room without making some attempt to help.

The woman ran her tongue along her lower lip, cleared her throat twice and then spoke in a voice so faint Sam had to move to the chair next to the bed.

"I'm pleased to meet you. Danny told me you offered to help him find his father."

Sam nodded.

"Are you a private detective?" Emily asked.

Sam hesitated before replying, "Not exactly, but I am experienced at finding things." She quickly added, "To tell you the truth, I'm not certain I can be any help at all."

A frown settled over the pale face. "All this has taken me by surprise. Danny just told me the whole story yesterday. How he happened to find you on the Internet and your offer to help." She paused to catch her breath.

Not quite the whole story, Sam was thinking. She looked at Danny sitting in the chair on the other side of the bed, but he was engrossed in a magazine. Or at least pretending to be.

"I don't expect you to have much luck with this," Emily added.

Danny's head shot up.

"It's been so many years. I haven't heard from Daniel since just before I…" She stopped and glanced at Danny.

"Hon, could you go get me a can of ginger ale from the nurses' station? No ice and one of those bendy straws."

He looked as if he was about to say something but changed his mind. As he left he shot Sam a glance, as if it was somehow her fault that his mother wanted to speak privately.

"I'll try to be quick," his mother said as soon as he left the room. "Just that it's embarrassing…you know…in front of my son. I met Daniel when I was waitressing at a diner up in Greenwood, not far from where Danny and I live now. You ever been to Woodland Park zoo there?"

Sam shook her head. The north end of Seattle was foreign territory to her.

"It's nice. I used to take Danny there when he was little." She broke off for a moment, her small front teeth biting down on her lower lip. Then she took a deep breath and went on, "The first time Daniel came in for coffee I was kinda put off by him, looking like a biker 'n all. But we got to talking after a while and I found out he was real nice. Different from what I expected. He talked like he was educated. You know? Anyway, one night he was still there when we closed up and he asked me to go for a drink at a bar down the street." She stopped and turned her gaze upward. "One thing led to another—if you know what I mean. I didn't even know I was pregnant until after he left."

"He *left?*"

Emily shifted her head on the pillow. Her eyes looked sad. "He just vanished. Didn't come in one day and I thought maybe he was sick or something. I waited a few more days before calling the phone number he'd given me. He was living in a rooming house. The man who answered said Daniel had up and gone. Didn't pay his last week's rent and he swore at *me,* thinking I was his girlfriend or something." She smiled wistfully.

"What was his last name?"

"Daniel's? Oh, he said it was Winston."

"Do you think that was a fake name?"

"After a few days of calling every Winston in the phone book, I figured it musta been. I wish I could help you some more but…"

"Do you have a photograph of him?"

"No, sorry." She broke into a spasm of coughing and tried to reach for the glass of water on the table next to her. Sam jumped up and held the glass for her. The very act of sipping seemed to exhaust her and she fell back against the pillows, panting as if she'd just finished a race.

"I guess Danny told you I don't have much time," she finally whispered. "He's been staying with Minnie Schwartz, our neighbor. But that's only till…well…till none of us has to wait anymore."

Sam saw tears well up in her eyes and looked away, afraid she'd start to cry herself.

"This is his idea—looking for his father," she went on. "I don't think he'll find him. But I think he should try. No harm in that, is there? For him to have a little hope for a bit longer?"

Sam blinked rapidly and shook her head. "No. No harm at all." She waited a few seconds and then asked, "Is there anything else that you know about him?"

Emily thought for a minute. "He told me his family came from Seattle. He was an only child, like me. That was one of the things we had in common." She cast Sam a rueful glance. "There wasn't much else, 'cept we had a couple laughs together whenever he came into the diner. Like I said, we only went out that one time." She paused. "He was very attractive. There was something special about him. I could see that right away." She stopped then, turning her head away.

"How about his age?"

"He was five years younger'n me. He used to tease me about being an older woman. At first, that's why I thought he left. Especially after that night. Maybe he was afraid, you know, of getting trapped into something." She gave a wobbly smile. "But looking back now, I think there was something goin' on in his life."

"Like what?"

Emily shook her head. "I dunno. Just that he didn't like talkin' about his past or his family, that kinda stuff."

"So how old would he be now, then?"

"He was twenty-four then and Danny just turned twelve so…"

"Thirty-six or -seven?"

"Yeah, I guess. I sometimes wonder what might have happened if…"

Just then he appeared in the doorway and his mother let her sentence trail off. He was holding a can of soda and he hesitated, staring first at his mother, then at Sam.

It seemed like a good time to leave. "I have to go now," Sam said, adding quickly at the alarm in Danny's face, "but I'll see what I can do to help. I have some contacts and people I can call." She saw relief wash over Danny's face. "But I can't promise anything. There's not a lot of information to go on."

"That's wonderful, isn't it, Danny?" Emily smiled at him.

Danny nodded. His eyes were red and Sam guessed he didn't trust himself to speak. Samantha watched the silent interchange between mother and son. She stood up. "I'll call you here at the hospital as soon as I find out anything."

As she walked to the door, her single thought was how much she feared breaking that slender thread of hope she knew she'd just cast out to them.

CHAPTER TWO

SAM WONDERED how much longer she could sit and stare at the telephone. She'd put off making the call since returning from the hospital yesterday afternoon. And although she'd intended to catch up on some work, she'd been unable to do anything but sit, stare and think.

As much as Danny's attitude had annoyed her, she doubted she could have been as gutsy at twelve as he was, facing his mother's death on his own and being placed in a foster home. Making a few phone calls, as she'd told him, might be all she could do for him. Yet here she was hours later, unable to make one particular call.

Unnecessary office tasks had filled some of the hours. She'd calculated the time in Washington D.C., convincing herself that Skye would be at lunch. Assuming that she was even *in* D.C. and not out in the field "nabbing bad guys," as her twin used to say—back when they were still speaking to each other. When Sam was still engaged to Todd, blissfully unaware of what lay ahead.

Then she thought of Danny's pale, brave face and his mother's eyes. She picked up the receiver and tapped in Skye's work number, rather than her cell phone. Keep this whole thing business, she told herself.

The phone rang long enough for Sam to think the voice mail might pick up and she'd have a reprieve of sorts. Just as she was about to disconnect, Skye answered.

"Agent Sorrenti. How may I help you?"

Sam cleared her throat. "Uh, hi. It's Samantha."

There was a moment of dead silence. *"Sam?"*

"You know another Samantha?"

"Well, this is a surprise. To say the least."

Sam hesitated, then plunged in. "I'm calling for a favor," she said.

"Oh?"

The uplift at the end of the word told Sam her sister was not only doubly surprised but also apprehensive. "I met this boy—he's twelve—and his mother is dying of cancer. There's just the two of them, no other family, and he—Danny's his name—is going to have to go into foster care." She paused to catch her breath.

"Uh-huh?"

Sam quickly went on before Skye could ask what any of this had to do with her. "He wants to find his biological father and he asked me to help him."

"Oh, *yeah?*"

"You don't have to say it like that!" Sam blurted, in spite of her intention to avoid any digression.

"Like what, Sam? I'm feeling a bit mystified."

"I was wondering if you could give me any tips on finding someone." Sam pictured her sister's grin. "I told Danny that I probably wouldn't be able to do much for him, so I'm not expecting miracles. Just maybe a lead on some places I could call."

"I thought your business was finding *things.*"

Sam closed her eyes, revisiting her first conversation with Danny. "He found me through my Web site and after I met his mother, I couldn't turn him down. I said I'd see what I could do."

"So what do you want *me* to do?"

Sam stifled her frustration. "As I said, maybe you could

tell me who to call. Any agencies or places that might have records—besides the usual ones, of course."

"What's this guy's name? The father."

"Daniel Winston. But Emily—the mother—doesn't think it's his real name."

"What else have you got on the guy?"

"When Emily knew him, he rode a motorcycle, had long hair and a tattoo."

"Sounds like the real fatherly type."

Although her own immediate reaction had been the same, Sam resisted commenting, wanting to get to the point. "Emily thinks his family comes from the Seattle area."

"So if you're in Seattle and he's from there…"

"Look, Skye, if you can't help, just say so. I've already checked the phone directory and as I said, the name could be false."

"Frankly, Sam, I don't know how much I can do."

"I already explained to them it might be impossible to locate him."

"Don't suppose you got a DOB?"

"A what?"

"Date of birth."

"No, but he was twenty-four at the time and that was twelve or thirteen years ago."

"Does the guy have a rap sheet? A record?"

"I've no idea. Emily never mentioned it."

"It'd make the job a bit easier anyway. So look, why don't you see if this Emily thinks of something else and we'll talk again in a couple of days?"

"Sure. Great. Thanks, Skye." The silence that fell between them was long and uncomfortable. *How sad that I can't think of anything else to say to my twin sister.*

"So how's Mom doing?" Skye eventually asked.

"Fine. Same as always. Her sixtieth is coming up next month. Remember? She'd love to hear from you."

"I've been busy," Skye snapped. "Just got back in town a few days ago after six weeks undercover."

Sam pursed her lips. As always, the implied reprimand struck home. Finding rare art objects paled next to the dangers of her twin's job. The weight of the many months of silence between them ground the conversation to a halt. There was nothing to do but get off the phone.

"Well, I appreciate whatever you can do, Skye," Sam said.

"I'll touch base with you soon."

"Thanks, Skye," Sam said as the call was abruptly disconnected from the other end. Sam sat for a long time staring at the phone. Willing her sister to call right back? Maybe with a long-overdue apology? It wasn't going to happen. Sam powered up her computer and got back to work.

But an hour later, after she'd found and purchased online a Civil War sword for a client, she closed her laptop. She'd take her sister's advice and go back to the hospital to see Emily Benson. If she was lucky, Danny wouldn't be there and she could have a private conversation with his mother.

THE NURSE at the palliative-care station frowned.

"Ms. Benson's not having a good day," she said. "But I suppose, if you're not long…"

"I won't be. Is her son here?"

"He came in early this morning, but his mother sent him to school." The frown turned disapproving. "He shouldn't miss so much."

"His mother is dying. I imagine getting down to schoolwork is pretty difficult."

The nurse flushed. "Of course. But…you know…with

no other relatives on the scene, Children's Services could step in even before his mother passes away."

Especially if people like you keep talking about the situation. But Sam knew better than to alienate someone who was looking after Emily Benson. "Yes, he'll need to lead as normal a life as possible…." she said vaguely.

The nurse nodded. "And as I said, Emily's not having a good day today, so if she looks tired…"

"I'll leave. Definitely. Thanks." Sam walked down the hall and paused outside Emily's room. There was a spasm of coughing from within that sent chills up Sam's spine. When they subsided, she tapped lightly on the partially opened door and stepped inside.

Emily was stretching to reach a tissue from the box at her bedside. "Here, let me," Sam said, and leaped toward the box. She snatched up a handful and thrust them at Emily. "How about some water? Can I help you with that?"

Emily sagged back against the pillows and dabbed at her mouth. After a few seconds, she said, breathlessly, "No. It might trigger another spasm. I'm okay for now. Thanks." She closed her eyes, as if the mere act of speaking was too much.

Sam guessed it probably was. She waited until the other woman was ready.

Finally Emily opened her eyes and managed a weak smile. "Sorry about that. Not a good day."

"I should have let you know I was coming."

"It wouldn't have made any difference. I suppose it's too soon for any news?"

Sam hated to dash the hope in those sunken eyes. "I need to find out a few more things."

"It was hard to talk yesterday, with Danny here. Like I told you, I don't expect much. This is all just for Danny." She spoke in halting fragments, taking in gulps of air in between.

Sam nodded. When she felt she could safely speak, she asked, "Do you know if Danny's father had a police record?"

"He was secretive about his background, but he didn't seem like a criminal...or a biker, despite the way he looked. It made me curious about him. You know, why he acted the biker type. Made me wonder if he was running away from something...or someone."

Sam edged forward in her chair. Emily's voice was so very weak. "What do you mean?"

"I remember when I told him I had no family at all, he said that might be a good thing. I figured he'd had a falling-out with his. I mean, if he was in Seattle and they were, too, why wasn't he seeing them?"

Sam knew the question was rhetorical. She guessed Emily had asked herself it many times, especially after she knew she was pregnant.

"Did you try to find him when you found out you were pregnant?"

"Kind of. Thing is, I knew that what happened between us was just going to be one night." She turned her head to the window at her right.

Sam followed her gaze. The late-afternoon spring sun was rich and golden, ripe with the promise of summer. Was Emily wondering how many more days like it she'd see?

"When he came into Baywicks—that's the diner—the day after that night," Emily went on, "I could tell we weren't meant to be. He apologized." Her smile was more like a grimace. "So when I discovered I was pregnant, I didn't really make a lot of effort to find him. By then he'd stopped coming to the diner, and when I finally went to his place—he'd told me where he was living—I learned he'd moved out. No forwarding address. Maybe whatever he was running from caught up to him." She closed her eyes.

There was one more question Sam had to ask, though she hated to. When Emily reopened her eyes, she said, "What happens if I do find Daniel and he doesn't want to meet his son?"

"Yeah. I've thought about that a lot. Do me a favor, Sam?" Her eyes were imploring. "Don't tell either of us. Just say you couldn't find him. It would be better than knowing he wanted nothing to do with Danny or me."

"I don't know if I could do that," Sam murmured, appalled at the idea of lying to a dying woman and her soon-to-be-orphaned son.

Emily struggled to sit up. "You *have* to," she gasped. "It's bad enough Danny will be raised by foster parents. I don't want him knowing his daddy didn't want him. This way, he can always have his 'what-if' to hold on to." She fell back, exhausted. "Besides, I couldn't tell Danny the truth about his father and me—our one-night stand. I let him think we'd been dating…."

Sam studied the pattern of shadows cast on the wall by the sun filtering through the open slats of the Venetian blinds. There was no way out. She'd taken on an impossible quest and knew she couldn't live with herself if she failed. When she met Emily's gaze again, she said, "I'll do what I can for Danny. I won't hurt him."

Emily's eyes were filled with tears and Sam looked away. After a moment, she said, "My sister works for the FBI and she said she'd try to find Daniel in their database. If he has a record, it'll be easier. That's why I asked."

"Thanks, Sam, for anything you can do," Emily said quietly. "I appreciate it." Then she frowned. "Can you tell me what you charge?"

"Please, don't worry about the fee."

"I have some money set aside. I can pay."

"Let's not worry about that for now."

"But it's your business and you deserve payment. Please don't think we're poor."

Sam flushed. She'd been thinking exactly that. She saw the pride in Emily's eyes and was ashamed. "It's just that I have no idea what to charge," she said lightly, "since this kind of search is new to me. Let's see how it goes first."

Emily nodded. "Fair enough." She closed her eyes again.

Sam watched the bedcover rise and fall gently for a few moments.

Slowly Emily's face settled into repose and Sam knew she was dozing. Then she rose quietly from her chair and tiptoed out of the room.

BALANCING HER briefcase and lunch bag on one hip, Sam opened the mailbox in the small foyer of the building where she worked. It was a triplex that had been renovated five years ago into offices, and the owner was Nina Sorrenti. Her mother had bought it several years ago with money inherited from her parents.

Sam had been a regular paying tenant for the past two years, but her first year setting up Finders Keepers had been rent-free. Although she'd appreciated her mother's generosity, she was grateful to be earning enough money now to pay the same rent as the other tenants. Besides, her free year had come with strings. Lots of advice from her mother and a few digs from Skye about being on the family payroll. As if Skye had never taken a parental handout!

Sam grabbed an elasticized bundle of catalogs from her mailbox and headed up the stairs. When she reached the top landing and turned right toward her office, she stopped.

"What are you doing here? Isn't this a school day?"

Danny got up from where he'd been sitting cross-legged in front of her office door. He ignored her question. "Your sign says the office opens at eight-thirty. It's almost nine."

He had a knack for evasion that was formidable in a child his age. Sam brushed past him to unlock the door and had barely deposited her armful onto her desk when he plopped into a chair.

As she turned around, he said, "You went to see my mother yesterday."

His tone made her pause. She took her time replying, closing her office door and slinging her jacket over the coatrack. He followed her every movement, and when she finally sat down across from him on the other side of her desk, he asked, "What did you talk to her about?"

Time to set some boundaries. "I had some questions to ask your mother about your father. If you want to know what we discussed, you'll have to ask her."

"This whole thing was my idea and I was the one who found you."

"Yes, but you're a minor and can't employ someone to look for another person."

"Even if that someone just looks for *things?*" He jumped to his feet.

"I'm not going to quibble about this. I repeat—ask your mother."

"I already did and she acted like you two didn't talk about anything. It's not *fair.*" He sat back down, arms folded across his chest.

In spite of that last petulant word, Sam could tell from the fire in his eyes that he wouldn't leave until he had some kind of satisfactory answer. "Basically I had to find out if your father had a criminal record, because it would make the search a lot easier."

"So what did my mom say?"

"She didn't know, but she doubted it."

He thought for a moment. "Is someone helping you?"

"Yes."

"So my mom is okay with what you're doing?"

Obviously his concern had been about informing Emily. "She's okay with it but you really need to talk to her. About everything. You two need to make plans about—"

"See, that's what really bugs me. The way adults are always telling us kids what we should do or shouldn't do, like we couldn't figure out stuff ourselves. My mom…she didn't even tell me…" He stopped, swiping at his eyes with the back of a hand.

Sam looked down at her desktop. All she could give him right now was a chance to compose himself, though she wished she could offer more.

Huskily he went on. "I never knew until things got really bad. She didn't want me to worry. And I know she's letting me do this just to get my mind off things, to make me think there's a way out of going to a foster home."

Sam looked at him in surprise. He obviously *could* figure out stuff for himself. Smart kid.

As if reading her mind, he said, "I may only be twelve but I'm no kid. Not really. So I don't really need an adult, some social worker, telling me what to do. So far no other adult—except maybe for Minnie—has really done anything for my mom and me."

Sam took in the angry face across from her. "Fair enough, Danny. All I can promise is that I'll do my very best to help you find your father."

He nodded, got to his feet and held out his right hand, which she clasped in hers. "Deal," he said, and left the office without another word.

Sam brought her hands up to her face and massaged her forehead, the faint stirring of a migraine beneath her fingertips. The day's beginning didn't bode well for the tasks she'd planned for the morning. She decided to finish some paperwork first. Perhaps she'd feel up to a cheerful conversation with her contact at Christie's in New York later in the day. Right now, she had to keep her mind on ordinary things to keep from crying over the plight of a kid who was anything but ordinary.

The tactic was a good one in theory, but emotion kept its own rules. When the phone rang an hour after Danny walked out, Sam grabbed for it gratefully. "Finders Keepers."

There was a slight muffled sound on the other end, and for a second, Sam was afraid she'd connected with a telemarketer. "Who is this?" she asked.

At last a voice replied, "It's *me,* your sister."

"I couldn't hear you."

"'Cause my mouth was full of muffin. I wasn't expecting you to pick up the phone so quickly."

"Muffin? Isn't it past your lunchtime out there?"

"Yep, but I forgot to eat breakfast, so I'm working my way toward lunch. Probably have it just before I leave for the day."

Sam kept silent. Skye's erratic schedules had more to do with her personality than her job, which was merely the convenient excuse.

"You still there?"

"Just waiting for you to stop chewing."

"Okay, okay. Listen, I'm off to a conference tomorrow and wanted to get back to you while I had the chance."

Sam clenched the receiver. "Did you find him?"

"Yes and no."

"Skye, no games please. This is important."

"Relax. I just want to explain what I did because I can't really give any more time to this. But I got a start and it looks promising. The rest you should be able to take care of."

Yeah, right. Sam wished she had as much confidence

in her sleuthing abilities as her sister seemed to have. "Go on."

"You told me this Emily person figured the guy was using an assumed name, and if he had no record, I figured he'd probably do what most amateurs do when they pick an alias."

"I thought you were in a hurry."

"Give me a break, Sam. Most people pick a name they're already familiar with. Makes it easier. So I decided to run a search for 'Daniel Winston', thinking at least one of those names might be the right one. I didn't get anything until I asked for all names with Daniel Winston in them and I came up with two for the greater Seattle area."

"And?"

"One was a kid and the other was for a Winston Daniel Sullivan, but…" She paused.

"What?"

"He's dead."

Sam exhaled slowly. So, it was finished almost before it began. Maybe it was better this way. Finding out your father was dead might be a preferable option to being rejected by him.

"You still there?"

"Yes. Just thinking about Danny and his mother."

"Right, well, don't go calling them up with the bad news yet, 'cause Daniel Winston Sullivan died about twelve years ago when he was sixty-six."

"*Sixty-six?* Then…"

"Not your man."

Sam closed her eyes, wishing she was close enough to grab hold of her sister and squeeze. "For God's sake!"

"There's more, though. When I called up his name I drew a flag here."

"A what?"

"A flag telling me the name was connected to an old case."

"What kind of case? Drugs or something?"

"No. Fraud. Ironically it was one of my cases when I was working there."

"You mean, when you first signed up with the agency?"

"Yep. It really wasn't much of a case though. I'm looking at it right now—downloaded the old file when I got the flag. Hmm—seems it was initiated after a couple of anonymous phone tips. Uh-huh. It's kinda coming back to me now."

"Could you just give me the basic details, Skye?"

"Relax, Sam. I'm just skimming through it here. Winston Sullivan, as he was called, was one of the owners of a company called Trade Winds—import and export operation—accused of scamming the government on contracts."

"Hold on a sec, I want to write this down." Sam reached for the pen and notepad on her desktop. "All right, go on."

"Okay, so this might have been a serious charge, but we couldn't find any real evidence. The tipster never came forward and people we interviewed had nothing much we could use."

"So why even bother? Do you normally follow up anonymous tips like that?"

"Not often, but like I said, it was my first year and my boss thought it would be good experience for me. We didn't expect anything to come of it and nothing did."

"Then why the flag?"

"Not sure… Oh, yeah. Here it is. A key witness was unavailable for interviewing. I guess I flagged it, intending to follow up, but then I was posted to D.C. shortly after and the agent who took over my caseload closed it, but kept the flag on in case the witness reported back."

Sam scribbled on the notepad. "And the witness?"

"None other than Chase Daniel Sullivan, son of Winston Daniel Sullivan."

"Chase?" She tried—unsuccessfully—to attach that name to her mental image of Danny's father.

"Fancy, eh? At the time he was working in the company's accounting department. When I went in to check the company's books, I found out the woman who'd been the manager had just resigned. And this Chase guy was away on a business trip or something."

Sam chewed thoughtfully on the end of her pen. "Isn't that a bit odd? That both important witnesses would be away at the same time?"

"I thought so, too, but the big bosses at the company were very open to my looking at everything."

"You mean, the father?"

"And his brother, Bryant Sullivan. They both inherited the business from their father. I just Googled the company name, and it seems the brother is still running it with his two sons."

"And what about Chase?"

"I can't tell you anything more about him. No phone listing under that name. I know someone in Transport who can check if he has a driver's license, but I haven't had a chance to call her yet. He has no credit card—at least, not in his real name and not in the alias he was using with this Emily person."

Sam closed her eyes, picturing "this Emily person" lying in her hospital bed. Sometimes Skye's professional detachment was too much. But she didn't want to get side-tracked by another quibble with her sister. "So you're telling me Danny's father might be this Chase Sullivan, but you have no idea where he is."

"No, I'm not telling you that." Sam flinched at the irritation in her twin's voice. "He has no military record and I didn't have time to see if he's ever filed an income-tax return, but I've got one lead you can follow up easily enough yourself."

"What's that?"

"Papa Sullivan left a widow and she's a resident at a nursing home in Seattle. It's called Harbor House—in Magnolia. I'll e-mail all this to you. Her name is Martha."

"Thanks, Skye. I really appreciate it."

There was a slight pause on the other end. "I hope it helps. So, say hi to Mom for me, okay?"

"Sure. And I'm hoping you'll help plan her sixtieth."

There was a brief silence. "I'm away at a conference tomorrow and things can get busy real fast here. I'll get back to you as soon as I can about that."

Sam had heard that line before. Still, Skye had come quickly to her help regarding Danny's father, and if she had to hassle her about the party, best to do it later. "Keep it in mind, though, okay?"

When she spoke, her sister's voice was decidedly cooler. "Sure. Talk to you soon."

The line was disconnected and Sam had the unsettling feeling that perhaps she ought to have taken the opportunity to have a real talk with her sister. But once again, she'd chickened out.

CHAPTER THREE

HARBOR HOUSE must have been a private mansion in the days of the timber barons. An imposing Victorian-style house, it perched on a hilltop far above Elliott Bay, off Magnolia Boulevard. Sam guessed that a hundred years or so ago, when the house was new, it had had a spectacular view of the harbor. Now other modern palatial homes checkered the hillside, and the nursing home's upper balconies looked down on rooftops and skyscrapers in the distance.

Still, if a nursing home was in your future, this would be the one to choose. If you could afford it. A glimpse of the circular driveway leading to a portico surrounded by large terra-cotta pots of brightly colored annuals and groomed gardens beyond confirmed the place was well-funded. Of course, inside was what really counted.

But five minutes later Sam realized she wasn't going to see any more of the inside than the large foyer with its polished marble floor and the frowning, fiftysomething woman sitting behind an imposing oak desk.

"I'm sorry," the woman repeated, "but if your name isn't on Mrs. Sullivan's guest list, then you won't be able to see her."

Guest list? Sam stared at the austere woman in her dark, tailored business suit and curbed an impulse to be flippant. "I don't understand. I told Chase I'd be seeing his mother and I thought he'd take care of it."

The woman abruptly raised her head from the binder she'd been referring to. Sam caught the slight hesitation in her face and quickly added, "My parents are old family friends and I'm just in town for a few days. I left a voice message for Chase to say I'd meet him here, but perhaps he didn't get it."

A narrowing of steel-gray eyes hinted that Sam may have made a mistake.

"Mr. Sullivan's regular visiting time is ten in the morning on Mondays, so he's due here tomorrow. I'll ask him if he'd like your name placed on the list." Her quick smile indicated the matter was finished.

Sam struck a thoughtful pose, extending it as long as possible. "I suppose I could arrange to stay another day. Thanks." She started to leave, eyeing the elevator beyond the desk and wondering if she could reach it before the Dragon Lady could stop her.

"What was the name again?"

"Uh…Winston. Samantha Winston."

The woman wrote a Post-it and placed it on the cover of the binder. "I'll make sure this comes to Mr. Sullivan's attention when he arrives tomorrow."

Oh, it'll come to his attention, all right. Sam smiled and walked out the etched-glass main door.

ON MONDAY MORNING, Chase pulled into a space on the street. He never used the Harbor House visitor parking lot at the north end of the property because he suspected the sight of a battered pickup would draw complaints. The last thing he wanted was to have any negative attention directed at his mother. Not that she'd be aware of it, but it was the least he could do, considering. He grabbed the small box of peppermint patties—his mother's favorite treat—and climbed out of the truck.

It was a bright sunny day and he hoped to be back at his workshop in time to give the cabinet he was making a last coat of stain. The oak cabinet had been a rush order and he knew it wasn't going to measure up to his personal standard, but as long as the customer was happy, that was all that mattered. The bonus for quick work was going to be a down payment on a new truck. As he walked through the gated entry to Harbor House, his attention was caught by a red Acura parked over the yellow line marking the start of the driveway.

The owner was going to get a ticket if the vehicle was left there for any length of time. He'd seen it happen many times while visiting. The management was very strict about things like that. It was one of the many reasons he'd chosen Harbor House for his mother. The rules were always taken seriously, which meant that security was never compromised. That was of utmost importance.

Chase debated informing the receptionist but decided against it. When he pushed open the massive glass door, the woman behind the front desk looked up, smiling.

"Morning, Mrs. MacDonald," he said. "How're you today?"

"I'm great, Mr. Sullivan. And you?"

"Couldn't be better. How's my mother?"

"Doing well, I understand. She's waiting for you in the conservatory."

Chase smiled at the phrase. As if his mother remembered his regular visiting days. Yet the routine seldom varied. All a part of the incredible pretense of the place, he thought. Forget this is a home for sick old people who don't know their own children anymore. He forced aside the bitterness, wondering what had suddenly brought it on. He'd been doing this for almost two years and should be used to it.

"Great. Thanks." He started for the elevator when she stopped him.

"Oh, Mr. Sullivan. There's someone else here to see your mother." She stood up, tilting her head slightly to the right.

Chase noticed a woman sitting in a wing chair at the end of the hallway, a few feet beyond the elevator. On cue, the woman headed his way. As she emerged from the shadowy interior, Chase realized at once this was no one he knew.

"Hello, Chase. It's been a while. I can see you don't recognize me."

Chase squinted, as if that might jog his memory. Her raven hair swayed slightly against a slender neck rising out of a crisp white shirt topped by a torso-hugging, sky-blue sweater. Her tight black jeans emphasized long, slim legs. She certainly had his attention.

"Samantha *Winston*," she said.

He felt a sudden tightening in his chest and hoped he didn't look as confused as he felt. "Uh…" He stammered, uncertain if this was just a big coincidence or something far worse.

"Relative of *Daniel Winston?*"

Chase stared blankly at the bright red lips curved in a knowing smile. No coincidence, but what exactly was her game?

"I came to see your mother, but perhaps we could have a little chat first?"

She glanced at Mrs. MacDonald, listening in from her desk.

"Feel free to use the front parlor," the receptionist said with a slight sniff.

Chase couldn't take his eyes off the woman standing in front of him, someone who had dredged up a name from the past and yet was a complete stranger. Finally he responded, "Thanks Mrs. MacDonald. Uh…I'll pop in to see my mother in a few minutes."

"Of course, Mr. Sullivan. I'll tell the nurse you'll be arriving shortly."

Chase headed for the room to the left of the elevator. The parlor, designed as a small but comfortable living room in someone's home, was one of several in the establishment for patient visits with family members and was usually full on the weekends. But on Mondays it was relatively empty, one of the reasons he chose to make his weekly visits then. As soon as he entered the room, he set the box of chocolates down on a table and closed the door behind her.

"All right," he said. "Who are you and what do you want?"

She paid him the courtesy of dropping the coy act. In fact, he was surprised to see her face redden.

"Sorry for the ruse," she said, "but I thought you might not want the receptionist to hear what I have to say." She paused. "My real name is Samantha Sorrenti."

"Go on," he said. Her unexpected nervousness calmed him. Whatever she was about to spring on him, he decided he could handle it.

"Maybe we should sit." She pointed to a grouping of furniture around the fireplace.

Chase glanced at it, then back to her. A cozy chat wasn't what he had in mind. "I'm fine." He was almost enjoying her discomfort, but he knew not to let his guard down. She had, after all, used that name for a reason.

"Contrary to what I told the receptionist, I haven't come here to see your mother. Sorry about that. It was you I wanted to meet."

No kidding. He waited for her to continue.

"Do you remember Emily Benson?"

He hesitated. It wasn't the question he was expecting.

"She used to waitress at a diner in the northwest part of the city. I think it was called Baywicks."

"Yes, I remember the diner. And Emily." He had a sudden image of her. Pale, almost too thin. She was a chain-smoker and always running out to the sidewalk on her breaks. But she'd been a friendly face in a turbulent time for him. And a good listener. God, how many times he must have bored her with his incessant philosophizing. In those days he'd still had something to be idealistic about—before his indulged life came crashing down around him.

"How is Emily?"

"Not good."

He frowned. "How so?"

"She's dying. Lung cancer." She cleared her throat and looked down at the Persian carpet.

It was a moment before the words registered. The Emily he remembered had been a hardworking young woman whose lack of formal education had restricted her opportunities. Yet she'd had spirit and was always positive about her future.

"I'm very sorry to hear that," he murmured at last. Their eyes connected suddenly—Emily linking two strangers. Chase turned away and closed his. He was in Emily's apartment, taking in the Salvation Army furnishings and the quirky decor. He even remembered what she'd said: *It's not much, but it's all mine.* Poverty hadn't diminished her pride. He'd liked that about her. No apologies. And now she was dying of cancer.

"Is…uh…someone looking after her?" He dearly hoped so.

"She's in the palliative-care ward at Our Lady of Mercy Hospital."

She hadn't really answered his question. "I meant... does she have someone? A family member?"

When she didn't answer, he met her gaze. There was a peculiar expression in her face. "Emily once told me she had no family," he clarified. "That's why I'm asking. Does she have a partner?" He thought he saw tears in the woman's eyes and for the first time, wondered if she was related to Emily.

"No. She's a single mom."

"Oh?"

"She has a twelve-year-old son. His name is Danny. For his father."

His eyes were fixed on her face, but all he saw was the wall shifting behind her. The framed paintings seemed to project outward and the floor moved beneath his feet. Not an earthquake, he told himself as he backed into a wing chair and sat. *Just your past rumbling toward you.*

She was talking, but he couldn't make out what she was saying over the buzzing in his head. *You have a son. Emily's dying of cancer. A son.* When he could focus again, she was standing in front of him, her eyes narrowed.

"I'm sorry if this is a shock," she was saying.

A shock? That was rich. "Who are you?" His voice sounded hollow, disbelieving to his own ears.

"Samantha Sorrenti."

He shook his head. "No, I mean, what's your connection to Emily Benson?"

"Well, I have this business. Kind of an agency. I look for—"

He jumped to his feet. "You're a private investigator? Who are you working for?" He was starting to put it together now. Of course. It made sense. He pointed a finger at her. "Who sent you here? What do you want from me?"

She stepped back.

"Is everything all right?"

They both looked toward the receptionist holding open the door. "Mr. Sullivan?"

"It's okay, Mrs. MacDonald," he replied.

"All right." She looked from Chase to Samantha and hesitated, as if reluctant to leave.

"If you don't mind…" he prompted, turning his attention to Samantha.

"Of course." She closed the door quietly behind her.

Chase stared at the woman standing mere inches away. Up close, he noticed her gray eyes were flecked with green and their appraisal of him was unflinching. That was good, he thought, because nothing unnerved him more than a tearful woman, and there was no way he was going to be deterred from finding out what the hell was going on. "Sit," he said, pointing to the love seat behind her.

She hesitated, as if she didn't like his tone, but did as he asked. "Look—" she began.

"No, you look," he said, cutting her off. "I've no idea what you have to do with Emily Benson, but—"

"If you'll give me a chance," she said, her voice rising, "I'll be happy to explain."

He sat on the edge of the wing chair opposite her, leaning forward with his elbows resting on his knees. "Go ahead."

HIS VOICE WAS LOWER, calmer. He had the upper hand now, Sam thought, and he knew it. She was embarrassed at how badly she'd blown the whole thing. What had possessed her to use that Winston name? There'd been no point, other than putting him on the defensive right away. Maybe the recent memory of Danny's pinched and anxious face had compelled her to take the offensive—just in case Chase Sullivan proved to be one of those deadbeat dads. Yet the sudden blanching in his face when she'd told him suggested otherwise. Plus, he hadn't rushed to deny the possibility of paternity. And, he'd seemed just as shocked and upset that she might be a private investigator.

"I'm waiting," he said.

Samantha took a deep breath. No more games. All she had to do now was give him the facts and leave the rest to him. *Oh. And one more thing.* Try to get a commitment from him to see Danny so she could report back immediately. She had a feeling that might take longer than a few minutes in the parlor of a nursing home.

Sam moistened her lips, wondering why she felt so nervous. He certainly didn't look as scary as her mental picture of him from Danny's description. The long hair was shorter, scraping the collar of his polo-style shirt and he was clean shaven. Her glance drifted to his right arm, encased in the sleeve of his worn tweed sports jacket. Tattoo tucked away.

He was taller than she'd expected and heavier. But then, she only had Emily's description, and that was from thirteen years ago. But from the way the shirt stretched across what she could see of his chest, the weight was mostly muscle. He kept in shape. His eyes caught hers and she realized right away he knew she'd been checking him out.

"Confirming I'm the right man?" he asked.

The tone was not amused. Neither was the glint in his eye.

"Who are you working for?" he asked again.

"Emily and Danny…your son." She thought she saw him flinch when she added that. "And I need to clarify something. I'm not a private investigator."

"You said you had an agency. Looking for…?"

"Things. Items people might want to buy."

"What kinds of things?"

She sighed. "Rare books. Art objects. Coins. Whatever."

"And how long have you known Emily?"

He'd skipped the Danny connection, she noticed. Maybe still processing that. "I just met her a couple of days ago. I—"

"So how come you're working for her?"

"If you'll let me explain—"

"I've been waiting for you to do that," he said testily.

"Then why do you keep interrupting?"

He didn't respond, but Sam thought she saw a trace of satisfaction in his face. Angrily, she said, "Danny found my agency on the Internet. Unfortunately he overlooked the fact that I search for objects, not people. Anyway, he persuaded me to meet his mother and later…after…well, I agreed to help him out even though this is not what I do." She had to stop to calm herself, his unblinking gaze unnerving.

"Go on," he said.

"Time is running out for Emily." She cleared her throat and waited a moment. "They're desperate." She paused, thinking he might interject. He sat so still she wondered if he'd heard her. Then she noticed one of his fingers tapping silently on his knee. A metronome keeping time with his heartbeat?

"They have no other family," she went on. "When Emily…goes…Danny will have to be placed in foster care. That's why he decided to look for you."

He got up and moved to the large bay window in the center of the room. It looked onto an enclosed garden patio, and for the first time Sam realized there were some people sitting outside, bundled up against the fresh spring air. She wondered if his mother was one of those people and had a sudden pang of conscience. Had she spoiled *her* day, as well as her son's? Too late for guilt now, she told herself.

"Okay," he said, without turning around. After a long moment, he added, "You can go, then."

"Pardon?"

He pivoted on his heel. His face was set in stone. "Your job is finished now, right? You've done your bit."

"Well I...I suppose...I guess..."

"So you can go."

Reluctantly, she got up from the love seat. "What about Danny?"

"Danny's my business now." His expression was so intimidating she turned meekly toward the door and pulled it open.

His voice stopped her. "Unless you feel you're owed something more."

Frowning, she looked back at him. "What?"

"Maybe you think you ought to be paid more money. In that case..." He paused to dig into the inner pocket of his sport jacket and pulled out a small billfold.

"For your information," she said, fighting to keep her voice even, "I haven't been paid a cent and don't expect to be. I came here for Danny and Emily because I wanted to help them. They don't have some wealthy, blue-blood family to fall back on like you do." She spun around and walked out, slamming the door behind her.

Her brisk march along the carpeted hall to the main door was met by raised eyebrows from Mrs. MacDonald, sitting behind the reception desk. Sam passed her with scarcely a glance and exited onto the front steps, where she stopped to catch her breath.

He was right, of course. That was what bothered her so much. She'd completed the task she'd been asked to do and had no further reason to stick around. It was his peremptory dismissal of her that rankled. As if she were a delinquent student and he the school principal. She felt embarrassed at how passively she'd left, without a single word of reproach. But then, she'd never been good at the smart comeback. That was Skye's forte.

She continued on to her car, wondering exactly what she'd tell Emily and, especially, Danny, about Chase Daniel Sullivan. She wished she'd pinned the man down, made him say exactly when and where he'd meet Danny. Then she pictured that meeting. A cool, perhaps reluctant father and his desperate, vulnerable son. *Someone a lot stronger than Emily Benson needs to be on the scene, too.*

By the time Sam reached her car, she'd decided to be that person, and even the sight of a parking tag fluttering beneath her windshield wiper failed to dampen her resolve. Then she realized that she had no idea where Sullivan lived or, worse, if he would actually follow through and meet with Emily and Danny. She snatched the parking tag off the window and got into the car.

Her options were to go back and demand some kind of commitment from the man or drive on meekly home. Not much of a choice. A third option occurred to her. She quickly started up the engine, backed out and drove to the street, where she parked about fifty feet from the Harbor House driveway. When he left, she'd see him and follow.

She saw the front door of the nursing home open. A tall figure stood in the doorway, his back to the street. It was him. Sam slouched down in the seat as Chase headed for the sidewalk. She raised her head enough to watch him through her side mirror. He stopped for a second at the foot of the circular driveway, and Sam stiffened when she saw him look at the space where she'd originally parked. There was no way he knew what her car looked like because she'd arrived at the home ahead of him.

After a few seconds, he strode up the street away from her. Sam sat up and watched him. He seemed to be examining all the vehicles parked on both sides of the street. Looking for her? she wondered. Would he turn around and come back her way? Her heart thumped a bit more vigorously. But he stopped beside a pickup truck, his hand on the door. Suddenly he spun around and headed her way again.

Sam ducked her head enough to watch him walk back up the circular driveway and into Harbor House. She considered her next move. Assuming the truck was his, at least she could get the license-plate number for Skye to check out. She turned over the Acura engine and, with one last glance at the nursing-home front door, drove toward the pickup.

She stopped just short of it, jotting down the plate number on the back of her parking tag before driving off. She had no doubt at all that she'd be meeting up again with Chase Sullivan. No way was he going to have the last word. Metaphorically, anyway, she thought, recalling her last words to him. Something about wealthy blue bloods. Judging by the sad shape of that pickup truck, the "wealthy" bit wasn't apt.

"DID YOU FIND what you were looking for?" Mrs. MacDonald asked pleasantly as Chase entered the front door.

"Hmm?" he asked, preoccupied with how Samantha Sorrenti had vanished so quickly. He still had no idea why he'd run after her. Just that the instant she'd walked out the door he'd realized he really knew nothing about her. He hated the feeling of someone having information about him while he was left in the dark. Suppose he wanted to get in touch with her—God forbid!—or at least needed to contact her?

"Whatever you left in the truck?" Mrs. MacDonald prompted.

"Oh." He'd already forgotten the excuse he'd given her for his sudden rush out the door. "I was afraid I'd left the keys in the truck, but I hadn't. A bit forgetful today," he explained, and started down the hall to the conservatory.

"Mr. Sullivan?"

He turned around. The receptionist was standing up and grinning. In her right hand was the box of patties. Chase hoped he didn't look as ridiculous as he felt.

"Thanks," he said, striding back to the desk to collect the chocolates.

"She'll be expecting them," she said with a soft smile.

"For sure. Thanks again." He was grateful for the long, winding hallway to the conservatory, as it gave him time to compose himself. His mother was keenly sensitive to the moods of others and would mentally shut down if she detected a whiff of stress.

He stood at the entrance to the room whose decor mimicked a small concert area, with a highly polished piano in one corner and a musical stand beside it. Several folding chairs were stacked along one wall to accommodate patients and their guests when musical events were held. But now the area was scattered with wheelchairs, their occupants staring passively out the floor-to-ceiling bank of windows that looked out on the grounds behind the home.

Spotting his mother, whose chair was angled inward, Chase headed her way. Although he waved his fingers as he approached her wheelchair, she didn't focus on him until he was standing directly in front of her.

"Hi, Mom," he said, leaning over to kiss her cheek.

She didn't respond to the kiss, but at least she didn't flinch, as she did occasionally. "For me?" she asked as she noticed the box of patties in his hand.

Chase smiled. The weekly routine had begun. "For you," he said, handing the box to her. He unfolded one of the chairs and set it beside her wheelchair. Then he reached over to help her take the plastic wrap off the box. After he opened it and she held a patty in one trembling hand, her watery blue eyes met his and she asked, "Who are you again?"

He stroked the back of her other hand, resting on her lap. "I'm Chase, Mom."

She frowned. The name obviously triggered some faint memory, but not one she could connect to the man sitting next to her.

"The peppermint patty man," he clarified.

She smiled sweetly. "I love peppermint patties," she said, and nibbled delicately on the one she was holding.

Chase watched her savor the chocolate. He still remembered the first time he'd brought her a box and the gleam of delight in her eyes. The confection was the only bond between them. That fact had saddened him in the beginning, but now he accepted it and was content to simply watch her enjoy herself. He knew the nursing staff, for nutritional and health purposes, managed to spirit away the leftovers every week. His mother likely forgot about them, anyway, the instant they were out of sight. But he clung to the ritual, afraid of losing even that link with her.

When she finished eating a couple, he dabbed her lips with a tissue from one of the ubiquitous boxes in every room and made an attempt at conversation. But as always, her attention drifted. After a few minutes, he bent over to kiss her goodbye. "See you next week, Mom," he whispered. He set the box with the remaining patties on a table and headed out the door. He never looked back to see if she noticed he was leaving.

By the time he got to the truck, he'd decided to forgo his weekly latte fix. He needed some quiet time away from people to think about what had happened that afternoon. Driving away, he impulsively made a right at the first intersection.

The tree-lined street wound up the hillside above Harbor House and Magnolia Boulevard. He hadn't been along this route for years, but little had changed. Some of the larger homes had been subdivided into apartment units, but the cul-de-sac he turned onto hadn't changed at all. Especially the house at the very end. Chase pulled over and switched off the engine.

Funny that he could view the vine-covered stone exterior and the wrought iron gate with so little emotion. Even now most of the memories of the place were unhappy ones. He wondered who lived there now. Not that it mattered. When he'd been away all those years after his father's death, sleeping in grungy boardinghouses or sometimes in the rough, he'd often imagined the dark, wood-paneled interior and polished hallways. The quiet, too.

As a child he'd seldom had friends visit. His mother had suffered from migraines and couldn't bear the noise and exuberance of children. When he was a teenager, he began to spend more and more time away until he'd eventually disappointed everyone—or perhaps no one—by moving out altogether. Then he couldn't get enough noise and bright lights and loud, raucous people.

Chase wiped a hand over his face. He'd awakened that morning anticipating the customary routine of his weekly visit. Mother first, then a stop at the nearest Starbucks for his latte. On to his favorite hardware store to browse or perhaps pick up an order. If he had time, he'd stop at the market and buy croissants at the bakery he loved best.

Over the past few years impulse and spontaneity had given way to order and routine. He'd made a new life for himself. Not the one he'd expected to have as a teenager, but still…a life he could handle. Now it was going to be blown apart, shattered and reformed into something he had no vision of, much less feeling for.

He'd given up on the notion of a family for himself years ago. That acceptance had led to a couple of broken relationships, which he'd regretted at the time. It was ironic that the one-night fling he'd had with Emily Benson had produced exactly what he'd sworn never to have. A child. Chase lowered his forehead onto his hands, clutching the steering wheel. Omigod. *A twelve-year-old son.*

CHAPTER FOUR

SAMANTHA WAS DUE at her mother's for dinner by six, so, figuring that would give her enough time for a visit with Emily Benson, decided to drop by the hospital on her way. As she rode up to the palliative-care ward, she hoped that Danny would not be there. She thought he might have a lot more questions than his mother and she wanted to avoid having to answer one in particular. *Why didn't you get Chase Sullivan's address and phone number?*

Of course, she could explain that she'd immediately called her FBI sister and left a message asking her to get an address from the license plate. But she had a feeling Danny would consider the excuse lame. And it was.

Sam was relieved to find Emily alone, sitting up in bed and leafing through a magazine. She looked a hundred percent better than she had the last time Sam had seen her.

"Hi, Emily."

"Sam, I wasn't expecting to see you so soon," Emily murmured, a look of apprehension in her face.

"Mind if I close the door?"

"Leave it open a crack. The nurses like to be able to look in on me."

Sam did so. She ought to have thought of that. A patient in palliative care could have a crisis at any moment. When she sat down, Emily turned the magazine over on her lap and quietly asked, "Good news or bad?"

Right to the point, Sam thought, just like her son. "I've found a man called Chase Daniel Sullivan whom I believe to be Danny's father."

"Chase?"

"Yes. His father was Winston Daniel Sullivan, but he died about thirteen years ago. He lived here in Seattle and was an owner of an import-export business."

"Uh-huh. And this man...Chase? Have you met him? What makes you think he's Danny's father?"

"I have met him. Same eyes," Sam said at once. "Hair color, too. Plus, he remembered you."

Emily looked away. Sam waited for her to digest this very significant piece of information. Finally Emily asked, "How did he look?"

The question didn't really surprise Sam. Most women would have wanted to know what an ex had said about them. Not Emily. She either didn't care or knew it was irrelevant. Likely the latter, Sam thought.

"Short hair. No sign of a pierced ear, but I can't report on the tattoo because his arms were covered."

Emily smiled. "I remember that tattoo. Some kind of Tibetan prayer, I think. You'd have thought from his appearance, that it would be a snake or a big heart with MOM in the center." She waited a moment. "So...uh...what did he say when you told him about Danny? Or did you?"

"He was obviously shocked, but he didn't deny the possibility of being Danny's father."

"But what did he *say?*"

Sam played back the scene mentally, but it came out as a swirl of emotion rather than facts. She recalled her frustration when he peremptorily dismissed her. "He was more concerned about you," she said finally, telling herself that wasn't really a lie so much as an assumption.

Emily looked away toward the window again. "I've

been thinking about all of this the last couple of days. Now I'm not so sure I want Danny to meet him."

Those quietly spoken words bounced around the room. "Why not?" was the only response Sam could manage, but she was thinking, a bit late for second thoughts now.

Emily gazed out the window a few seconds longer, then returned her gaze to Sam. "I don't know if you'll understand."

"I can try." *Or I could scream,* which wouldn't do in a palliative-care ward.

"As much as I hate the thought of Danny being in foster care, I'm scared about him being with a man who may be torn about having a son suddenly forced on him. I mean, unless Danny—Chase—has drastically changed, I know he'd do the right thing by my Danny."

Sam thought back to Chase's end-of-conversation remark that Danny was his business now. *Business.* "I got that impression, too," she understated.

"So that's not the issue. It's more…what if he comes to resent Danny later? This is going to affect his whole life. And maybe he already has a family."

That hadn't occurred to Sam, and not for the first time, she marveled at how she'd screwed up. When Danny had pressed her to look for his father, he'd certainly had far more faith in her investigative skills than she deserved. Plus, there was the other thing—the small matter of an old FBI inquiry into the family business. She really knew nothing about Chase Sullivan. Maybe Emily was right. On the other hand, there was Danny, clinging to his dream.

"But isn't this about Danny? He's so determined to find his father and if Chase is his father, then he'll do the right thing. He'll adapt. Isn't that enough?" Sam's gut feeling was that Danny had to know.

"*Adapt.* I think Danny deserves more than a father who

just adapts. And he's a tough kid, you know? I think he can adapt, too. There are a lot of great foster homes out there and hopefully I'll have time to be involved in helping Children's Services look for one."

"But it's not the same, is it? As being with your own father?"

Emily's sigh indicated more fatigue than frustration. "No, it's not the same. But it may not be worse if that father really doesn't want you. And I don't want Danny to have to deal with that. I won't be here to help him."

Sam stared at the floor. She could say nothing about the undeniable truth of that last sentence, but she had to make one last pitch. "I just think Danny deserves to know. He's old enough to handle the problems that will come with this change in his life."

Emily thought that over for a moment. Finally she said, "Yes, but he's still learning how to handle losing one parent." She stopped then and looked down. A huge tear landed on the magazine on her lap.

Sam wanted to comfort her. But she also knew words would change nothing and, besides, she knew what Emily was saying. Losing his mother was going to be traumatic enough for Danny. Realizing the father he'd been looking for might be less than enthused about his newfound son would be devastating. Still…

"Emily," she said once she could trust herself to speak. "Give the idea some more thought."

Emily dabbed at her face with a tissue. "All right. I suppose I need time to absorb this, too. So let's not tell Danny just yet."

"No. But soon we have to tell him something."

Emily nodded. "Soon." She sank against her pillows.

Sam got out of her chair. "I'll come by in a couple of days, all right?"

Another nod.

Sam closed the door gently behind her. On the elevator ride down, she realized something that made her catch her breath. She'd have to find Chase Sullivan before he found Emily and Danny. And she doubted he'd be happy to see her again.

SAM KNEW the question would come but still braced herself when it did.

"So what's the latest with that boy?" Her mother was pulling items from the refrigerator and missed the look on Sam's face. "The one whose mother is dying. And how is she doing, by the way? How much more time does she have?"

As usual, Nina was tossing out questions too quickly for Sam to answer any of them. "I don't know, medically, anyway. I visited this afternoon. She looked better than the last time I saw her." *At least until I had my talk with her.*

Nina glanced up from salad preparation. "Does that mean you've decided to take on the case?"

"Yes, Mom, it does. And I took your suggestion and called Skye. She gave me some information."

Nina appeared to mull that over. "Good for you. So what's happening now?"

"Well, thanks to Skye, I think I've found Danny's father."

"Already?"

"It wasn't that hard."

"You said, 'think.'"

"There's been no DNA test, but he looks a lot like Danny and he didn't deny that he is the father."

"Still, it's not an indisputable fact."

Sam chewed the inside of her cheek. "No, it's not. Want me to set the table?"

Nina raised an eyebrow. "I thought we'd eat right here, at the counter. If you don't mind."

Sam shrugged. "Fine with me."

While she retrieved cutlery from the drawer beneath the work counter, Nina added, "So what now?"

"Well, it's complicated."

"How?"

"Now Emily isn't sure if she wants Danny to know I may have found his father. She's worried that the dad— his name is Chase Sullivan—will feel pressured to take him and will eventually resent Danny."

"Sounds like Emily's a smart woman."

"Oh, she is, but she's only looking at it from her point of view."

Nina frowned. "Yes, but she's the mother and she's dying. She wants what's best for her son."

"Even if it means Danny not knowing his father?"

"Sometimes those sacrifices must be made for the good of the child."

Sam stared at her mother. She wondered if they were still talking about Emily and Danny. "Is that why you didn't take Dad back when he asked?"

Nina paled, but didn't hesitate to answer. "Yes, because I didn't want my children to grow up in an atmosphere of distrust and betrayal and bitterness."

"But maybe Skye and I could have handled that."

"Perhaps, but I knew *I* couldn't. And I thought better to have one parent and live in peace and harmony than to be around two adults who'd grown to dislike one another. I had to make a choice, Samantha. Just like Emily."

"But what if it's not the right choice?"

Nina sighed. "Maybe it won't be. People can only go with their instincts. With what feels right to them."

"Is that what you did?"

Nina placed her hand on top of Sam's. "I hoped it was the right choice." She looked into Sam's eyes. "What do you think?"

Sam wasn't sure she wanted the talk to go this way, but it was too late to back out now. "I'm not sure. I never had the chance to find out otherwise."

"No, you didn't. But I never stopped your father from seeing you girls."

Sam bit down on her lip. It always came to that. The irrefutable fact that he never had.

"Does it still hurt?" her mother asked.

"I don't know, frankly. It shouldn't, now that I'm all grown up." She forced a smile.

"Maybe that's why you care so much about Danny. Why it's important for you to have him connect with his father."

Analyzing again, Sam thought, but she had to admit how close to the mark her mother might be. "Maybe," she whispered.

After a few seconds her mother said, "I think the lasagna's ready."

SAM LEFT her mother's condo early. She had an appointment at ten the next morning, but needed to make a few phone calls to organize the final details of the sale and shipment of a Thai Buddha for the client. The report confirming the provenance of the Buddha was supposed to be e-mailed to her office before nine and her transatlantic phone call agreeing to the vendor's terms had to be placed by nine-thirty. The adrenaline rush of such tight scheduling was a part of the job that Sam loved and a contrast to the long, sometimes dull, hours spent searching the Internet or obscure catalogs for items.

When she noticed she had voice mail, she was tempted to ignore it. Her gut feeling was that Danny had found out she'd visited Emily and wanted to pump her for information. Not that she *had* to return his call until the next day, anyway, but she bet he'd be waiting by the phone and she doubted either of them would get any sleep if she didn't call him back.

But the message was from Skye. "Hey, Sam, got your call about the plate number for Chase Sullivan. I must admit, I am impressed. Didn't take you long to rustle him up at all. Maybe you missed your calling. So here's the info. The guy lives on Bainbridge Island. Cool, eh? Remember how we always wanted to open up a little toy shop there when we were kids? Anyway, he has a carpentry business called Sullivan's Fine Furniture on Primrose Lane, wherever that is. I don't imagine the island has grown too much in the last few years, so it shouldn't be too hard to track him down. Listen, kind of off topic, but I've got an idea. My conference sucks, so I've decided to blow off the last two days, go back to the office and schedule some holiday time.

"I haven't seen Mom since…um…Christmas, and you said you'd like some help with her sixtieth, so I think I'll fly out there for a week or two. And like I said, since you've tracked down Chase Sullivan, maybe I'll pop into the office there and have a look at the old case, see if anything's been done on it since I left. So I'll call Mom and tell her she's going to be having a guest for a week or so. See ya soon. Bye."

Sam jotted down the address, deleted the message and slumped onto the sofa. Great. All she needed was Skye added to the mix of Emily, Danny and now, Chase Sullivan. It was typical of her sister to butt into her business. *First she compliments me on my detective work and then she decides to come and take over.*

And in spite of the recent phone calls, Sam knew she couldn't go through the whole Christmas thing again with Skye. The accusations and the expressions of wounded innocence. *How could you think that? What kind of sister do you think I am?* The kind who kisses her twin's fiancé. With passion. That kind.

Sam groaned and headed for bed, sensing that the next few days were going to get a lot more complicated.

CHASE WAS IN THE BACK of the shop when he heard the tinkle of the doorbell, indicating someone had just entered. He'd hated the cuteness of that bell when he'd bought the place a year ago, but knew he'd be spending a lot of time in the workroom and common sense—*business* sense—had prevailed. He was clamping two sections of a chair together and rather than have to stop, he leaned forward to peer around the door frame. A woman was closing the door. Something familiar about her. When she turned around, Chase quickly withdrew his head. It was *her*. He couldn't believe it. And how had she found him? Irrationally he convinced himself that if he stayed quiet, she just might leave.

"Hello?" she called out.

Any second she'd wander into the back and catch him perching on his stool. Chase swore under his breath, set the clamp down and headed into the showroom part of his small shop.

"Oh," she said. "I wasn't sure if anyone was here."

She was either a skilled liar or a fool, and Chase doubted the latter. "Bainbridge isn't so far from the city that we can leave our businesses unattended," he said dryly.

"Oh? But it has the reputation of being such a tight-knit community. Neighbors looking out for each other."

The look she gave him indicated she was up to the challenge of a sparring contest. Chase was having no part of it. "Miss…uh…"

"Sorrenti. Samantha Sorrenti." Her tone and the look

on her face told him she knew he hadn't really forgotten her name.

"I've no idea why you're here," he said, leaning against one of the handmade oak display cases. "I'm sure you're not just touring the island, and I have nothing more to say to you. If you've come to hound me about contacting Emily's son—"

"And *your* son."

"If you say so."

"That's not what you said yesterday."

"I don't recall saying anything about being the father of the boy."

"His name is *Danny*."

Chase held his breath, fighting to keep calm. She was doing it again, drawing him into a verbal wrangle that he knew could only end badly for him. It wasn't his kind of game.

"And you know in your heart he's your son," she added.

He did, but he wasn't going to admit that to her. "I told you I would contact Emily and I will. Now I'd like you to leave my shop."

The features in her face seemed to tighten and she turned her head. Bingo, he thought. That got to her.

After a moment, she quietly said, "I went to see Emily yesterday afternoon and told her about our meeting."

A surge of anger rose inside him. What was it about this woman that she felt no impunity at all about interfering in his personal life? "I specifically asked you—"

She held up a hand, cutting him off. "I know what you *told* me. I also know that I don't take orders from you. Once again you're not letting me explain."

"But that's the issue here, isn't it? Why you feel you even need to explain. You found me and you passed on some information to me. Yes, significant information that affects me in a deeply personal way. And the key word there is *personal,* Miss Sorrenti. So now that I have that information, my question to you is, why are you still around?"

"I'm still *around,* as you so nicely put it, because Emily made a request of me that meant I'd have to contact you again."

Judging from her expression, Chase guessed the request was not one she'd agreed with. He waited for her to continue, refusing to be drawn into any more talk than necessary. Besides, he could see that she was struggling to keep her voice steady and he wasn't certain if that pleased him—in a petty way—or not.

Finally she said, "Emily isn't certain now that she wants you to meet Danny. She'd like some time—not that she has a lot of it—to think things through. And she definitely wants to talk to you first, alone."

It wasn't what he'd expected. He'd spent the whole night tossing and turning over in his mind all the scenarios of a face-to-face with Danny. *His son.* By daybreak he'd accepted the very real possibility of Danny being his son and had even begun to accept that he'd have to bring him into his life in some way. The suggestion that this might not happen was something he couldn't take in, at least not at the moment. He turned his back on her, hoping she'd leave. He needed to be left alone with this news—to digest it and decide what his options were.

After what seemed an interminable length of time, she said, "So now that I've done what Emily has requested, the ball is back in your court, Mr. Sullivan. Goodbye."

He waited for the door to close before moving nearer to one of the windows to see her climb into a small red Acura parked in front of the shop. So that was *her* car parked illegally at Harbor House.

WHO WAS SHE KIDDING? Not that there was anyone else around to impress, anyway, but there was work to do. It was just that for the past few days she'd done little more than go through the motions. She seethed every time she thought back to the beginning of the week and her visit to Bainbridge Island. Her intentions had been good, she rationalized. She was doing Emily a favor and had expected that she'd be bringing a message he'd be happy to receive. But all expectations ceased the second she stepped out of her car.

She'd had to double-check the address because the chic simplicity of Sullivan's Fine Furniture didn't fit with the battered pickup truck he'd been driving. And the austere, almost stark exterior of the place also jarred against the whimsical cuteness of the neighboring stores, decorated with fake gingerbread and seafaring motifs. But the real surprise was what was inside.

The carvings of birds and pieces of exquisite hand-crafted furniture were as good, if not better, than any she'd seen in online catalogs, or even in any exclusive furniture shop. The place was a gem tucked away out of public view on Bainbridge Island. Sam doubted the locals could afford his pieces and wondered how Sullivan advertised off-island? Perhaps he didn't. Perhaps clients found him by chance. Perhaps he preferred it that way.

The thought reminded her of Skye's investigation into the family business. Maybe part of Chase Sullivan's hostility had more to do with that than with the discovery that he'd fathered a son. Whatever the reason, he obviously couldn't get rid of her fast enough and she was all too happy to oblige. Though why she was still fuming about the visit three days later mystified her. She'd called Emily right away, giving her an edited version of events and passing on the address of the place. There was no directory listing for Chase, but she decided to check out the Internet and found a Web site for the shop that was as austere as the place itself. An e-mail address and phone number were also provided.

Sam gave up pretending to work and decided to leave for the day. The phone calls she needed to make could be done at home and besides, she was happy to defer the last step in her most recent job. A man from Portland had e-mailed photographs of a twelfth-century Indian Buddha he'd recently purchased and wondered if she could find another one for his collection. She'd forwarded the picture and description to a curator at a Seattle museum who moonlighted as an appraiser. Her report indicated the Buddha was most probably a fake. Now Sam not only had to inform the man that he'd spent a small fortune on a twentieth-century reproduction but convince him of that fact.

She locked up, thinking her trip to Bainbridge had left her "prickly and snarly," as her sister used to say in their adolescence, when arguments were a daily occurrence. Thoughts of Skye reminded Sam to call her back and tell her not to bother coming home just yet. As far as Sam was concerned, the whole Sullivan-Benson affair was finished, and their mother's sixtieth was still a month away. She was still forming the voice-mail message she'd leave Skye when she stood in front of her condo door and realized it was unlocked. Either she'd forgotten to lock up when she'd left that morning or someone had broken in. Well, not exactly broken in, since there was no sign of forced entry. Someone with a key, then. And only two other people had keys to her condo. No, wait. Three? Had Todd returned his after their breakup? Damn.

She cautiously opened the door and noticed two things. The shower was going full blast and a black duffel bag was sitting on the foyer floor. She didn't recognize the bag but wasn't alarmed. Burglars didn't usually shower. Still, she tiptoed toward the bathroom and reached it as the door swung open. Sam felt her stomach plummet.

It was like looking at her mirror image. Almost. Except this one was wrapped in her bath towel and dripping on the tiled floor.

"Hey, sister," Skye said, flashing a big smile.

CHAPTER FIVE

"MY SURPRISE evidently has left you speechless," said Skye.

"I wasn't really expecting you. I thought at first some-one had broken in."

"And taken a shower while burgling the place?"

"Ha ha," Sam muttered.

"Come on, lighten up," teased Skye.

"You might have let me know you were coming."

"I left a voice mail."

"You said you were coming home. Not to *my* place."

Skye stared at her long and hard. "So I guess I should get dressed and leave you to *your* place." She went back into the bathroom and closed the door behind her.

Damn and double damn, thought Sam. We haven't seen each other for six months and we're already pushing each other's buttons. She retreated into the kitchen and put the kettle on for tea. When Skye emerged from the bathroom minutes later, Sam called out, "Want some tea before you go?"

Skye appeared in the doorway. "Tea? It's almost five. Got any wine?"

"I'm surprised you haven't already checked."

"I was going to do that after my shower."

Her sudden grin tugged Sam back to their childhood, before adolescent rivalry had reared its ugly head. Sam turned off the stove. "Wine it is," she said, pulling the refrigerator door open. She glanced at her sister while opening a bottle of Riesling. "When did you cut your hair?"

"A couple of months ago. When did you cut yours?"

"About the same time."

They smiled at each other, understanding the weird connection of coincidence with identical twins. Their lives had been full of such parallels, until distance made any comparisons impossible. Distance and the fact they'd scarcely spoken to each other in the last six months. Sam frowned.

"Okay, so what's *really* the problem?" asked Skye, picking up her wineglass.

Now wasn't the time, Sam knew. "Nothing. I wasn't expecting you so soon. Just wondering if Mom knows you're here already. "

"Not yet. Thought I'd—"

"She hates surprises," interjected Sam.

"I was going to say I planned to call her from here."

"Oh." Sam peered into her glass, thinking she was always making assumptions about Skye and having them fizzle in her face. *Maybe the problem is with me. No. I wasn't going behind her back with* her *fiancé.*

"Living room?" Sam cocked her head toward the L-shaped area off the galley kitchen. She led the way, taking the armchair opposite the couch.

"No changes here," said Skye.

Sam glanced around the small apartment and its simple furnishings. In spite of a couple of expensive art pieces—an eighteenth-century Chinese porcelain bowl and a one-of-a-kind Lalique vase—the place was almost spartan. She thought suddenly of Chase Sullivan's shop and the few pieces of furniture she'd seen there the other day, wondering what his reaction might be were she to turn up again, only this time as a customer.

"Why the smile?"

"Hmm?" Sam looked across at Skye. "Oh, nothing, really. I was just thinking that except for a few things, the apartment is pretty bare."

"Yeah, but the few things are really beautiful."

"I guess." Sam sipped her wine. The dead stop in the conversation was merely another confirmation of the widening gap between them. The Christmas-Todd thing seemed destined to be the "elephant in the room" no one would talk about, consigning their conversation to small talk. She wanted to say, "Look, if you'll just say you're sorry, then I can forgive you," but she knew Skye was no more capable of apologizing then she was of forgiving. They'd established this pattern sometime in early childhood, and age had only entrenched them.

"What're you thinking about?" Skye suddenly asked.

Caught out, Sam felt her face heat up. "Oh, nothing much," she said, turning her head toward the window. She glimpsed Skye's face as she did so, noting her sister knew she was lying. The silence stretched.

Finally Skye said, "I guess I should be going."

"Are you going to call Mom?"

"I'll call her on my cell in the taxi."

Sam hesitated, then said, "I can give you a ride."

"It's a bit out of your way, Sam. Unless you were planning to see Mom tonight, anyway."

"No, I wasn't."

"Well, then." Skye slapped her palms on her thighs and got up from the couch.

Sam sat motionless, listening to Skye gather up her things from the bathroom and when she heard the zip of the duffel bag, she forced herself out of the chair to say goodbye.

Skye was standing at the door, her bag in hand. She looked expectantly at Sam.

"Sure you don't want a ride?"

"Nah. I can grab a cab at the corner." Skye paused. "I like your hair."

Sam smiled. "Thanks. I like yours, too."

"Almost identical."

"Almost."

Skye opened the door and suddenly stopped. "I got sidetracked a bit. Meant to ask how that case of yours is going."

"Case?"

"You know—the boy, his father and the dying mom."

Sam felt her skin prickle. *Trust you to phrase it so casually.* "Uh, well, okay."

Skye leaned against the door frame, obviously in no hurry to leave. "I took some holiday time—I think I mentioned that in my voice mail. If you like, I could give you some help with it."

Sam looked her sister in the eye. "I'm fine, but thanks, anyway. Case is solved—or resolved."

"Oh? Father acknowledging paternity?"

"Basically."

Skye nodded thoughtfully, then said, "Well, that's good for the kid…I suppose. I'm still curious, though."

"About what?"

The sharpness in her voice made Skye straighten up. She gave Sam a puzzled look. "About the fraud thing. With the guy's family's business."

Sam waved a hand. "That's history. The important thing is Danny linking up with his father."

"Maybe. Unless…"

"Unless what?"

"Unless the father could potentially be a felon."

Sam stared at Skye in disbelief. "No way."

Skye arched a brow. "You sound so convinced, sis. Is he attractive, this Sullivan?"

"What are you suggesting, Skye?"

"Nothing. Just picking up a certain tone in your voice."

"Not everything boils down to the simple equation of man and woman," Sam retorted.

Skye's gaze traveled across Sam's face. "You sure about that?" She stepped into the hall, adding, "Anyway, as I said before, I've got some time on my hands. Might be worth checking out." She closed the door before Sam could reply.

Not that she had anything to say. Except for a slow mental count to ten to calm herself. She downed the rest of her wine and pondered her next move. Knowing Skye, she wouldn't be distracted from her goal. The key was to preempt her somehow. But then, what if Skye was right and Chase Sullivan *was* guilty of some past crime?

If Emily were in good health, Sam could discuss the problem with her and let her decide. Introduce the man to Danny and take a chance that he wasn't going to be hauled off to jail, or wait and see. Maybe Skye wouldn't find anything linking him to a crime. Hadn't she already investigated the family business—what was it called? Winds something—and ended up dropping the matter for lack of evidence?

Sam took the empty wineglasses into the kitchen and rinsed them. *You worry too much, Samantha Sorrenti.* That was what Skye always used to say, and some of the time, she'd been right. Yet in her dealings with others—especially her family—Skye herself didn't seem to worry *enough.* Chances were this idea of hers would never get off the ground. No point in keeping Danny from his biological father on some whim of Skye's. Sam reached for the phone to call Emily at the hospital and find out if she'd made a decision about seeing Chase. If things sped up a bit, Skye might backtrack or change her mind. *Maybe.*

When a young voice answered, Sam almost hung up. *Danny.* "Uh, could I please speak to Emily?"

There was a brief silence, followed by, "Who's calling?"

"Samantha Sorrenti."

"Have you found out something?"

The blurted question sounded both excited and apprehensive. Sam closed her eyes, debating whether to lie or evade. She opted for the latter. Emily could do the lying if it came to that. "I really need to speak to your mother, Danny," she said in a voice that permitted no argument.

His silence was long enough for her to consider other strategies when Emily abruptly came on the line. Sam heard her telling Danny to please leave the room *now.*

A few moments passed, then, "Samantha?" Emily sounded tired.

"Sorry. I didn't think Danny would be there."

"It's okay. Not your problem. He keeps forgetting I'm still his mother." There was a weak laugh. "I think we've reversed roles a bit these past few weeks."

"I guess that's understandable," Sam said, "and I suppose he's been anxious to hear some news."

"Mmm." A pause, then Emily said, "I feel bad, you know? I've been kinda lying to him. I tell myself they're important lies to protect him, but I've decided I can't do it much longer. If you hadn't called me, I was going to call you and tell you to go ahead."

"Go ahead?"

"You know, tell Daniel—I mean, Chase—that I'd like to see him."

Sam hesitated, wondering if she ought to tell Emily about Skye and what *she* was thinking of doing. But Emily had enough to deal with right now—keeping Danny from finding out about Chase until Emily had a chance to meet with him first. "Okay. I suppose that's a good idea."

"You sound doubtful."

Sam sighed. How to explain that contacting Chase Sullivan again was the last thing she wanted to do? "Not about him seeing you." She paused, knowing there was no way out of this one. "I guess I could call him for you."

"Would you mind? I'm not good with phone talk— especially for something emotional. And I don't think they're going to give me a day's leave to visit him." There was a sharp cackle of laughter mixed with the dry, uncontrollable cough that often overcame her.

When the horrible hacking finally stopped, Sam asked, "Meanwhile, what will you tell Danny?"

"That he'll just have to be patient."

Right. He'll really buy into that. "I'll get back to you then," Sam said.

When she hung up, she sank into the chair and dropped her head into her palms. *Was this ever going to end?*

"HE'S NOT OPEN YET."

Sam turned to the fiftysomething woman watering the flowers in the window boxes of her souvenir shop.

"Ten," the woman said, gesturing with her free hand to a sign on the door that Sam only just noticed.

Sam checked her watch. It was barely past nine and she was already regretting her decision to see Chase Sullivan, instead of calling him. On the ferry ride over, she'd wondered why the impulse had struck her at all. Hadn't she found the man totally irritating the last time she'd been on Bainbridge? Furthermore, she had to get back to the city in time for a noon phone call from an East Coast client. Perhaps she wanted to see his face when she told him Emily wanted to meet with him. She didn't have to be a real private investigator to know you could tell a lot from someone's face, especially at an emotional moment.

The woman stepped closer to the knee-high picket fence surrounding her tiny storefront and said, "If it's really important—and I know Chase can use the business—he's down the street having his morning coffee. Make a right just before you hit the main intersection. A few doors in from the corner. The Primrose Café. He's there every morning."

"Thanks, I appreciate it." As she headed for her car, the woman called out, "Easier to walk. It'll take ten minutes and parking in that section can be a hassle."

"Okay, thanks again." Sam hitched her shoulder bag higher and walked briskly toward the central shopping and tourist area of Winslow, the island's official town.

The short walk brought back memories for Sam, when she and her sister came here on school visits and, sometimes, with Nina and out-of-town guests. The community, with its arts-and-culture focus, pretty marinas and tourist shopping was a convenient thirty-five-minute ferry ride from the Seattle docks and many people who lived on the island commuted into the city to work.

Until yesterday, Sam hadn't made the trip to Bainbridge in more than fifteen years. The noticeable changes were along the main drag, with a profusion of tourist shops competing for space with longtime stores that provided the basic necessities. If Bainbridge was bigger, Sam guessed the big-box stores would start sprouting up as they had on the mainland. Perhaps they already had, somewhere beyond the central area. Still, she could see why someone with artistic talent and a penchant for a quieter life might opt to live here. Or perhaps someone with a past he wanted to forget.

As soon as she spotted Primrose Café, Sam stopped to think about how she was going to tackle the meeting. He'd be surprised of course, and not pleasantly. So he'd either take the offensive right away and try to get rid of her as quickly as possible, or he'd refuse to speak to her altogether. Her best strategy would be polite insistence. Besides, he didn't seem the type to make a scene in a public place.

She saw him as soon as she stepped inside. He was sitting in a corner booth, facing the door and reading the *Seattle Times*. She hesitated, reminding herself that she was here for Emily and Danny, not to score points in the game of getting the last word. And if she managed to keep the talk polite, she might even find out something about his past. Something she could use to persuade Skye to leave the man and his family alone.

He didn't look up from his paper for a full thirty seconds while she stood in front of him. When he did, his expression of shock was immediately followed by apprehension. No, thought Sam, more like fear. *He thinks I'm stalking him.* Although the notion amused her, she didn't dare smile. Instead she got right to the apology.

"I'm really sorry to bother you again, Mr. Sullivan, especially here in the middle of your...uh—" she glanced down at the half-filled coffee mug and plate of crumbs "—breakfast, but I spoke to Emily Benson last night and she's changed her mind."

He frowned, but said nothing.

"She would like to see you, after all, as soon as possible."

His face remained impassive, though she noted a slight tightening around his jaw. He folded the paper and set it on the bench beside him. "You came all the way here to tell me that?"

Sam shrugged. "Unfortunately I neglected to get your phone number yesterday." It was almost the truth, she told herself.

"Getting the facts must be lesson one in the private eye's manual," he said.

She forced a smile. "Probably, but like I said, I'm not a private investigator. Mind if I sit?"

"Suit yourself, but I have to open up at—"

"Ten. That gives us forty minutes."

He raised an eyebrow.

"The woman who runs the store next to your place."

"Ah, that would be Marjorie."

"Very helpful," Sam said as she sat on the banquette seat across from him.

"Our local neighborhood watch," he muttered. He was about to say more when a waitress appeared to ask Sam if she wanted coffee.

"Chase?" She turned away after getting Sam's order. "More coffee?"

"Sure, Laura." After she left, he placed his elbows on the table, intertwining his fingers while studying Sam. "Why the sudden change of mind from Emily?"

He was getting right to the point—and beating her to it, as usual. "She can't put Danny off much longer. Plus, she doesn't like deceiving him."

"What do you mean?"

"He doesn't know about you yet. I mean," she added at the confusion in his face, "he doesn't know that I found you."

He frowned. "This is all very very strange. Almost disorienting. I keep thinking I'm going to wake up to find it's all been a…"

"Bad dream?"

"Yes. And I don't mean because my life has suddenly been turned upside down or that I'm afraid to accept responsibility for a foolish act when I was younger—none of that. Just that I don't have a clear picture of any of this. I don't know how or where it started."

The dark circles under his eyes and his sober, unshaved

face said it all. The man was suffering and, unexpectedly, Sam felt sorry for him. Until she wondered how Emily would react to the description of Danny's conception as a "foolish act."

"Look, Mr. Sullivan…"

"Make it Chase. We may not be friends, Miss Sorrenti…"

"Samantha. Or Sam."

He nodded. "Samantha, but it's apparent you know much more about me than the average acquaintance."

And maybe more than you think, Chase Sullivan. "Not really," she lied, "but you're right. I should start from the beginning. I think I told you when we first met that I have this business—I find things for people—and Danny found my Web site when he was searching for local private investigators."

"And he persuaded you to help him."

"He's a pretty persuasive kid," she said. The waitress came then with a mug for Sam and the coffeepot. Sam thought he looked grateful for the interruption. Chase insisted on paying and after she left with the money, Sam went on to say, "Once I met Emily, I couldn't refuse. They were both so desperate for…for something to hang on to. Some hope."

At that, she busied herself with her coffee. She didn't dare look up, fearing he'd think she was trying to pull his emotional strings. But when she risked a peek, she saw that he was still stirring his coffee, staring into the mug.

After a long moment, he raised his head and asked, "So how did you manage to find me so quickly? I'm not in the phone book."

Now comes the tricky part, thought Sam. Keeping Skye out of the equation. "Well, I Googled 'Winston Sullivan' and got your father."

His coffee mug stopped midway to his mouth. "Why that name? Emily knew me as Daniel Winston."

"Why the alias?" she countered.

His face took on a faraway look. "It's a long story," he said, sipping his coffee. When he set it down again, he checked his watch. "And there's no time for it today, I'm afraid. You've got fifteen more minutes to fill me in."

Sam felt a surge of annoyance. "And likewise mine is a long story. Let's just say I have some connections."

That got his attention. "Oh? What kind of connections?"

Sam decided the talk had taken a wrong turn. "Is that really important right now? The fact is that Emily would like to see you and time is running out."

He rubbed his forehead. "I don't really know what she expects, other than child support. And if Danny is my son, of course I'll pay it. Somehow."

She recalled the neighbor's comment about how Chase could "use the business". Still, the man must have some money if he was paying for his mother's care at Harbor House. She watched him fidget with his spoon. He seemed nervous. But then she pictured Emily, pinning her hopes on this man.

"I think Emily's not worried too much about money, though I'm sure her medical bills are huge." Sam leaned forward, stressing the point she wanted to make. "I believe she and Danny are more interested in *father* support."

He looked up, his dark brown eyes large in his drawn face. "*Father* support. Yeah, I can relate to a kid wanting that." Then, as if he'd said too much, he finished off the rest of his coffee and stood up. "I have to go."

Sam followed him out of the café. His stride was long and brisk and she trotted at his heels like a puppy. "When do you think you'll be calling her?"

He stopped. The look on his face made her add, "Just that she'll be waiting to hear from you."

"What's your stake in all this?"

The question took her aback. She wasn't sure she could even explain. "I just…as I told you…I was touched by both of them." She stepped aside for a woman pushing a stroller and when she turned her face to him again, something in his eyes made her blurt, "I don't know why. I can't seem to let it go."

He nodded. "Well, that may be the first honest thing you've said to me this morning." He resumed walking.

Sam was speechless. She slowed her pace, not trusting herself to say another word, assuming that was even possible. A few feet shy of the shop, Chase halted again. His neighbor, Marjorie, was sweeping the sidewalk in front of her store.

He waited for Sam to catch up to him and in a low voice asked, "What floor at Our Lady of Mercy?"

"Ten. The palliative-care unit."

"Thank you," he said, and marched up to the front door of his shop. Marjorie said something to him while he was unlocking the door, but Sam could tell he wasn't interested in making small talk. He nodded at her and stepped inside, closing the door.

Sam stood on the sidewalk, feeling as if she'd been ditched on her high-school dance floor.

Marjorie looked her way and smiled brightly. "Changed your mind?" she asked.

"Hmm?" Sam frowned. "Oh…er…yes."

"That's a shame," the woman said. "He does wonderful work."

"I'm sure," Sam murmured, and headed for her car, catching a glimpse of Marjorie's curious face as she did.

CHASE PAUSED in the open doorway. Emily was lying propped against two pillows and watching something on the small overhead television. He took in the oxygen tank at her bedside, the tangle of translucent plastic tubing and the solitary plant perched on the windowsill. A confusion of emotions overwhelmed him. *Thirteen years ago I would have hightailed it.* It was a shameful admission, but he also knew he was no longer that self-centered young man. He'd made amends in many ways. This was just one more.

Inhaling deeply, he tapped lightly on the door frame. Emily's head slowly swung his way. Her face paled even more. Chase cleared his throat. "Hi, Emily," he said, and walked toward the bed.

Her blue eyes were huge in the sunken cheeks of her face. Chase stood staring down at her, at a complete loss for words. Then he pulled a chair closer to the bed, sat down and gently lifted her hand from the bed, wrapping it tenderly in his.

CHAPTER SIX

SAM WAS PRINTING out a bill of sale for a client when the phone rang. As she reached for it, she noticed Our Lady of Mercy Hospital on the call display. She stared at the number, letting the phone ring twice more before summoning the courage to pick up.

"Sam?"

"Hi, Emily. Everything okay there?"

"Yes. Great. He came to see me the day before yesterday."

"Chase?"

"Chase. Daniel. I'm still not used to calling him that."

"Has he met Danny yet?"

"Yesterday. I told him Danny would be by after school and he came, too, just a bit later. Gave me time to tell Danny he was coming."

"And how did it go?"

There was a long pause, followed by a sigh. "Not the way I expected."

"What do you mean?"

"Danny seemed real subdued. When I told him you'd found Chase, he seemed almost scared and when they met, he barely said a word."

Sam wasn't surprised. "I think that's a natural reaction, don't you? I mean, now that his fantasy has been realized, he may be questioning if it's what he really wanted, after all."

"You think? I never thought of it that way. Another reason I was calling you is that Minnie came to see me today and—"

"Minnie?"

"My neighbor, the one who's taken Danny in while I've been here."

"Oh, right."

"She got a call from his school—seems he's been playing truant a lot more than I suspected."

That didn't surprise Sam.

"Anyway, the principal wants Minnie—or Danny's guardian—to go to some meeting about this. The problem is that Minnie has real bad arthritis and to tell the truth, I think she's at the end of her rope with Danny. I'm not sure how much longer I can impose on her."

Sam had a bad feeling where the talk was going. She decided to step right in. "Then I guess it's a good thing you've found his father."

There was another silence. "Yeah, but…it seems unfair to put this on Chase, don't you think? I mean, he's still getting used to the idea of having a son at all, much less having to deal with a problem and I was wondering, since you know Danny already…" Her voice trailed off.

"Emily, I hardly know Danny. Don't you think he's better represented by a school counselor or someone?"

"I was thinking more of someone not connected to the school who could, you know, advocate for him."

"Where and what time is this meeting?" She jotted down the details and before hanging up, said, "Please tell Danny I'll meet him in the principal's office."

"Of course and, Sam, thank you so much. Really."

"Glad to do it, Emily."

"And you know what?"

"What?"

"He's really changed. Not at all like he was thirteen years ago."

Chase, she meant. "I guess that's a good thing."

"For sure. I mean, he was always a decent person, but now he doesn't seem so uptight."

Really? I hadn't noticed myself. Sam wondered how Emily felt emotionally about seeing Chase again but didn't have the nerve to ask.

"Anyway, seeing and talking to him made me feel that he'll do right by Danny." Her voice fell. "I don't know what the future holds for them, but I think things will work out. And it was good for me in another way—made me realize the Daniel I knew would never have been a good match for me." Her chuckle ended in a coughing fit.

Sam waited, wishing there was something she could do to ease the woman's suffering.

"Sam," she said when she'd recovered somewhat, "please let me know what I owe you—"

"Emily, I'm not even a real P.I. Forget about it— please!"

"It could never be enough, know what I mean? You've made the next few weeks more…more hopeful for me and Danny."

Sam reached for a tissue on her desk and dabbed at her eyes. "That's more than enough payment right there, Emily."

"Thanks, Sam. Listen, I'm kinda tired now. Call me tomorrow—after the meeting, would you? And again, Sam, thank you."

The line disconnected abruptly. Sam sat very still for a long time before calling the one person in the whole world she wanted to see right then. Her mother.

"I'M IN THE KITCHEN, dear," Nina called out as Sam, shouting a hello, walked in the front door.

Sam threw her purse and jacket onto the closest chair and joined her mother, who was arranging flowers in a vase.

"Those are pretty," she said.

"Yes, they are. I love the first tulips of spring. Skye brought them."

"Oh? Is she here now?"

"Not yet, but I'm expecting her soon. After you called, I thought it would be nice for all of us to have dinner at Domani's."

"I wasn't expecting to stay for dinner."

Nina looked up from her flowers. "Do you have plans?"

"No, but—"

"Then you must come. The three of us haven't been together since Christmas."

Christmas. "Look, Mom, I need to talk to you about something."

Nina moved closer to Sam, concern in her face. "Are you okay?"

Sam smiled. The serious business of the world always faded in importance when Nina's daughters might be in trouble. "Yes, I'm fine. It's about that boy and his mother—Emily and Danny Benson."

"Oh, yes! Skye said you met the father."

She did, did she? What else did my meddling sister have to say? Sam's jaw tightened.

"Is there a problem?" her mother was saying while anxiously searching Sam's face.

"It's Danny," she said.

"Uh-huh. Look, dear, let's sit in the solarium. Shall I put the kettle on? Or would you like something stronger?"

The Sorrenti family cure for whatever ailed you. Tea and talk. Sometimes something stronger than tea. Sam thought back to the other day when Skye was at her place.

For a few minutes the tension had been lifted by the chit-chat and wine—until Skye's parting comments.

"Nothing, Mom," she said, deciding to try to finish the talk before Skye came home.

They sat in the small solarium in the L at the end of the living room. A small terrace separated this area from the kitchen, and as Sam sat on the love seat she realized she was facing the same view as she had been at Christmas. When Skye was finishing the last of the pots and pans and Todd had crept up behind her, encircling her waist with his arms and spinning her around to plant a long—very long—kiss on her lips. Lips that were identical to Sam's. *But not Sam's.*

"What is it?" her mother asked. "You look so pensive."

"Emily called me this afternoon and apparently Danny's been truant from school. She asked me to go to a meeting with his principal—as his advocate."

"Surely the father…"

"Exactly what I said, but Emily thinks it's too soon to drag him into a problem with Danny. Maybe she's worried it'll put him off—you know, make him rethink the whole parenthood thing."

"A bit late for that."

Sam smiled. "Yes, I agree. But I feel obliged to help."

"Dear, what's the basis of this relationship you seem to have established with Emily and her son?"

Sam slumped back onto the love seat. "Mom, I really don't need any analysis at the moment, trust me. I think Danny needs counseling and I want to know if you can get him a referral to someone. Hopefully someone inexpensive."

"Unless Emily has private insurance…"

"I think she must have some kind of plan—she's got a private room in the palliative-care ward. But all that can be worked out later."

"Obviously her son has a great deal of anxiety about what the future holds for him, hence the acting out at school."

Sam couldn't resist teasing. "Gee, Mom, you think?"

Nina smiled. "Stop mocking me, Samantha. All right. I'll see what I can do. I mean, I'd offer to help the boy myself, but I don't think it's appropriate."

"Not arm's length enough?" Sam quipped. It was a line she and Skye had trotted out as teenagers whenever Nina tried to counsel them.

"No, and now I'm going to speak to you as your mother. I believe you've taken on quite a lot with the Bensons. Don't interrupt. Let me have my say before you dismiss well-intentioned advice. Part of me is pleased that you're a caring person willing to help someone at such a painful time, but another part is worried that you're becoming embroiled in that family's troubles and you may have difficulty extricating yourself from ongoing responsibility for them. When the time comes—when this tragic situation unfolds, as you and I both know it will—will you be able to deal with it?"

Sam reached over and took her mother's hand. "Mom, I assure you that I'll be fine."

"What do you think of the father? Is he a decent man? Will he stand by his obligations?"

Sam smiled. Nina often reverted to her own rearing with its focus on old-fashioned values when dealing with personal issues. She recalled many would-be boyfriends being grilled in just such terms. *And one who probably ought to have been.*

"I haven't quite figured him out, but he hasn't shirked the whole paternity thing, so I've a feeling he'll be there for Danny."

Nina's gaze was fixed on Sam. "Well, that's a start.

But don't you think you've done all you can do for that family now?"

"Of course. The rest is up to them."

"Yes." Nina paused a second. "Then why did you agree to go to this meeting about Danny?"

"Did I say I agreed to go?"

Nina smiled indulgently. "Yes, dear. You said you felt obliged."

Sam smiled ruefully. "I did, didn't I. I don't know why exactly I felt obliged, but I'm sure that'll be the extent of my ongoing responsibility."

"How can you be sure?"

"Because Danny now has a father to support him."

"That's not a certainty. And then there's Danny. He may reject this new person in his life."

"But it's what he wanted! He was obsessed with finding his father."

"That's when the letdown can happen. After the finding part."

Sam sighed. "I came here to feel better, not more confused."

"Confused? Who's confused?"

Sam and Nina turned as one to where Skye was standing in the entrance to the solarium. "Have I interrupted something?"

For once Sam was grateful for her sister's timing. "Nope. We were just discussing a mutual acquaintance," Sam quickly said. "And Mom's treating us to dinner. At Domani's."

"Ah, just like old times."

Sam kept her eyes fixed on Skye. She had no intention of bringing Danny, Emily and especially, Chase Sullivan, into any further conversation with Skye. She also knew her mother's professional discretion would kick in. Nina had always managed a fine balance in negotiating arguments between her daughters while respecting their confidences. It was a trait Sam had learned to appreciate over the years.

As Nina got up to get ready to go out, she turned to Skye. "And how did you spend your day, dear?"

"Catching up with some old friends," she answered, following her mother into the living room.

It wasn't until much later, on the drive back to her apartment, that Sam realized during the entire dinner Skye had not referred to her day again. Nor to the "old friends" she'd supposedly contacted. By the time she was turning out her bedside light, she'd convinced herself that those friends might have been former business colleagues. Skye was up to something, and she had a feeling it was going to end in another quarrel. Or worse.

THE NEXT MORNING Sam was almost out the door of her office to go to the meeting at Danny's school when the phone rang. She paused, debating whether to let it go to voice mail. She was running late and didn't want to get stuck in a long conversation with a client. On the other hand, she'd been expecting important information from a dealer in New York and hated to extend the matter with an endless game of telephone or e-mail tag. She strode back to her desk and looked down at the phone. The call display flashed Sullivan.

Sam froze, then grabbed for the phone. "Chase?"

"Hello, Samantha." He got right to the point, as usual. "I was talking to Emily last night, arranging for Danny to spend the weekend with me, when she mentioned the meeting you're going to this morning. I'd like to tag along."

"How did you get my number?"

There was a slight pause followed by a low chuckle. "Well, I guess you're not the only one good at sleuthing. I helped myself to a Seattle directory."

"You're his father. Why don't you go to the meeting instead of me."

The voice became a bit chillier. "I suppose I was thinking of Danny. He's only met me once. I thought maybe he'd feel more comfortable if you were also there. I simply wanted to be kept informed on what's happening."

Sam had to give him credit for that. "Does Emily know you want to go, too?"

"No. I didn't think of it until after I talked to her last night. I assumed she wouldn't mind."

Grudgingly Sam said, "I'll meet you at the school then. The meeting's in forty-five minutes. Can you make it from the island in time?"

"I'm already in the city."

Sam gave him the address for the school and rang off. Traffic was light, but the school was in the northeast area of the city, in Greenwood. A long way from Emily's hospital. Sam thought of Danny going all that way on his own on public transit. The kid had gumption.

The idea that she was attending a school meeting as a substitute parent for a boy she'd known less than a couple of weeks was bizarre. The Benson family business had taken up a lot of her personal time, but then again, what would she have been doing otherwise? It was a sad commentary on her life post-Todd.

Yet, it struck her that as much as her life without Todd was more solitary, except for the first few weeks after the Christmas debacle, it hadn't been unhappy. The thought had slowly been forming that she might be better off without Todd. Hadn't she sometimes thought they had little in common? If she was really honest with herself, hadn't she occasionally suspected he was a little too attentive to other women? That he might even have cheated on her? Of course, none of that excused her sister. Todd might not have known which one he was kissing—as he'd protested—but Skye most definitely had.

Sam spotted the two-story, yellow, stucco school building on her right. She swung into the semicircular driveway that fronted the school, parking right behind a rusting white pickup. As she got out of the car, Chase was climbing out from the truck.

He'd obviously taken some effort with his appearance. He was clean-shaven, and his gray crew neck pullover was topped by the pale-yellow collar of a shirt. Black jeans accentuated long, lean legs, which Sam noticed for the first time. All her other encounters with the man had been centered on her mission for Danny and Emily. Now, in such a neutral context, she could see that he was a very attractive man. If only he'd lighten up a bit. The smile he gave as she walked toward him was promising, suggesting this meeting with him might not begin as badly as the others had.

"Shall we go in?" he asked without any preamble. He headed for the door, holding it open for her.

A sign requesting visitors to report to the office and with an arrow pointing straight ahead was posted on the wall opposite the main door. They walked silently along a corridor lined with bulletin boards displaying samples of children's art and writing until they reached the glass-walled office.

A fortyish secretary sat at a desk behind the office reception counter and looked up. "May I help you?" she asked, smiling.

"We have a meeting with the principal," Chase said. "About Danny Benson."

The secretary got up and walked to the counter. "Oh, yes. And you are…"

"Chase Sullivan," he said, pausing slightly before adding, "Danny's father."

"Oh. Very good. Danny's mother called to say someone would be coming in on her behalf. Please have a seat Mr. and Mrs. Sullivan, and I'll let the principal know you're here."

Sam couldn't help smiling, though she didn't dare look at Chase. When they were ushered into the inner office, she quickly introduced herself as a friend of Danny's mother. The principal, a short, stocky man in his early fifties, shook hands and asked his secretary to call Danny from class.

As the door closed behind her, the first thing he said was, "We're aware of Danny's situation at home and have been giving him plenty of latitude regarding his behavior. But I regret to say there's been little improvement. Unfortunately Danny was involved in a physical altercation yesterday and I have no option but to suspend him for a couple of days."

Chase leaned forward in his chair and asked, "What was the reason for the fight?"

"I believe he was called a name and he retaliated physically. We try to teach our students to use words to express their feelings, rather than fists but…"

Sam's immediate thought was that Danny must have been pushed to the limit. She didn't see him as a child who'd use violence. She was about to ask what name he'd been called when Chase beat her to it.

The principal looked embarrassed. "I believe the boy who provoked Danny called him a bastard. And although he was the one who was injured, he was reprimanded very severely for using such language."

While the principal was talking, Sam watched Chase's reaction with interest. He paled visibly at the word *bastard*. Then a dark stain crept up from the collar of his shirt, suffusing into his face. His fingertips curled under his hands, resting on his thighs as if he were struggling not to leap across the desk and grab the other man. Or so it seemed to

Sam, but when Chase finally did speak, he sounded very much in control.

"I will certainly speak to Danny about the appropriateness of his actions and will have him write an apology to the boy he attacked. And I would like that boy to write an apology to Danny for what he called him."

The principal nodded. "Yes, of course. But given the physicality involved, I'm afraid the suspension still stands. Danny may return to school on Monday." He buzzed the intercom on his desk to have Danny sent in.

Danny walked in, closing the door behind him. He saw Sam first and flashed a sheepish smile. When he noticed Chase, the smile vanished. He perched on the edge of a chair next to the door. While the principal reiterated their conversation, Sam noticed that Danny kept taking sidelong glances at Chase.

As soon as the principal finished, Chase stood up, extended his hand and said, "Thank you sir, for informing us about this matter. I'll see that Danny's letter is sent off right away." Then he tapped Danny lightly on the shoulder, signaling him to stand.

Sam blurted a thank-you, as well, and followed Danny and Chase out of the office. When they reached the front door, Chase abruptly turned around and asked Danny if he needed to get anything from his classroom before leaving.

Danny's sullen no was a surprise to Sam, who'd always seen a much spunkier side to the boy. Chase simply said, "Fine, then let's get on our way."

Once outside, he stopped again. "You've got two days before the weekend. I spoke to your mother yesterday about your coming to my place on Friday, staying for the weekend. However, given that you can't go to school and your neighbor..." He paused, obviously forgetting her name.

"Minnie Schwartz," mumbled Danny.

"Right. Anyway, it sounds as if she might need a break from, well, supervising you so—"

"I can stay by myself at our apartment. I've done it before," blurted Danny. His face was red and he was frowning.

Sam couldn't tell if he was on the verge of tears or an angry outburst.

Chase looked down at Danny's bent head. "I don't think so, Danny. That's not an option."

No one spoke until Sam couldn't hold back any longer. "Actually I was wondering if Danny might want to come to my place. Or rather, my mother's house. She told me she'd like to meet you and—"

Chase shot her a withering look. "Perhaps the three of us should grab some lunch and talk about the next step."

Feeling foolish now, Sam said, "If you like. How about it, Danny?"

He shrugged.

Chase expelled a loud sigh. "Okay, lunch it is. There used to be a takeout burger place in the park at Greenlake. Not far from here. At any rate, I'm sure there's some kind of fast-food place around the lake. Danny, why don't you ride with Samantha? I'll lead the way." Without awaiting a reply from either of them, he headed for the pickup, climbed in and started the engine.

She shook her head, wondering why she'd come to the meeting only to have him very competently take charge. "C'mon, Danny."

As she followed the truck out the driveway and onto the street, Danny said, "Sorry you had to come all this way, Sam. But that guy had it coming. He's been bugging me for weeks."

Sam glanced at the boy, slumped on the seat beside her. "It's okay, Danny. I'm sorry you didn't tell anybody about that boy if he's been bullying you."

"I tried to, but no one would listen," he said, his voice rising. "Anyway, none of that matters anymore. I'm just sorry I made problems for my mom."

Sam reached out a hand to pat his arm. "Your mom understands."

"Yeah, I guess." He turned his head to look out the window. After a moment, he said, "What do you think of him?" He jutted his chin to the windshield and the truck in front of them.

She had no idea what to say. The question was so similar to her mother's she opted for a similar answer. "I'm not sure, to be honest. But I think if he didn't care about you, he wouldn't have come to the meeting today."

He thought about that. "Maybe. He's probably pissed—sorry—ticked off about me. Maybe he's even wondering how he can get out of, you know, the whole thing."

He didn't have to clarify what the "whole thing" was. And Sam didn't have the courage to insist otherwise. Danny might be right.

As the truck pulled into a parking lot adjacent to a burger stand, Sam turned to him and said, "I meant what I said about meeting my mother, Danny. She's a psychologist and knows a lot of people who are trained to counsel kids who…well, kids who…"

"Whose mothers are dying?"

She parked beside the truck and turned off the engine. "Kids who need to talk about their feelings. People need to do that, Danny. When they're grieving."

He raised his head, flicking back the hank of hair that seemed to perpetually droop across his forehead. "I'll think about it," he said, opened the door and got out.

Midweek, the park was virtually empty except for a few dog walkers and joggers. But the burger place was open. They took their orders to a picnic table under a tree and wolfed the food down silently. Danny finished first and, after tossing his refuse into a bin, wandered along the edge of the water. Hands in pockets and shoulders slumped, he seemed small and vulnerable against the larger backdrop of the lake.

"I sometimes forget he's only twelve," Sam said, watching him.

"It's a pivotal year," Chase said. "Once he's a teenager, greater expectations and responsibilities will be heaped on him."

He sounded so wistful Sam turned to him and asked, "Is that what happened to you?"

"How do you mean?"

She was startled by the suspicion in his voice. "Was more expected of you when you became a teenager?"

"There was more expected of me the instant I was *born.*"

Sam looked at him, caught by the bitterness in the reply, but he was staring off into the distance. Or into the past, she decided. Except for the scraps of information Skye had passed on, Sam knew little about his background. Scion of an old wealthy Seattle family. Hint of scandal or wrongdoing in the family business. Mother in exclusive nursing home. The only paradox in the whole mix was Chase himself.

Former motorcycle rider and current fine-furniture maker. Owner of beatup truck. Bearer of tattoo, now hidden under long sleeves. New father.

Not exactly the markings of a rebel, but Sam supposed that, set against where he came from, Chase Sullivan was a bit of an anomaly.

Her curiosity about him prompted her to ask, "I assume Greenwood is where Emily and Danny live, since his school is here. Is this where you were living and working when you met Emily thirteen years ago?"

"Yes," he said, still gazing out at the lake and Danny. "She was working in a diner when I met her. I was working at a construction site nearby."

Construction. Not the family business. She wanted to know more, but he abruptly stood up and said, "We should call Danny back and figure out where he's going to be for the next few days."

"I was talking to him about my mother on the way here," Sam said. "Mom is a clinical psychologist and she might be able to refer Danny to someone. Just so he can talk about Emily and…and everything." She felt suddenly nervous under his scrutiny.

Finally he said, "Yeah, that'd be good for him. He may not think he needs it now, but he will later." He glanced at Danny, slowly walking toward their picnic table. "But I guess he'll have to be the one to decide."

"Yeah, I'll leave it up to him—he has enough pressure right now."

"For sure."

The moment stretched between them and Sam felt an urge to fill it. "You were good with him, in the principal's office. Setting the record straight about the other boy's part in the fight. And you didn't jump on Danny."

He turned sharply from the lake to her. "I'd no right to jump on Danny. I may be his biological father, but I've yet to become the father he needs. Besides, if that had been me in Danny's place, I'd have done the same thing."

He flashed a smile that altered his whole face and Sam felt herself smiling back. When Danny reached them, they briefly discussed the next few days, finally agreeing that he would stay with Minnie until the end of the day on Friday and then go to Bainbridge with Chase for the weekend. Chase also suggested Danny ride home with him in the truck now, so that he could see where Danny lived, and the boy agreed. Reluctantly, it seemed to Sam.

"Don't forget to call if you decide to take me up on my offer," Sam reminded Danny as he was about to get into Chase's truck. "You know, what we discussed on the way here," she added at his frown.

"Oh, yeah, sure," he said. Then he grabbed her arm. "Hey, why don't you come to Bainbridge this weekend, too?"

"Oh, well, heavens, Danny…" Sam was at a loss for words. She glanced quickly at Chase, whose face was impassive, though she thought she saw a flicker of alarm in his eyes.

"Please?" He looked at Chase. "It would be all right, wouldn't it?"

Sam realized the boy was nervous about the trip. "I don't know, Danny. This is a chance for you to get to know your…well…Chase."

The man in question finally spoke up. "Why don't you come for lunch—maybe Saturday?"

Danny smiled expectantly at her as Sam struggled to find a way out. In the end, she could think of no excuse that wouldn't sound lame or mean-spirited. "Sure, that would be nice."

As she waved goodbye, she recalled her promise to her mother only yesterday. *That's it for my involvement with the family. Now the rest is up to them.* Yeah, right.

CHAPTER SEVEN

SKYE TOSSED the photocopied file onto the passenger seat of her mother's car and, starting up, pulled out of the parking lot of Seattle's FBI field office. She'd had no trouble getting the file, especially since she'd been the investigating agent thirteen years ago.

Many of the agents who'd been working there with Skye then had either retired or been transferred or promoted elsewhere. Except for the clerk in Records who'd teased, "Tying up loose ends, eh, Skye?" when she'd requested the file.

"You never know," she'd replied. "Anyway, gives me something to do in my holidays." She'd instantly regretted that because the clerk had given her a pitying look and said, "Don't tell me you've turned into another workaholic agent."

"Occupational hazard," she'd joked as she scooped up the file and headed for the copy machine.

If only it were a joke and not the pathetic truth, she thought as she drove. Although she'd tried to convince herself and Sam that she had to make the trip west for her mother's birthday, anyway, she knew arrangements could have been done by e-mail. The birthday itself wasn't for another month, and Sam had had every right to be suspicious of her motives for returning home so much earlier.

She bet her twin was seething about the interference

with her current project—the Benson/Sullivan family—and she couldn't blame her. Skye would never have thought of looking into the old inquiry if Sam hadn't called up asking for assistance. It was a lot easier for Skye to use that as an excuse to spend holiday time at home without having to spell out the main reason—she was tired of the estrangement from her sister and was hoping to put the whole Christmas-and-Todd fiasco to rest.

Yet now she was home, she had doubts that any reconciliation was possible. Whenever they were together they were like two alley cats. Fur raised, claws bared. Sam took everything she said the wrong way and all conversation inevitably led to that thing with Todd. The bane of Skye's life for the past six months. And it hadn't even been a good kiss.

Skye took another swig from the plastic coffee cup in the holder and contemplated her next move. A good cup of coffee seemed the first step—it was a crime that the office coffee could be so foul in the birthplace of Starbucks. Then she'd go back home, reread the file and make some notes. Next, she'd pay a little visit to Trade Winds, the import-export company Chase Sullivan's father had partly owned. After that, Bainbridge Island. In the original inquiry, she'd never interviewed Chase. He'd been off at a conference or out of the country somewhere. And after observing Sam's face when she'd teasingly suggested she might be attracted to the man, Skye's curiosity was significantly aroused. *Yes. Haven't been to Bainbridge in years.*

The light changed and she made a sharp turn, heading for a coffee outlet two blocks away. A large latte, cozy up on the couch in the solarium for a good read and then she'd toss a coin to see which came next. Trade Winds or Bainbridge. Sounded like a plan.

CHASE STOOD BACK for a better view of the room. He had two more days to rig up space for Danny and the task was proving to be a real challenge. No matter where he moved things, the problem remained. His place was just too damn small. Ironically it had been the size that appealed to him almost two years ago when he signed a lease agreement to rent the shop and the cottage behind it. It was definitely a huge change from his childhood home in Magnolia. That fact alone—as well as the price—had clinched the deal.

He'd spent most of the morning moving things from the small room off the kitchen that had served as storage and distributing them between the cottage and the shop. His neighbor, Marjorie, had watched from the backyard of her gift shop.

"You're not moving, are you?" she'd asked, peering over the waist-high fence.

Chase had stopped, shifting the carton in his arms. There was no point in being too vague about what was happening, because Marjorie would keep digging until eventually she'd mined all the gossip potential she could. After a few seconds, he'd explained, "I'm having company for the weekend—maybe longer."

"Oh? Someone from out-of-town?"

"No, someone from the city." He'd seen right away she wasn't going to be satisfied with that, so he'd set the box down and walked over to the fence. "My son." The words bounced around in his head. Their meaning had yet to sink in.

She'd gaped. "I'd no idea you were even married."

"I'm not—not anymore." he'd added quickly, recalling the epithet that Danny had been taunted with at school.

"My goodness! How old is he?"

"Uh…twelve…going on thirteen."

"For heaven's sake! Aren't *you* the dark horse!"

Chase had had no doubt that the news would spread rapidly up and down Primrose Lane, which was probably a good thing, saving him from making the explanation over and over again.

Most of the day had been a write-off. Even Marjorie lost interest after a while. By late afternoon, Chase had emptied the storage room of everything but a small table. He'd have to go into the city tomorrow to one of the chain stores to buy a cheap single bed and mattress, along with some other accessories to make the place look like a room and not a renovated storage area.

Still, the work had been a good physical diversion from the questions that had been plaguing him since the day he first met Samantha Sorrenti at Harbor House. Questions like, how did he get to know a twelve-year-old boy who, a week ago, was a complete stranger and who, now, was his son? Or, what would the two of them do for a whole weekend? And the biggest question of all—how would his life change?

He knew the answer to the last one. *In more ways than you can even foresee.* He was ashamed to admit to himself that a mere few years ago, that realization would have filled him with self-pity. But now that the initial shock had passed and the truth had registered—the instant he saw Danny, Chase knew he was his son—he'd come to accept that this was one responsibility he would not be able to walk away from. He remembered an old saying his father had thrown at him several times—"You've made your bed, now lie in it."

As a teenager, he'd loathed hearing that. Not just for its implicit dismissal of any and all troubles, but for its cold-ness. The underlying message was always clear: *You'll get no help from me.* The adult Chase Sullivan had grown to understand the reasons his father had uttered it. Which led to the question Chase feared the most.

Would he be a better father to Danny than his own father was to him?

He checked the time. A tourist was dropping by just after five to pick up a carving of a great blue heron. He'd started carving birds and other animals in the dark days of winter more than a year ago and had been surprised at their popularity with tourists. It made sense to diversify a bit. Not many people wandered in off the main drag to buy a cherrywood cabinet or a black walnut table. Most of his furniture sales were orders or commissions from specialty shops in New York or San Francisco. Some pieces had been sent as far away as Toronto, Canada. He could live modestly on Bainbridge on the sales of just three or four of these commissions, but the carvings drew the tourists into the shop.

He thought about Marjorie's reaction to the news he had a son and guessed that most of the residents on the lane would be equally surprised. He'd lived on the island for almost two years and had had no visitors. In fact, he seldom had company at all. When he'd first arrived, Marjorie had tried to set him up with a couple of women, but she'd eventually given up. Other than a handful of acquaintances, there was really no one else to be shocked— or pleased—at this new person in his life. The only person he knew who would have loved to know Danny was his mother. Sadly she didn't even recognize her *own* son anymore.

He closed the cottage door and walked up the stone path to the shop. He still had a few minutes to make up a shopping list for his trip into the city in the morning. The first thing he did was to turn over the Closed sign and unlock the front door. He noticed a car parked in front of Marjorie's place and wondered if she, too, had a late customer. The tourist season wouldn't pick up until late May so many stores closed at five, rather than six or even nine.

He recalled his remark to Samantha Sorrenti the other day about Marjorie as the local neighborhood watch and realized that he himself wasn't very good at noticing the comings and goings of the people on Primrose Lane. In many ways, full-time residence on Bainbridge was like living in a village. Especially given that the permanent population was only about twenty-five thousand or so, and most of those lived in Winslow.

He was just finishing the list in the workroom when he heard the doorbell tinkle. "Be right with you," he called out. There was no reply, so he set the paper and pencil down and peered into the showroom. When he saw a woman looking at a carving, her back to him, his immediate response was annoyance.

Samantha Sorrenti. What now? They'd already agreed that she'd come for lunch on Saturday. The woman was impossible. And obviously she wasn't here for any emergency, because she now had his phone number and so did Danny and Emily. Which meant she'd probably come to belabor some point or remind him to do something. Determined to hide his irritation, he forced a jocular tone into his greeting.

"Samantha," he said, walking toward her, "you're a full three days early. You're—"

She turned around, smiling.

He stopped. She looked like Samantha, though the hair seemed a bit different.

"Chase?"

She sounded like Samantha. She tilted her head and the smile became a tease.

"—not Samantha," he finished. He felt disoriented. How could she not be Samantha?

"You're quite right," she said, extending her hand. "I'm her twin sister, Skye. And you must be Chase Sullivan."

"Samantha didn't tell me she had a twin," he said.

"No? Well, perhaps she felt it wasn't important."

And of course it wasn't, he thought. Most of their talk had been centered on Danny or Emily. He searched her face for any telltale difference, still not quite sure how he'd guessed.

"And you are very good," she went on, "because few people can tell us apart, especially so quickly. Tell me," she said, moving closer, "what were the clues?" She fixed her gaze on his.

That was one right there. That almost provocative boldness.

"Just intuition, I guess."

"Uh-huh," she said. She studied him a bit longer and then, indicating the showroom, added, "You've got some wonderful pieces here. How're sales?"

That was another one. He doubted Samantha would have been so blunt. "Not bad, Miss Sorrenti."

"Please, under the circumstances, call me Skye."

"And what circumstances are those, Skye?"

"Well, you know Sam and..." For the first time, she seemed to falter.

She'd come to check him out, he realized. But why? For her sister? "Are you touring the island, or visiting my shop in particular?" he asked.

"I'd like to see around the island—it's been years since I was here last. But unfortunately I don't have the time today. And although your place is lovely, I actually came to speak to you."

Aha. She was checking him out. Anxious to ensure that her sister was not getting involved with some deadbeat dad? Or maybe this was some trick cooked up by the two of them. Fool Chase and see what admission he might make about…what? That was what stumped him. It wasn't as if he denied being Danny's father.

"About what?"

"About your family's business—Trade Winds."

Her reply was so unexpected that for a moment he couldn't speak at all. Every nerve and pulse in his body came to a complete halt.

When he failed to answer, she said, "In particular, an inquiry instigated some thirteen years ago by the Seattle FBI field office."

Ignoring the drumming in his ears, he asked, "What does my family's business have to do with Samantha?"

She smiled. "Not much. The big coincidence here is that *I* was the investigating agent at the time."

He'd have sat down at that, except he didn't want to appear weak. Besides, there was nothing handy.

"I no longer work out of that office," she went on, "but recently…well, a decision was made to reopen the inquiry."

"What? Why?"

She shrugged. "Maybe the office is just reviewing some cases, who knows? Anyway, since I never had the chance to interview you back then, I thought I might be able to ask you a few questions now."

His mouth was dry and his head teemed with far too many questions of his own. And he didn't want to address any of them to Skye Sorrenti. What he wanted was to get rid of her as quickly as possible.

The front door swung open then, the bell echoing in the silence.

"Hello," said the woman hesitantly, standing in the doorway. "You're still open, aren't you?"

Chase could not have greeted a customer more

warmly. "I've got the bird all packed up," he said, moving away from Skye.

"That's great. I hope I'm not taking you from anything?" She glanced from him to Skye.

"Not at all." He turned toward Skye, noting the pursed lips and frown. "Perhaps we could talk again, another time?"

She either didn't hear or was refusing to budge. He was about to repeat himself when she nodded curtly, muttered, "Definitely" and strode out the door.

Later, with a double scotch in hand, Chase sat down in his cottage and reflected on an afternoon that far outweighed, in potential for calamity, his first confrontation with Samantha at Harbor House. He had no idea why his past had been resurrected and was now poised and ready to dash his current life to pieces.

He didn't believe for a second that Samantha Sorrenti's twin sister—*an FBI agent!*—was coincidentally on the scene less than two weeks after the whole nightmare began. Obviously they had planned and prepared this, but to what avail? There was no connection that he could see between Emily and Danny and Trade Winds. Except, of course, that if the FBI inquiry had never occurred, he would never have met Emily. *And never had a son.* The endless possibilities of *if* spiraled through his mind. He downed the scotch and turned off the CD player. In three days he'd be seeing Samantha. Then he'd get some answers.

SAM KNEW SOMETHING was wrong the instant she walked into the shop on Saturday. Chase was talking to customers and his eyes flicked over her as she entered, but shifted without trace of a welcome immediately back to the couple. Not that she was expecting an effusive greeting, but a quick smile would have been nice. Perhaps the visit with Danny was not turning out well and for some reason, he held her responsible. No, she thought at once, he's not that petty.

She browsed idly around the display cases until Chase, on his way to the cash register, muttered, "Danny's in the cottage, behind the store. Go out the rear door in the workroom and along the path."

"Okay. Thanks," she muttered back, thinking, *you were the one who invited me for lunch!*

When she stepped outside, she felt as though she'd entered another world. A narrow but long yard, bordered on one side by a fence draped with a flowering vine and on the other by a row of tall pine trees, sloped gently down to what seemed to be a narrow river or channel. A stone cottage stood at the end of the pine trees, a few yards from the water. As Sam drew closer, she saw a makeshift wooden dock and an overturned red canoe.

The day was warm for early May and the screen door of the cottage was open. It was the kind of old-fashioned door Sam had seen in country-home magazines, with white-painted scrollwork framing the mesh. Perhaps Chase had made it himself. She walked up two stone steps to the door and tapped lightly.

"Danny? It's me, Samantha."

"I'm in the kitchen," he called out. "Straight through the living room and to the right."

Inside, the cottage was all that the screen door had suggested. Simplicity, style and comfort. The floors were hardwood and instead of a fireplace, there was a black woodstove against a wall lined with shelves of books. A tan-colored sofa and matching armchair were the only places to sit, though a magnificent, gleaming round coffee table, on which sat an enamel pitcher of daffodils, was definitely the showpiece of the room. The whitewashed stucco walls were bare except for a poster-size framed photograph of a northern landscape. A floor lamp stood beside the armchair and the stack of books and magazines on the floor next to it suggested this was where Chase spent time.

The living room ended in a large picture window that overlooked the river. A door to the right led into a sunny kitchen where Danny stood at a counter, chopping vegetables. The kitchen was half the size of the living room but large enough to contain a small harvest table along one wall. There was an exterior door, opened to reveal a screen door identical to the one at the front of the cottage.

"Well, Chef Danny," said Sam, smiling. "Are you preparing lunch today?"

He gave a token scowl, but Sam could tell his heart wasn't in it. "Just the salad. Does…uh…Chase still have customers?"

Sam heard the hesitation. At least he wasn't calling him Mr. Sullivan. "Yes. So, how's it been?"

He shrugged, but didn't look up from his chopping. "Okay, I guess."

"What did you do last night?"

"Not much. He doesn't even have cable! He said maybe we could rent some DVDs today."

"Has it been boring, then?"

Danny raised his head. "At first. But last night he helped me with a carving, and then today's been okay. We went out in the canoe early this morning and saw some neat birds. Stuff like that. And he said maybe sometime he'd teach me how to do some things around his workshop. You know, like sanding."

"That would be interesting."

The scowl returned. "I guess." He went back to the salad.

Sam waited a few moments before asking, "Have you thought some more about the counseling idea?"

"Yeah, but I haven't decided yet."

She knew not to push the issue. At least he was thinking about it.

"Can I help?" she asked.

He turned his hands, palms up. "I don't know. Chase said to chop this stuff for salad and there's a bowl on the counter over there. I don't know about dressing or anything."

"I'll look in the fridge." It was well stocked for a bachelor, she thought, but then realized he must have shopped with a teenager in mind as there was a lot of milk and a big bottle of cola. A platter with an assortment of cheeses was on a shelf and she pulled it out, along with a bottle of salad dressing.

Danny had finished his task and was leaning against the table, his head bowed and his arms folded across his chest. He seemed a bit lost, and Sam knew that the events of the past week must be overwhelming. She set the items from the fridge on the counter and went over to Danny, touching his forearm.

"It'll be okay, Danny. One day at a time."

He raised his head, his eyes shining with tears. "Yeah," he said huskily, "that's what Mom says. And I try to do that, but sometimes, you know, in the middle of the night I wake up and…"

Sam pulled him into a hug. They were still standing like that seconds later when Chase walked into the kitchen.

He paused, then went to the fridge. "Salad looks good," he said as he pulled out some cold meat and condiments.

Sam patted Danny's back and withdrew, then helped to transfer the lunch items from the counter nearest the fridge to the table.

"What would you like to drink?" Chase asked. "I've got wine, iced tea, milk, water, soda, juice. The usual."

"Iced tea sounds good," said Sam.

"Water," said Danny, adding "please," a second later.

Chase put a bread board with two crusty loaves on the table and gestured for them to sit. Sam couldn't recall the last time she'd felt so uncomfortable. She tried to kickstart a conversation, but every attempt fizzled.

Suddenly Chase suggested that Danny go up to the workshop and bring the carving he'd started the night before. The instant Danny left the kitchen, Chase said, "I had a visitor a couple of days ago."

"Oh?" Sam was more mystified by the expression on his face than the comment itself.

"Your sister."

"Skye?" Sam dropped the piece of bread she was buttering onto her plate.

"That's the name she gave. And I admit it was a bit of a shock, since I didn't know you had a twin."

The accusation in his voice rankled. "Look, it's not as if we've exchanged CVs or anything."

"True enough, though I think you already know quite a lot about me. Maybe it's time you reciprocated."

"Is that necessary now? I mean, you know I have a twin."

"A twin?" Danny stood in the doorway. "Cool. How come you never told me?"

Sam caught Chase's smirk as she looked from him to Danny. "'Cause it never really came up, Danny. What's that you've got?"

He held up a block of wood roughly shaped like a boat. "I started it last night." He handed the piece of wood to Sam.

"It's gonna be a tugboat."

"Why don't you get the drawings for it?" Chase suggested.

Danny looked from him to Sam and back again. "Sure," he mumbled, and headed out again.

"You haven't asked the big question yet," Chase said to Sam.

She knew at once what he meant but was hoping Danny would return fast and save her from answering. "What question?"

"Why your sister was here." He kept his voice low.

"I've no idea why she came here," she replied.

"Oh, I think you do." He glared at her across the table.

"Actually, I don't."

"You expect me to believe that? You have a twin who *happens* to be an FBI agent who *happens* to have investigated my family years ago. If you're telling me this is all some weird coincidence, I'm not buying it."

Sam stood up and pushed back her chair. "I don't know why she came to see you. And I have no intention of being grilled like this. I'm not the criminal here."

"What did you say?"

She didn't dare look at him. "I better leave," she muttered. She reached for her purse slung over the back of her chair.

"Sam? What's the matter?" Danny stood in the kitchen doorway. He looked very upset.

"I'm sorry, Danny. I have to leave. Something's… come up."

She scarcely glanced his way as she brushed past him. "I'll call you Monday. Good luck at school." As she marched into the living room, she heard Danny's voice behind her.

"What happened, Chase? What did you say to her?"

CHAPTER EIGHT

SAM GOT AS FAR as the sidewalk and stopped, still hearing the dismay in Danny's voice. She was behaving like a child, running off when things got tough. She couldn't do that to Danny, and whatever Skye was up to, she owed it to Chase to at least set the record straight.

So she turned around and followed the path along the side of the building, back into the yard and down to the cottage. Humiliation time. The kitchen was so quiet at first she thought they'd left. They both looked up, surprised. Danny's grin made up for her embarrassment.

"I…uh…changed my mind," she said. "I don't have to get back after all. I see you haven't gone on to dessert yet, so that's a good thing." She slung her purse back over her chair and sat down. Chase got up and without a word, set another plate in front of her. Danny passed her the salad and they finished the lunch with a minimum of small talk. After a dessert of fruit salad, Danny insisted on washing up.

"Chase will show you around the yard," he prompted.

"That won't take long," Chase said, "but there's a bench by the river."

Sam got the hint. "Well, it's a lovely spring day and I'd like to see the river."

When Chase closed the door behind them, she added, "Almost thirteen and going on thirty."

"I'm beginning to think so. Maybe thirteen is the new thirty."

Sam laughed. When he grinned back, she was struck by how much he resembled Danny. And because of that, she felt a sudden connection with him.

But then his face turned serious. "Thanks for coming back. I was worried for a moment that the whole weekend was going down the tube."

"It was silly of me to run off like that, as if I'd done something wrong."

He just kept looking at her. "Shall we head for the bench?" he finally asked and, without waiting for her reply, led the way to the river's edge and a small white bench under a sprawling willow tree.

When they were seated, Sam stared at the narrow river with its weedy shore, then at the cottages and homes jutting out of the trees on the other side. Craning her neck, she could see a bridge downriver and the beginning of the large marina that served the town.

"It's very pretty here," she said. "When I came to Bainbridge as a child, I only saw the main drag and regular tourist places. Though once we came by car and drove out to the one of the beaches. I can't remember the name."

"Tell me about your sister," he said.

Okay, so small talk isn't going to distract him.

"She's an FBI agent and once was stationed in Seattle. Now she's in Washington, D.C."

"She said she investigated my family. What do you know about that?"

"Not much." Sam met his eyes. "There was an allegation of fraud or something. She said the inquiry didn't turn up anything and the case was closed. End of story."

"I wish," he muttered.

"Look," she said, "whatever happened years ago has nothing to do with you and Danny."

He looked across the river. "Maybe not, but I'm confused by the timing of all this. Why now?" He turned back to Sam. "Danny's told me some of it—how he found you and so on. What bothers me is your sister's part. You said she no longer works in Seattle, so why has it happened that when she visits Seattle, the case is suddenly reopened? I can only think that it was at *her* initiative. What's she after?"

Sam took a deep breath. "To tell you the truth, I don't know. You've got to believe me," she said at the change in his face. "I called her to ask for some help right after I met Emily. I wasn't really expecting to find you at all, but finding you turned out to be much easier than I thought."

"Because of what your sister told you," he said quietly.

"Yes. I probably would never have found you on my own because the only name Emily knew you by was—"

"Daniel Winston."

"Right. Why did you use an alias? Did it have something to do with the case?"

"In a roundabout way. Frankly, I don't want to discuss that at the moment. I just want to find out what your sister intends to do."

And that was the crux of the problem, Sam thought. "I don't know. Skye is one of those people who—you know the saying—marches to the beat of her own drum. She and I haven't been as close as we were when we were kids. And until she arrived a couple of days ago, I hadn't seen her since Christmas."

"Really? Why is that?"

"I don't want to get into that right now."

"So we both have our secrets." His dark brown eyes revealed no hint of irony.

"I guess we do," she said. "But the important thing in all this is Danny. He needs to know that he'll have a father to look after him when Emily…"

"Precisely," he said. "Which is why I'm asking you to find out exactly what your sister is planning and to do whatever you can to prevent her from pursuing the case."

His face was dead sober. Sam had the feeling that the request was more of an order. Then Danny's shout broke the spell. They both turned toward the cottage. He was standing just outside the cottage back door. "I'm finished," he announced.

Chase waved, signaling they were coming. He stood up and offered a hand to Sam, helping her to her feet. His grasp was strong and his fingers callused from his trade. He continued to hold on to her hand.

"Danny wants us to go to the center of town with him. Perhaps we can get back to our conversation later?" He applied more pressure and Sam knew for sure that his request was an order.

She wrenched her hand free. "Of course," she said.

Danny gave her a questioning look as she came up to him. Wanting to know if whatever had happened between her and Chase was now resolved? she wondered. Sam tousled his hair and said, "Let's go do some sightseeing."

"You two go ahead. I should probably open up the shop again," Chase said as he caught up to them.

"Are you sure?" Danny asked.

"Of course." Chase looked from him to Sam. "Don't forget to pop in and say goodbye before you head back to the city."

She almost saluted, but settled for a quick "sure" as she looped her arm through Danny's and headed up to the street.

They walked silently for a bit until Danny said, "I'm

glad you came back, Sam." He paused, then added hesitantly, "Did he say something to upset you?"

"It was a misunderstanding," she said, "and it had nothing to do with you."

"But I thought you hardly knew him."

"Well, that's true. Oh, look, isn't that cute?" She pointed at a window display of a miniature fishing village.

Danny either saw through her diversionary tactic or wasn't interested, because he scarcely glanced at the window. "I guess you must know more about him than I do, because you searched for him."

She knew right away what he was hinting at. "Danny, the best person to ask about Chase is your mom. And of course, the man himself."

"He's pretty quiet," Danny said. "He asks me stuff about myself and my mom, too, but he never talks about himself. Just about his business mostly."

"Where did he learn to carve and make furniture?"

"He said he traveled around a lot after he and my mom broke up. He lived in Alaska for a long time and worked for a carpenter there. That's when he learned how to make furniture."

Like Emily, Chase had apparently given Danny a version of the relationship that made him feel part of something real, not just the byproduct of a one-night stand. It was obvious the man was both insightful and sensitive—which certainly was a major contrast with the way he grilled her about Skye. Definitely a man of contradictions.

"He must have told you something about his own family," she said.

"Only that his father is dead and his mother is in a nursing home."

"I see." But she didn't really. Why the mystery? Sure, his family business had been investigated for fraud, but hadn't Skye said Chase wasn't even questioned? That there hadn't been enough evidence to take the inquiry further? What could the man possibly be hiding?

"Sam?"

"Hmm?" She looked down at Danny's frowning face.

"I asked if you'd like an ice cream from the best place in all of Seattle."

"Oh. Sorry, Danny. Yes, I'd love to. How sweet of you."

He gave a sheepish grin. "It was actually Chase's idea. He gave me the money."

"In that case, I think a double is in order. Lead on."

They ate their waffle cones while walking back to Primrose Lane. Just as they reached the front of Chase's shop, a woman from the adjacent store was saying good-bye to someone in a car at the curb.

Sam recognized her immediately from her last visit to the island.

The woman turned to them as the car pulled away. "Hello, there," she said. "You must be Chase's son," she said to Danny and, smiling at Sam, said, "We haven't officially met, but I've seen you a couple of times."

"Oh, right. I'm Samantha Sorrenti and this is Danny."

"I'm Marjorie Lawrence. Chase told me he had a son coming for the weekend. Such a private guy, isn't he? I mean, we've been neighbors for almost two years and I just found out he had a son the other day!"

Sam smiled, but said nothing, recalling Chase's referral to the woman as the "neighborhood watch."

"How do you like Bainbridge so far?" Marjorie asked Danny.

"It's cool. Different."

"Not as much to do here as in the city, I suppose."

He shrugged. "The city can get boring, too," he said.

"True enough," she said, laughing. Then turning to Sam,

she said, "I know you like it because you keep coming back. That's a good sign. I waved at you when you were here the other day, but I guess you didn't see me."

Skye. Rather than get into a tiresome explanation—and she'd had enough of Skye for the day—Sam said, "No, I didn't. Sorry about that." She looked at Danny. "We'd better let your father know we're back," she said, ushering him up the sidewalk.

Chase was in the back of the shop working and got up to greet them.

"Thanks for the treat," Sam said, holding up the remains of her cone.

"Glad you enjoyed it," he said.

Rather than have to go through another question-answer period about her sister, Sam said, "I should get going. I have some work to do in the city. Thanks for inviting me. Lunch was great."

They walked her out to her car and while Danny's attention was caught by a passing group of teens, Chase quickly spoke in Sam's ear. "Don't forget to talk to your sister."

Sam pulled her head back to look him in the eye. "As soon as I can."

He nodded. "And, uh…I'm sorry if I seemed a bit intense earlier. It's…" He paused, as if at a loss for words.

"A long story?"

He gave a half smile. "Yeah. Someday I hope to fill you in on the rest of it."

The admission took her by surprise. She smiled back. "Good. I'd like that."

It was a strange end to a strange day, she thought as the ferry headed back to the mainland. She couldn't say for certain that she knew Chase Sullivan any better, but she'd definitely learned more. As soon as the ferry docked she headed straight for her mother's place to see Skye.

Fortunately Nina wasn't home. Sam knew how much Nina disliked bickering, especially between her daughters. When they were teenagers, she'd often remind them that friends would come and go in their lives—as would lovers, but a sister would always be there. Sam wasn't sure that was a good thing.

She got to the point as soon as she found Skye in the kitchen making a pot of coffee.

"I've just come back from Bainbridge Island."

Skye looked up from the coffee machine. "Oh?"

She sounded nonchalant, but Sam noted the quick flash of guilt. "You might have told me you saw Chase, instead of setting me up like that."

Skye set the coffeepot on its stand and pushed the start button. When she turned around, her eyes were blazing. "Why is it always about you, Sam? This has nothing to do with you, okay? There was no setup, no entrapment. I went to see him in a line of inquiry—"

"That you established, Skye. You have no official backing for any of this. It's your own personal obsession."

"Obsession? What kind of psychobabble are you spouting now?"

"You didn't find anything thirteen years ago, yet you still can't let it go."

"That's ridiculous. I came home to see Mom and hopefully patch things up with you—though I'm beginning to realize that's an impossibility—and I decided to spend some of my free time reexamining an old file. Where does *obsession* fit into that scenario?"

Sam counted to ten. Skye had always been an amazing spin doctor, and her rationale would have convinced anyone who didn't know her as well as Sam did.

"Skye," she said, purposely lowering her voice, "you know very well that Chase Sullivan would never have entered your FBI radar if I hadn't asked for some assistance."

"What are you suggesting, Sam? That I'm doing this out of some desire to get back at you? A personal vendetta or something? Do you realize how that sounds?"

They were on the brink, but Sam refused to back off. She couldn't now. "I know how it sounds and how it looks, Skye. We've been through this many times since we were teenagers."

Skye turned away to get a coffee mug from the cupboard. "Yeah, yeah. The old competition thing. I was the bad twin and you were the good one."

"You were the only person who thought that, Skye. No one else did. Not ever."

Skye remained silent, just poured the coffee and gestured to the pot.

Sam shook her head but didn't take her eyes off her sister. They were going to finish this years-old argument at last.

Skye took a long sip, staring thoughtfully at Sam the whole time. "I *am* competitive," she finally said. "It's true. But I'm like that with everyone and everywhere. Not only with you."

"Okay, but there are times when you're supposed to back off."

Skye set her coffee mug down on the center island counter. "I know that, too. But…I can't explain it. I just can't seem to back off. My life's a constant race. Every situation I'm in, it's as if there's a guy waving a checkered flag in front of me."

"Come on, Skye. That sounds like the 'just can't help myself' syndrome."

Her sister's eyes flashed. "And you sound like Mom."

"That's a low blow. Beneath even you."

Skye grinned. "We did promise never to quote Mom to each other, didn't we?"

Sam felt a rush of warmth for her sister, remembering suddenly the times when they giggled late at night in their bunk beds. Way back when. Then she remembered other promises they'd made. One in particular—*thou shalt not steal your sister's boyfriend*—that Skye had blatantly broken. The surge of affection was instantly replaced by despair. Were they ever going to get on track again as sisters?

"So where do we go from here?" Sam asked.

"Regarding?"

Us, Sam wanted to say. But there were other priorities. A twelve-year-old boy who'd just found his father. It would be too cruel if Danny were to lose Chase, as well as his mother.

"Chase. His family's business. That whole thing."

"Oh." Skye moved away, flicking off the coffee machine and putting her empty mug in the sink. "Right. Back to that."

Sam heard the disappointment in her voice. Had she misread her sister? "There's a time limit here, Skye. Danny's mother. She needs to know he'll be okay. That his father will be around for him. That he won't have to go into a foster home."

"Sounds like a Dickens' novel," muttered Skye.

"Don't trivialize this."

Skye raised her hands in surrender. "Okay, okay. What's your point?"

"I'm asking you to drop it. To forget about reexamining the case."

Skye kept her eyes on Sam as if waiting for her to change her mind or to back off. Then she abruptly spun around and left the room.

Sam headed for the sink to splash water on her face. What was her next step if Skye refused?

Seconds later Skye was back, holding a large brown envelope in her hand. She tossed it onto the counter by the sink.

"Here," she said, her voice sharp and decisive. "I'll let *you* decide what to do. Read this and get back to me."

Sam picked up the envelope and pulled out the papers inside. The cover page was stamped with the FBI logo and file number. Beneath was a date from thirteen years ago. Sam looked up, but her sister had already left the room.

SAM POURED HERSELF a second cup of coffee and sat in her favourite chair, staring at the thin sheaf of papers on the table next to her. She hadn't had the nerve to read the photocopied file at her mother's place, not wanting Skye looking over her shoulder. So she'd waited till today— Sunday—just to prove to herself that she, unlike her sister, was not obsessive and the file was no big deal.

And after reading it, she thought perhaps it really wasn't a big deal. The gist was that the FBI's Seattle field office had received two anonymous phone calls from two different public phone booths. A male voice had suggested the office might want to investigate a local import-export company called Trade Winds, which had received several government contracts. The caller said the company was defrauding the government.

A memo recommended that, in light of other recent cases of government fraud, the calls should be followed up on. A case number was assigned and the file handed over to the new recruit, Skye Sorrenti. The remaining reports on file belonged to her.

Sam was fascinated by the terse, bureaucratic jargon that her sister had used. At the time, she'd only been in the Seattle office less than a year, and Sam knew Skye didn't talk like that in her personal life. But somewhere in the past thirteen years her professional and personal styles merged, so that her speech and mannerisms at work and at home were the same now. The realization saddened Sam. Had Skye's job changed her that much, or had the potential for such a change always been there in Skye? Perhaps it didn't matter how the change occurred. The real issue was, could the old Skye—the one she remembered from their early adolescence—be resurrected?

A few employees had been interviewed, along with the two men who owned and ran the company—Winston and Bryant Sullivan. Sam was intrigued by the notation that Bryant and his two sons actually ran the business. Though only in his midsixties, Winston was considered semi-retired due to a heart condition.

A sample of contracts, along with invoices and receipts, were also reviewed. People who'd signed some of the receipts were interviewed, but one person whose name appeared on a few papers had been unavailable. Chase Sullivan, only child of Winston. Sam picked up the file and shuffled through the loose papers until she found a handwritten note by Skye to contact Chase Sullivan on his return. It was dated two weeks before Skye was transferred out of Seattle. The last memo on file was a recommendation to take no further action in the inquiry.

It didn't take an FBI agent to see that there wasn't much of a case. Sam knew her sister had been right to close it. So why all the fuss now? she wondered. And why was Chase so insistent that Skye drop it?

Sam had no answers to either question. What she did know was that she needed a break from it all.

CHAPTER NINE

CHASE HUNG UP the phone. What rotten luck. A big order, one for a cabinet, and he'd had to turn it down. Mainly because of the timeline. Or so he'd began to tell himself as the customer described what she wanted. After he made his excuses and rang off, he realized that time was indeed the factor. Only it was Emily and Danny's time he'd been thinking about. The kind of cabinet the woman wanted would take at least three months. How could he devote himself to an intricate piece when Emily didn't have three months? Not according to her doctor, whom he'd spoken with after introducing himself as Danny's father.

That was why he'd invited Danny for the weekend right away, rather than allow for a slow and steady period of adjustment. They didn't have time for that, which was also why he'd panicked after Sam's sister dropped in on him. If the whole thing had come up six months or more from now, he might have been able to deal with it. But when he'd promised Emily he'd take care of Danny—*no matter what*—he'd no inkling that *all* of his past was going to come back with a vengeance.

He hadn't heard a word from Sam since she'd left on Saturday. Okay, he told himself, it's only been three days. She needed time to talk things out with her sister, and having met the sister, he figured that would be a challenge. She didn't seem the type to capitulate easily. They might be identical physically in almost every way—except that Sam had green flecks in her gray eyes and her sister didn't—but in personality they were different. He scarcely knew Sam, but could clearly see that difference. Chalk and cheese. Angles and circles. Maybe it was Skye's career that had created that edginess, or maybe she was simply made that way.

All he knew was that unless Sam could persuade her sister to drop whatever she was doing, his whole life could change. Again. And not just his, but Danny's. He hoped that Sam had some luck. A lot depended on that. More than anyone knew.

He'd realized almost at once that Sam hadn't known about Skye's visit, but something had driven him to keep at her, to find out exactly what was going on and how much she was involved. It was partly because he didn't *want* to believe that Sam was in on it with Skye; but if she was working with her sister, he didn't want Danny affected by it. Chase could see how much Danny liked her, and he didn't want the boy to get hurt.

The weekend had turned out better than expected, considering his stress after Skye's visit. He and Danny had apparently made the same vow: keep things as neutral and friendly as possible. Danny had phoned Emily a few times, filling her in on what they were doing. He'd heard the excitement in Danny's voice as he told his mother about their paddle along the channel and how Chase was going to teach him the J-stroke. It had seemed like a small thing to Chase, but he'd forgotten that Danny was a city kid who'd had little exposure to nature.

On the ride back into the city, they'd talked a bit about plans for the future, both of them shying away from the long-term and focusing on the day-to-day. Danny wanted to stay with Minnie until school ended, if she agreed. He wouldn't have to change schools and would be closer to the hospital. But he would spend weekends with Chase, giving her a break. Neither of them mentioned the summer or a time when Emily would no longer be there.

When Chase had dropped Danny off at Minnie's, there'd been a moment when Chase thought Danny expected a goodbye hug. But Chase held back, recalling himself at the same age and the embarrassment of public displays of affection. So they'd shaken hands, instead.

It was amazing how the mind adapts, Chase thought. Three weeks ago he had no clue how his life was about to change. His only connection to family was his weekly visit to a mother who no longer knew him. He hadn't been involved romantically with a woman since his sojourn in Alaska, and when he'd found out his mother had Alzheimer's and was in a nursing home, he'd left the state and the relationship quickly and permanently. Proving what he suspected about himself long ago—the whole idea of commitment to a family structure terrified him. One dysfunctional family in a lifetime was more than enough. Why risk it happening again?

Now he had a twelve-year-old son. The start of a family. The idea attracted and frightened him at the same time.

The doorbell drew him from the workroom to the front of the shop. Chase froze when he saw the man in a business suit looming inside the doorway. It had been years since he'd seen his cousin and, although Howard Sullivan had filled out considerably, Chase immediately recognized the patronizing smirk.

"Nice place you got here, Chase," said Howard. "Long time no see." He moved forward, extending his right hand.

Unless Howard had undergone a huge personality change, Chase knew the gesture was pure formality. And considering their last meeting, hypocrisy, as well. "What do you want?" he asked.

The other man dropped his hand. "Not very friendly for cousins."

"Cut it, Howard."

"Sure. Okay by me. It's not as if we were ever close."

"So, what do you want?" Chase repeated.

"The old man wants to talk to you. Got a minute?"

"What about?"

"I'll let him tell you."

"Where is he?"

"Outside in the car."

"Tell him to come in, then."

"He can't. Bad legs. He's got diabetes and a heart condition. Be better if you came out to him."

"I'm working."

"Don't look too busy to me. C'mon, it won't take long. Then you can get back to your *work*." The sneer summed up his opinion of Chase's vocation.

There was no point in arguing. "Give me a second." He returned to the workroom to turn off the carving tool he'd been using. The sudden appearance of his cousin and uncle in almost two years was no coincidence. He had a sinking feeling the impromptu visit was connected to Skye Sorrenti, which meant that Sam had either been unable or unwilling to act on his request. He hoped the former, hating to think he'd misjudged her.

"Best lock up," his cousin said as Chase followed him out. "We're taking a little drive."

Chase flipped the sign to Closed and locked the door.

There was a large black Cadillac sitting at the curb. The front passenger-side window rolled down and Howard's brother, Terence, greeted him. Like his brother, Terence had grown in girth, though his receding hairline and wire-rimmed glasses gave him an air of maturity his brother lacked.

Chase hesitated. There was an implicit threat in the whole scene. His cousins had always been bullies, who had refined veneers they assumed in social settings. But he doubted his uncle would permit any harm to come to him. At any rate, there seemed little choice but to do as instructed. He opened the rear door nearest the sidewalk and climbed inside.

"Uncle Bryant," he said as Howard closed the door behind him and walked around to the driver's side.

"Chase," Bryant Sullivan rasped. "I see you got a haircut. Still got the tattoo?"

"What do you want, Uncle Bryant?"

His uncle ignored him, turning to the front seat. "Howard, take us somewhere nice and quiet. Preferably with a view."

"Sure, Pop. Any recommendations, Chase?"

Chase said nothing, keeping his eyes on his uncle. He'd always been a larger version of his brother, Winston, and Chase figured his father would have looked much the same had he still been alive. The past two years had aged the man dramatically. Ill health seeped out of every pore in his sallow face.

Chase had always been fascinated by his cousins' utter lack of social skills. Bryant and Winston, Chase's father, were the only sons of a Seattle family that was socially prominent at the turn of the twentieth century. Old money. Traditions. Etiquette. Chase had been indoctrinated from birth, and he'd assumed his cousins had been, too. But their parents had divorced and a string of stepmothers had failed to do what a nurturing mother like Chase's had done to act as a buffer against the father's bullying ways and teach the boys the niceties.

The car cruised down Primrose Lane, made a right onto the main drag and headed out of town. After a few minutes Bryant said, "We had a business agreement, Chase. I hope you haven't broken it."

"I keep my promises."

"We hope so," said Terence.

Chase ignored him. "What's this all about, Uncle Bryant?"

"I had an unexpected visit last Friday afternoon. End of the day. I was about to head to my club when a young woman insisted on an appointment."

Chase had a sickening feeling about what was coming. He swung his gaze to the window at his right, feigning disinterest.

"A woman from the FBI," Bryant said, "telling me she was heading an investigation into the business."

Chase closed his eyes. He couldn't have spoken if he'd wanted to.

"Do you know anything about this, Chase?"

He took a deep breath and looked at his uncle. "Not a thing."

"So you haven't been making any more phone calls like the one you made thirteen years ago?"

Chase didn't flinch from the watery-eyed stare. "No, I haven't. Now can we go back to town? I have work to do."

His uncle studied Chase's face long and hard. Finally he said, "Take us back, Howard."

"That's it?" asked Howard. "We could've settled this on the phone."

The tight smile that came and went in Bryant's face never quite reached his eyes. "Nothing like a one-on-one, Howard. The need to see for yourself. That's a business maxim you should know by now."

"Sure, Pop," he muttered, scowling at Chase.

Chase stared out the window on the short ride back to Primrose Lane. He knew his uncle might find out eventually about the connection to Skye Sorrenti. He just hoped he'd have time to plan what he could do about it, if anything.

When the Cadillac purred to a stop in front of the shop, Chase immediately opened the door. But his uncle stopped him one last time.

"How's your mother doing? I haven't seen her for ages. Must drop by for a visit."

Chase continued out the door, slamming it behind him.

SAMANTHA KNEW she couldn't put off contacting her sister and Chase any longer. She hated the position she was in, caught between two people who had a strong interest—for whatever reason—in something that happened years ago. The last couple of days had been spent catching up on some of the work she'd deferred as long as possible and frankly, she'd appreciated the break from the whole Trade Winds thing. Yet she'd found herself thinking about Chase at odd moments, picturing him on his stool at his workbench or putting together lunch in his small, sunlit kitchen.

Her opinion of him had altered dramatically since that first meeting at Harbor House, when she'd feared he'd deny all possibility of being Danny's father and find a way to absolve himself from any responsibility. And in spite of the fact that he'd been abrupt and almost hostile toward her in the next couple of meetings, she felt he was beginning to warm up a bit. What surprised her was how much that pleased her. And it wasn't just because she needed a positive relationship with him to maintain her connection with Danny and his mother, which was something she now realized she wanted. It was more than that, though she couldn't have said what, exactly. The only problem in the equation was Skye.

Sam stood up and stretched. She'd managed to get caught up on most of her calls and e-mails and knew she really could not postpone getting back to either Chase or Skye any longer. But which one? The phone suddenly rang, and when she looked at the caller display, she knew the decision had been made for her.

"I need to talk to you," he said, skipping a greeting.

Maybe she was deluding herself about the warming-up bit, Sam thought. "About?" she asked, though she knew even before he answered.

"Your sister. Meet me at the Starbucks at Pikes' market. I have some shopping to do there. Half an hour?"

As if he gave her a choice. Sam said, "Sure," and he hung up. She stared at the receiver for a moment in disbelief. The man was definitely challenged when it came to social niceties. She filed some papers and was about to leave when the phone rang. Caller display indicated it was Chase again.

"Listen, I—" she began.

"Just heard from Minnie Schwartz. The hospital called her to say Emily has taken a turn for the worse. I'm heading there now. Want to meet me?"

"I'll be there as soon as I can. Does Danny know?"

She heard him swear softly. "I'll call his school and arrange to pick him up on my way to the hospital."

"Is it bad?"

"Her lungs are filling up with fluids and they've had to put a chest tube in. That's as much as Minnie knows."

"I'll get there as soon as I can," Sam said, and hung up. She moved mechanically and quickly, grabbing her purse, cell phone and, at the last moment, a paperback, though she didn't expect she'd be relaxed enough to read.

The ward seemed especially quiet as Sam stepped off the elevator. Emily's door was partially open, so she was able to peek around it to see if she ought to enter or not. Emily was lying propped against two pillows, an oxygen mask covering the lower part of her face. The bedcovers were carefully arranged over a clear, plastic tubing system that went from her chest to a container hanging off the side of the bed. Her eyes were closed and Sam hesitated, almost afraid to go into the room. A nurse came along and stopped next to Sam.

"Are you family?" she asked.

"Not really."

"There's a waiting room down the hall," the nurse said, pointing.

"Her son will soon be here. Will he be able to see her?"

The nurse smiled. "Danny? For sure. She's come around quite a bit since this morning, but she's tired. Every crisis, no matter how small or big, is exhausting for her. Have Danny check in at the nurses' station before he goes in."

She started to walk on when Sam asked, "What does this mean? In terms of her ongoing condition, I mean."

"You'll have to talk to her doctor about that. He'll be making rounds in an hour or so. But unless you're an immediate family member…"

"Of course, I understand." As the nurse walked away, Sam realized that her unexpected feeling of exclusion arose from the fact that she felt as if she *was* family. She headed for the waiting room and halfheartedly skimmed her paperback, constantly checking the bank of elevators that opened into the area for sign of Chase and Danny. Half an hour later an elevator opened and the two exited.

Danny looked pale and dazed. He headed automatically for Emily's room, brushing past Sam as she stood to greet them. "Danny!"

He spun around. "Honey," Sam said, lowering her

voice, "the nurse said you should check in with them first. Your mother might be sleeping."

"Is she okay?"

She ached to wrap her arms around him, but knew what he needed right then was information—and his mother. "The nurse said she'd improved since this morning."

She caught Chase's eye over Danny's head, wanting him to step in.

"Come on, Danny. I'll go with you," he said, and placing a hand on the boy's shoulder, steered him toward the nurses' station down the hall.

Sam watched them, a lump forming in her throat. She noticed that they had the same way of carrying themselves. Straight-backed, shoulders squared. Resolute in the way they walked side by side, but somehow vulnerable, too. And in that moment a flood of affection for the two flowed through her. Crazy. On one level, she scarcely knew either of them, yet the connecting link of Emily and what she was going through had forged a bond.

They stopped at the counter and Sam watched as a nurse escorted them to Emily's room. They stood in the doorway a few seconds and then followed the nurse inside.

Sam began to pace. Moments later there was a flurry in the hall and a group of white-coated men and women trailing behind an authoritative man with a clipboard emerged from a room and headed toward Emily's. The doctor and his students making rounds. Sam watched as they stood briefly in the hall outside Emily's room while the doctor spoke to them. They went inside and once again, Sam was left waiting and wondering.

After what seemed ages, the medical group left the room and continued on down the hall. Just as Sam was considering going in to see Emily, Chase came out and headed her way. He was pale, his face drawn. He sank into a chair.

"How is she?"

"Better. But the doctor told me that these crises will escalate. Her lungs fill with fluid and have to be drained."

Sam sat in the chair next to his and bowed her head, overwhelmed by the implication of what he'd said. Escalate. Emily's suffering would increase. She felt his hand pat her upper back and then make slow, circular motions that were comforting and warm. She let herself drift with the movement until he suddenly pulled his hand away. She raised her head.

"We have to talk," he said.

She knew instantly he wasn't referring to Danny and Emily. "Yes," she said.

"Your sister went to see my uncle, at his place of business. She asked him some questions and then he came to see me." He rubbed his brow with an index finger. "Did you talk to her?"

Sam shook her head. "I tried, but it's still up in the air. To tell you the truth, I just wanted to forget the whole thing. Make it go away."

"Yeah," he said. "You and me both. I've spent the last thirteen years reconciling myself to the fact that I played a big part in the breakdown of my family and even my father's death. These past two years I finally managed to put together a life for myself and the promise of a future."

Sam didn't know what to say. The blunt facts in the FBI file she'd read had certainly not addressed the personal and emotional toll on the Sullivan family. She wished she could make it right for Chase, but knew it was too late for that.

"What happened?" she finally asked.

"It's…it's complicated, Sam. This isn't the time or place for explanations."

"I understand and I'm sorry, Chase," she said, pausing,

"but isn't it a good thing that you were still able to over-come all that?"

He got to his feet, and forked a hand through his hair. "That's the point. Things were going well until…"

"I came into the picture."

"Not just you. All of it. Emily and Danny and then your sister. Now my uncle and cousins have turned up and sud-denly my whole damn past is right in my face." He strode over to a window overlooking the hospital parking lot.

"Of course it is. What did you think? That you could just live your life and never have to account for what hap-pened? That all those unresolved issues would simply vanish?"

After a long moment, he said, "I paid for all of that. I exiled myself from my family—my mother—and tried to make amends as best I could. If it wasn't for your sister—"

Mentally she agreed totally. But loyalty to her twin sur-faced. Sam walked over to where he stood, his back still turned to her.

"Don't put this on Skye. She's doing her job. I don't know why she's decided to resurrect the whole thing with your family's business, but she has. If you're innocent, you have nothing to worry about, do you?" *Are you?* she wanted to add.

He turned to face her. "You don't know anything about my worries. You come into my life, playing the Good Sa-maritan or whatever, reuniting a boy with his father and then blithely set loose someone who can ultimately destroy everything."

The unfairness of his words angered her. "Set loose? Skye is my sister, not some pack dog. And if you'd dealt with these things the way you ought to have years ago, you wouldn't be in this situation now."

He grabbed hold of her forearms, holding her so close

she could smell the breath mint he must have been sucking on moments ago. "You know nothing about my problems nor what I've done about them."

"You walked away from Emily when she was pregnant."

He drew back, dropping his hands. "That's beneath you."

Sam flushed and bit her lip.

"I didn't know about Danny," he said. "If I had, I'd have…"

"What?"

The unexpected voice drew their attention to the entrance of the waiting area and Danny, staring at them. "What would you have done?" he asked again. His face was red and his eyes glistening. "Would you have married my mom and made her whole life different? Maybe she wouldn't have had to work so hard. Maybe she'd have quit smoking, because she wouldn't have been so stressed about making money and looking after me all by herself."

"Danny—" Chase moved toward him.

"No. It's too late to say you're sorry!" he cried. He spun on his heel and ran toward the bank of elevators. One opened and he jumped on.

Sam hurried after him. "Danny, wait! Come back." But the door closed.

"Please don't tell me this is my fault, too," Sam said, looking at Chase.

"No," he said with a sigh. "I should have talked to him honestly about Emily and me."

"He'll come back," she said, feeling suddenly sorry for him.

But when Danny didn't return after fifteen minutes, Chase went downstairs to the cafeteria and gift-shop area to look for him. While he was gone, Sam took the opportunity to see Emily. She was sleeping, but Sam tiptoed into the room. She stroked the back of her hand, resting on top of the covers, and whispered, "Don't worry, Emily. Danny will be fine. Chase will take care of him. And I will, too," she added. Then she left the room to return to the waiting area, arriving as the elevator opened and Chase walked out.

"Any luck?"

He shook his head. "I called Minnie to warn her he may show up there, angry and hurt. She promised to call if he did."

"Where could he have gone?"

"I don't know. I know so little about him. Who his friends are or where he hangs out." Chase chewed on a knuckle thoughtfully. "The park. Where we went last week, after the interview at his school. Greenlake."

"It's a long way from here. He'd have to take a bus."

"Yeah, but it's still on his way home. Anyway, he's been gone half an hour. We have to do something." He started for the elevators.

"I'll come with you."

He turned around. "You don't have to."

"I know. I want to. Is that okay?"

"There's not room for three in the truck."

"Why don't we take my car? I'll bring you back here for your truck."

"Sure. Let me tell someone at the nurses' station to call in case Danny comes back here."

They walked out to the parking lot. Sam thought back to everything they'd said, wondering how much Danny had heard. She was ashamed to think she'd accused Chase of running out on Emily when she knew he hadn't known she was pregnant. And as for her rebuke that he ought to have resolved the problems in his past, rather than flee from them…. *Well done, Samantha. Why haven't you taken your own advice?*

She was glad to be driving. Concentrating on the traffic meant no conversation, and she figured she and Chase had said enough for one day. Occasionally she glanced his way, watching him stare out the window, lost in thought. Yet some part of him seemed to be constantly moving. His fingers tapped on his thighs and his leg jiggled impatiently, as if he were mentally racing the car to the park himself. Fortunately she managed to hit every green light.

When she finally pulled in to the same parking area they'd been at a few days ago, Chase had the door open before Sam even turned off the engine. She watched him cover the asphalt lot with long, purposeful strides. He didn't bother looking back to see if she was following. By the time she reached the picnic area beyond the take-out burger stand, Chase was heading along the water's edge. In the distance, she saw a small figure hunched against the wind.

Sam stopped by a picnic table and watched as Chase caught up to Danny. Chase put a hand on Danny's shoulder and bent down, obviously talking. Danny threw off the hand and moved away. Chase waited, then extended an arm and drew the boy closer. Sam perched on the tabletop, shivering. It was past six and the temperature was dropping as the sun dipped toward the western sky.

Eventually the two began to walk her way. Danny's head was hanging and he shuffled along beside Chase, whose arm rested lightly across his shoulders. When they reached Sam, Danny looked up. His eyes were red and swollen.

"I'm sorry I ran away, Sam," he said.

Tears welled up in Sam's eyes. She opened her arms and wrapped them around Danny as he climbed up onto the table next to her. He lowered his head onto her lap and sobbed. Sam rubbed his back with one hand, using the other to wipe her own tears away. Chase sat on the other side of Sam and, without a word, draped his arm around her shoulders, drawing her closer to him. They sat like that long after the sun disappeared beneath the horizon.

CHAPTER TEN

IMPULSIVELY, driving out of Greenlake Park, Sam suggested, "Maybe Danny would like to spend the night at my place."

She looked at Chase, in the passenger seat. He caught her gaze and nodded. Turning to Danny in the rear, he asked, "That okay with you?"

Danny mumbled something that sounded like a yes.

"Thanks, Samantha," Chase said.

"My family and friends call me Sam."

"Sam it is."

She felt his eyes on her and wondered what he was thinking. She hoped that he no longer thought she'd been conspiring with Skye. When they arrived at her place and Danny got settled in front of the television, Sam decided to do something to prove to Chase that she wasn't teaming up with her sister against him.

They were having a glass of wine, sitting at the small table for two in a corner of the kitchen when Sam excused herself, went into the bedroom and returned with the file Skye had given her. Chase frowned as he registered the name on the cover page.

"Where did you get this?"

"My sister copied it from the archives at her old office."

His face told her he was wrestling with that. "Have you read it?"

She nodded.

"And?"

"I didn't see anything incriminating."

"May I?" he asked, indicating the file.

"Of course. That's why I'm showing it to you. And I'm hoping…"

"I can explain it?" His face cracked in a half smile, as if he doubted he'd be able to.

"Yes," she said, smiling back at him.

He opened the file and thumbed through it. "You're right, there's not much here. Nothing incriminating, as you said. But what's here raises a question, and the answer to that is what your sister missed when she investigated Trade Winds."

Sam was almost as intrigued by the fact that Skye might have made a mistake as she was by Chase's cryptic reply. "How so?"

He shuffled the papers, extracting two or three and showing them to her. "Here are two reports and an invoice all signed by me."

"Uh-huh." She felt an urge to tell him to get to the point, but was beginning to realize he needed to work through the steps himself.

"So if I were investigating this, I'd ask myself why a low-level clerk in a company was signing reports and invoices." He paused for a long moment and said, "I guess I should start from the beginning."

"That would be good. Let me just see if Danny needs anything." Sam went into the living room to check on him, though she really wanted to make sure the television was loud enough to drown out their conversation. But Danny had fallen asleep. She clicked off the TV and covered him with the throw on the back of the couch.

"He's sleeping," she said on her return.

"He's had a rough day." Chase rubbed his forehead. "We all have. Especially Emily."

She liked that he'd highlighted the person who made all the rest of their bad days seem minor. *We must never forget Emily.*

"Okay," he said, sighing, "to begin. My father and his younger brother, Bryant, inherited Trade Winds when I was just a toddler. It's been owned by Sullivans for more than a hundred years and was originally a shipping company. But at some point, my father and uncle decided to get into the import-export business. They got commissions and contracts from various agencies and companies to import or export goods. Basically to act as brokers. Something like what you do, I think, but in a broader context."

He flashed a smile that, unexpectedly, warmed her.

Then the smile faltered. "I don't want to digress by getting too far into the dynamics of my family, but they're relevant to what happened. I had a rocky relationship with my father. When I graduated from university—in arts, not business as he'd wanted—my main goal was to get as far away from Seattle as I could. My mother was secretly on my side, but she didn't have the wherewithal to stand up to my father. She gave me money for graduation and told me to see the world. I did, and came back two years later, broke. I couldn't get a decent job, so when my father urged me to work for the company, I caved in. His health hadn't been good and while I was away, he'd been diagnosed with angina. By the time I came home, he'd handed over the daily operations to my uncle, though he kept his title of president. Most of his time, however, was spent on the golf course and at his men's club." He paused to sip his wine, running a fingertip around the edge of the glass.

"What did you do in the company?" Sam asked.

"While I was away, my uncle's two sons—Terence and

Howard—came into the business. They started out in the mail room and spent time in every department. My father wanted me to do the same. Of course, by then they were already supervising—Terence was in accounts and Howard oversaw the administration part. Trade Winds has always been a family-run business. Back then, there were fewer than fifty employees. The smallness is important, because it meant that virtually all the important aspects of the business were controlled by family. Anyway," he said, "I started out in the mail room and after a couple of months was moved into accounting. Because I had no background in that, I was basically a file clerk." He grimaced. "My cousins felt I needed a lot more practical experience. I hated working there, but my mother persuaded me to give it some time. My cousins took every opportunity to give me a hard time."

"They were bullies," Sam said.

"Yeah. Always had been, even when we were little. They'd gang up on me and lie when I tried to tell my parents what they'd been doing. My mother suspected, but my father always took their side. I needed to toughen up, he'd tell me."

Sam recalled the school bullying incident with Danny and Chase's refusal to rush to judgment about Danny's role.

"That part's important, too," Chase continued, "to what happened later. One day Uncle Bryant came up to me and asked me to sign a document. He told me it had to be signed by a family member, someone other than the CEO. I didn't even get a good look at it and to tell you the truth, I didn't care. That happened a few more times and probably I'd have continued to blindly sign away until one day the chief accounting clerk, a woman who'd worked for the company for several years, came to me with one of the invoices I'd signed.

"It was from a company that Trade Winds had hired to do some consulting work as part of a government contract. Terence and Howard had both gone to private schools and had maintained a lot of powerful contacts. After they got into management, they used those old friends to secure some very lucrative government contracts. It was another thing my father threw up at me. They'd been networking for the business while I'd been backpacking around Asia. And I'd come home with nothing to show for my world travels but long hair and a tattoo." He grinned. "Both of which I've since outgrown, though the hair was the easiest thing to change."

He lapsed into thought. Thinking of other changes? Sam wondered.

"Anyway," he went on, "the accounting clerk approached me about this invoice and wanted to know what kind of company it was. She wanted to ask about a figure on the invoice but couldn't contact the company."

"What do you mean?"

"The phone number on the invoice was phony and when she sent something by mail, it was returned. She went through her records and found a handful of invoices from the same company and I had signed all but one of them. She was shocked when I told her I didn't know anything about it. She said my signature indicated that I had received the goods and paid the company. Then she asked me why I would sign something I knew nothing about." He sighed. "It was a good question and I had no answer except for my own ignorance and stupidity. That plus the fact that I really didn't care at all. But when Big Nance—"

"Who?"

Chase smiled. "Nancy Wicks, the accounting clerk. Those of us she considered friends called her that. If you saw her, you'd get the irony. She's a tiny thing, but very tough. Anyway, Nancy said that there might be something going on and if I had signed off on everything, I'd be implicated. So I thought about it and gathered up all the documents I'd signed and took them in to my uncle. He assured me everything was kosher and not to worry. But there was something in his manner that made me think he was lying. Things started happening quickly after that. I was sent off to a trade show in Portland, which surprised me because no one had had any confidence in my business sense up to that point. While I was gone, an FBI agent dropped in to the office—your sister, Skye. She told my uncle they were investigating a complaint of fraud against the business. Apparently there had been an anonymous phone tip. In the meantime, Nancy Wicks was advised that she'd been made redundant. I knew none of this until I came back from the show."

He rubbed his eyes and yawned. "It's getting late. I'll try to wrap this up quickly. To sum it up, I came back to find Nancy gone and my uncle, father and cousins furious about the inquiry. Uncle Bryant accused me of tipping off the FBI and my father believed him. Uncle Bryant spun the whole thing to make it look like I'd been involved with what was going on. And my name was on a lot of those documents. There was a huge fight and my father accused me of betraying the family. I took off, leaving the whole mess behind me. Running away from my problems." His mouth twisted bitterly. "I hung out in the city for a bit, got a construction job and that's when I met Emily. A month later, my father had a fatal heart attack." He stopped. Then, "I never had a chance to prove my innocence. After the funeral, I wanted to get as far away from Seattle as I could."

"When did you come back?"

"Two years ago." He stretched and yawned. "And that's another story, which I'm much too tired to get into now. I should go—have to get my truck."

"Oh, right, I'd forgotten all about it. I was going to drive you there, but now that Danny's asleep—"

"Leave him be. I can take a taxi."

She almost invited him to stay over, too, but held back. Although she now had a more complete picture of his past and who he was, it was best to not rush their developing friendship.

On his way out, Chase asked, "Are you busy in the morning?"

"At some point I should check in at my office, but I can drive Danny to school if that's why you're asking."

He frowned. "Oh, right. School. I guess I have a way to go before I automatically think like a parent."

Sam patted his arm. "You're doing just fine, Chase. Give it time."

His eyes connected with hers. "Thanks. But the reason I asked is that I'd like you to meet someone. Danny, too. I'll call his school to say he'll be in later."

"All right." She was intrigued.

"Great. Meet me at Harbor House about nine-thirty. You remember where that is?" His grin was teasing.

He wants us to meet his mother. "I do." She smiled.

"Okay, then," he said. "Tomorrow."

He grasped her hand and Sam stiffened, thinking he was going to pull her toward him. But instead, he held it lightly, as if he were about to lead her onto a dance floor. Then he gently let go, turned and left.

Sam stood by the closed door a moment, thinking that something had just happened between them. Exactly what, she couldn't say. But she realized a barrier had been removed. He was no longer an adversary, but someone she wanted to work with to help Danny.

Yet sometime in the middle of a restless night, she asked herself if perhaps she'd simply been conned. After all, she'd heard only one side of the story. As she finally dropped off to sleep, she could hear Skye's more skeptical voice reminding her that people—especially criminals—tell you only what you want to hear.

HE GOT THERE EARLY, mainly because his mother had good days and bad days. Plus his routine was off, this being midweek.

"She's having a good day so far, Chase," the receptionist told him. "Nurse Andrew said she ate some breakfast, and right now, she's sitting in the solarium. Do you want to visit with her there?"

"Yes, thanks, Mrs. MacDonald, but I'm expecting a couple more visitors, so I'll wait for them in the hall."

When Sam turned up with Danny in tow, Chase was amused by the expression in Mrs. MacDonald's eyes. She obviously remembered Sam—and not kindly, judging by the downturn of her mouth. But her professionalism took charge and she managed a thin smile as they passed her desk on the way to the solarium.

Outside the entrance, Chase paused to say, "My mother has Alzheimer's, Danny. I don't know if you know what that is but—"

"Yeah, I do," he snapped. He obviously wasn't happy about the visit.

Chase bit back a retort. He tried to think how he'd have felt at the same age, being forced to go to a nursing home to see an old woman he didn't know. But this old woman was Danny's grandmother, and like it or not, he was going to meet her. His gaze met Sam's, above Danny's head. She shrugged and gave a sympathetic smile.

"Why don't you go in first and we'll follow a minute later, give you time to greet her?" Sam suggested.

He felt an unexpected warmth for her, realizing not for

the first time in the past couple of days, how badly he'd misjudged her. "Good idea. She might be alarmed if we all troop in at once." He glanced at Danny, who was busy surveying the paintings on the wall. Chase smiled inwardly at this new interest in art.

He stepped into the solarium, scanning the small group of elderly people in wheelchairs until he saw his mother sitting in a wing chair in a corner. It was her favourite place, giving her a clear view of the gardens outside and angled away from the rest of the room. Martha Sullivan had always been an introvert and even now, in the mental fog of Alzheimer's, that part of her personality remained. He walked toward her, and as he drew near, said, "Hello, Mother," as he always did, so as not to startle her.

She turned her head slightly and he squatted to be at eye level with her. Her pale eyes stared blankly at him, as they always did, but he no longer felt the pain at her lack of recognition.

"I'm Chase," he said. "How are you today, Mother?"

"I'm fine," she murmured. "How are you?"

"Good. I've brought you a couple of visitors. Would you like to meet them?"

Her face remained impassive, though when he mentioned visitors, she glanced over his shoulder. He turned to see Sam close behind him, Danny ambling slowly in their direction.

Chase stood up. "This is my friend Samantha."

"Hello, Mrs. Sullivan," Sam said as she moved closer. She extended her right hand, but Martha ignored it, as Chase knew she would.

"Hello," said Martha.

She looked back at Chase and for a second, he thought he saw recognition in her eyes.

"Are you the man who brings the peppermint patties?" she asked.

"I'm sorry, I didn't bring you any this time."

Chase pursed his lips. Just then, his mother's eyes widened and an expression of absolute delight filled her face as she looked beyond him.

"Chase!" she cried, raising her arms in greeting.

Chase turned to see Danny, who was only two feet away. The boy stared at Martha.

"Come here, son," said Martha.

Chase caught Sam's expression and moved aside, gesturing at Danny to come forward. And when his son did so and stood before Martha, Chase couldn't tell if what he felt was pride that Danny didn't hesitate or pain that the first time he'd heard his mother say his name in two years had not been for him. All he knew for sure was that he couldn't speak over the lump in his throat.

He watched Martha reach out and stroke Danny's arm. He couldn't recall the last time he'd seen his mother smile like that. After a couple of minutes, he managed to say, huskily, "We can't stay long, Mother. Danny, er, Chase, has to get to school."

Danny looked at him, then back at Martha.

"Are you going, Chase?" asked Martha, beaming at Danny.

"Yes, I have to go to school," he said, "but I'll come back another day."

"Please do," she said, then looking at Chase, said in a sterner voice, "Don't forget my peppermints the next time."

He caught the glint of amusement in Sam's eyes, but nodded soberly. "I won't," he said, and leaned over to kiss her on the cheek.

As he ushered Danny and Sam out the door, he took one last glance at his mother. She was staring blankly out the solarium windows. *We're already forgotten,* he thought.

When they reached the foyer, Chase made a decision. "Danny, would you mind going on ahead for a couple of minutes? I'd like to have a word with Sam."

Danny's gaze flicked from Chase to Sam and back again. His expression shifted, too, from neutral to suspicious. "I'll wait outside, by the front door."

"Thanks, buddy," Chase said. "We won't be long."

As he headed for the entrance, Chase turned to Sam. "I don't mean to be mysterious," he said at the question in her face. "I just want to fill you in on some background about my mother, and I feel uncomfortable talking about it in front of Danny."

Sam touched his arm. "Okay, but maybe you should explain to Danny when we get outside. He hates being left out."

Chase nodded, but he kept seeing the look in his mother's face when she spotted Danny. "I left Seattle after my father died, but I kept in touch with my mother," he began. "She begged me to come home, but I'd promised Uncle Bryant I'd stay away from Seattle. He'd convinced me everyone was better off and that if anything happened to the business, my mother's livelihood would suffer as much as his own—her main source of income after my father's death was his share in the business. So I kept my word until about two years ago. I'd begun to think something was wrong with her while talking to her on the phone. She seemed more forgetful than usual. The letters she sent me became almost nonsensical. Finally I contacted Uncle Bryant and asked him to check up on her. A couple of weeks later he called to say she'd been found wandering the street outside our family home and had been hospitalized. I was living in Alaska at the time, but I left as soon as I got the call."

"Is that when she was admitted here?"

"Yes. To his credit, my uncle didn't leave her. He got her in here right away and she was already settled by the time I arrived. She didn't know me, of course—the disease had reached that point—but she was obviously content. My uncle wasn't happy about my intention to stay in Seattle. He made it clear that he was happy to pay for my mother's accommodation and care as long as I refrained from making any claim on the family business. I had no choice but to agree. So if he cuts the purse strings, she'll have to be moved to a state hospital." He paused. "I couldn't bear that."

"Chase, you have to do something about this situation."

He looked at her, unsure what she was referring to.

"With your uncle and the company. If there was something illegal going on, it'll come back to haunt you."

"Are you telling me this because of your sister's interest in the case?"

"No. But if it wasn't her asking questions, it'd be someone else."

He felt a rush of annoyance. "Why can't people just let it be?"

"Do you want to spend the rest of your life with this hanging over you?"

She was right, of course. There were days when he could forget all about it and others when he was filled with anger—at his father and uncle and especially, himself. He'd been prepared to carry the burden to protect his mother and perhaps, after she was gone, then he'd put things right. But now he felt differently. Things had changed.

"Oh, Chase," Sam murmured. He felt her hand touch his. Instinctively he clasped her hand and held tight. For the first time in a long time, he sensed a connection with another adult. He liked the feeling and didn't move away until he saw Danny looking at them from the other side of the glass front door.

"You have to do it for Danny, Chase," Sam said. "He's in your life now."

He watched Danny—his son—gesture impatiently. *I owe this boy something,* Chase thought. *Most of all, I have to start being a father.*

SKYE WAS BEGINNING to regret coming home. The fact was, she was bored. And as always, when boredom struck, her mind wandered to other tasks she'd rather do or other places she'd rather be. She'd been waiting two days for Sam to get back to her about the Trade Winds file and refused to call her.

Surely Sam had found what she'd noted in the file thirteen years ago. That the documents had been signed by Chase Sullivan, who had been little more than a file clerk at the time. And although she had no new evidence to warrant a request to reopen the case, she was still intrigued by Sullivan's role.

Skye sighed heavily, blowing out all her pent-up frustration. She leaned back in the swivel chair at her old desk and stared at the notes on her laptop screen. The conundrum was that if she stirred things up at the field office and the case *was* reopened, her own neglect of it would be all too obvious. If she hadn't been in such a rush to leave Seattle for her transfer to Washington, she would have followed up with Chase Sullivan on his return. Instead she'd left the task and the file to her replacement, who apparently had screwed up, too.

Now she was left with the same question she'd asked herself years ago. Why had Chase's signature been on those reports and invoices, as innocuous as they seemed, if he had not been in management? She wanted the answer to that question but knew it would inevitably lead to trouble.

In spite of her sister's vehement denial that she had no interest in Chase Sullivan beyond his role in his son's life. Skye had seen the color in her cheeks. No one knew her sister better than she did. And no way was she going to be blamed for another ruined relationship. Although, did she want her twin linked to someone who might be a cheat? She thought about last Christmas. Maybe responding to Todd's kiss had been a regrettable impulse, but underlying the impulse was a desire to reveal him as the consummate womanizer she sensed he was.

When the phone rang later that day, Nina called Skye to pick up. It was Samantha.

"We need to talk," she said. "You, me and Chase Sullivan."

"Okay. When and where?"

"My place, tonight at seven."

"Okey-dokey," Skye said. She hung up with a satisfied smile. The decision had been taken right out of her hands. Good.

CHAPTER ELEVEN

"WHAT, NO WINE?"

Sam hid her grin from her sister. "This is a business meeting, not a social one." She switched on the coffee-maker and began pulling mugs from a cupboard.

"You aren't dressed for a business meeting," Skye pointed out. "That top is a tad sheer, isn't it? And those jeans very tight, I must say."

"Cut it out. Here, put some of these cookies on a plate." Sam handed her a box.

"Store bought? Couldn't you at least have baked?"

"Ha ha." It was a family joke—no one in their family baked. Sam hoped the light mood would last, but had her doubts. She'd invited Skye to come earlier than Chase—she wanted to fill her in on what she'd learned from him yesterday.

Chase had dropped Danny at the school, but called Sam from his cell phone to continue their discussion about Trade Winds. Eventually Sam had persuaded him to talk to Skye, informally and off the record. Now she had to convince her sister likewise.

"He seems to be a bit late," Skye said, checking her watch.

"No, I asked you to come earlier."

"Oh, yeah?"

Sam saw the instant wariness in her sister's eyes.

"Come and sit down," she said, leading the way into the living room.

Skye perched on the edge of the couch. "What have you cooked up, Sam?"

"Come on, Skye. Surely when I said we were meeting with Chase, you figured out what it was going to be about."

"So I gather the two of you are going to try to persuade me to drop the inquiry." Her expression suggested she was up for the challenge.

"Not really. I was hoping you'd agree to work with us to find out the truth."

Skye's eyes narrowed. "The truth? Are you prepared for that?"

"Why wouldn't I be?"

"Just that—you know—you seem a bit attached to this guy and his kid."

Sam held up a hand. "Hey. They have names and I want you to use them. Okay?"

Surprise flickered across Skye's face. Then she shrugged and said, "Fine."

"Good. Now let me tell you Chase's story. I'd like you to think about it before he gets here. If you're not into helping us, there's no point wasting everyone's time."

Skye leaned back into the couch, crossed her legs and said, "Go ahead."

Sam wasn't fooled by her nonchalance. She'd caught the flash of anger in her twin's eyes. But she gave a condensed version of the story, because she wanted to finish before Chase arrived. To her surprise, Skye didn't interrupt once, and she managed to relate the gist of what happened years ago, ending with the visit to Martha Sullivan.

When she finished, Skye didn't speak for a long time, obviously digesting everything she'd heard. "So you're telling me Chase had no idea what was going on in his own family's business?"

"It seems unbelievable, but he was younger—twenty-three then—and he had no interest in the company. He didn't even want to work there and was just biding his time until he'd had enough saved to travel again."

"The woman who went to Chase with her concerns—what was her name again?"

Sam scanned the notes she'd made. "Uh…Nancy Wicks."

"Okay, so she couldn't find any record of a company that had been contracted by Trade Winds for these government commissions."

"Right, and when Chase confronted his uncle with the invoices, he was told everything was aboveboard."

"Huh. Sort of, butt out and don't worry your pretty little head about all this."

Sam smiled. "In this case, your handsome little head."

Skye arched a brow. "Like that, is it?"

Sam regretted the remark instantly. "Just joking. Back to business."

Skye stared at her a long moment before saying, "All right. Was there any mention of Nancy in my notes?"

"No, she'd already been let go by the time you went there."

Skye frowned. "So they could have purposely left me in the dark about other employees to interview. It does make sense if she was there when the scamming was going on."

"Scamming?"

Skye leaned forward. "This is what I think was happening. Trade Winds had received a lot of lucrative government contracts, right?"

"Right. Apparently Chase's cousins had government connections."

"Whatever. The point is, a company like Trade Winds simply contracts jobs and goods. They'd get some other business to provide the stuff they've been hired to obtain, pay them and then collect from the state or the federal government."

"Chase said it was similar to what I do."

"Yeah, it is. But suppose the company that provides the service doesn't exist? Suppose it's a company on paper only and is actually 'owned' by Trade Winds."

"But they have to provide something, don't they, in order to get the government to pay them?"

"I hate to tell you how easy it is to cheat the government, Sam. People do it all the time. Think about it— governments are huge bureaucracies with a lot of people working in them. Half the time, one department has no idea what another is doing. You wouldn't believe the stories I've heard or the scenarios I've seen."

"Are you saying that one department could be paying off an invoice without actually checking to see if the job was done?"

"Exactly. Or if the goods were provided in full. Perhaps only half of what was requested was received, but full payment was made." Skye reached out a hand. "Let me see my file for a sec."

Sam handed her the file and waited while Skye rifled through it.

"Here's something," she said, retrieving a slip of paper. "This invoice is for something called 'inventory consultation' by a business called H. J. Weiner and Company."

"What is that? Inventory consultation?"

"Who knows? My guess is that it's something to do with business investing. Maybe checking out business markets somewhere." Skye flipped through the file again. "Here's a report connected with that particular invoice. H. J. Weiner was contracted by Trade Winds to study import-export markets in China. You know, like the kinds of goods that would sell well over there and vice versa. And," she added, skimming the report, "it's been signed by none other than Chase Sullivan."

"Because his uncle, or maybe one of his cousins, got him to."

Skye shot her a withering look. "So he says."

"I believe him. He signed things without bothering to read them. He didn't care."

"Relax, Sam. I'm just reminding you there is another perspective here. In spite of what Chase told you, there's no proof that he's telling the truth."

"And there's no proof that he defrauded the government."

Skye waggled the invoice and report at her. "His name is on both of these documents. If it could be proved that there is no such business as H. J. Weiner and Company, then he's in big trouble."

"But…" Sam stopped, overwhelmed by the implications.

"There may be a way out of this for Chase," Skye said. "If we could persuade the local FBI office to reopen the case, new evidence may turn up."

"How?"

"Presuming the uncle and sons were cheating the government twelve years ago, they may still be doing so. And obviously Chase won't be connected to those new cases."

"Well, you've more or less been doing that, haven't you? Reopening the case?"

"More or less."

Sam waited. "Well, which is it?"

"I've been researching the file on my own time, Sam. I don't work in Seattle anymore. I don't have official sanction to review the case."

"But you could get it, couldn't you?"

"Not without new evidence or information turning up to warrant a review."

"Then why have you been checking this out on your own?"

Skye looked away. "I'm not clear on that."

"What's that supposed to mean?"

Skye's gaze shifted back to Sam. "Well…for one thing, I knew I'd need something to do while I was in town. Also, I was curious. Your phone call brought it all back and I wondered if I could find anything new. Plus…" Her voice trailed off.

"What?"

"Just that I knew I hadn't done a great job with the inquiry the first time around. I was a rookie and tended to believe what was staring me in the face and not question what I didn't see."

Sam was surprised at this admission of weakness from Skye. She didn't know how to respond, but was saved from doing so by the front-door buzzer.

"That must be Chase," she said, getting up to ring him in. "Help yourself to coffee while I get the door," she said over her shoulder. She thought she heard Skye mutter "Whoopee" on the way.

Sam didn't expect the sudden flutter in her midsection when she saw Chase standing in the doorway. He held out a bottle of wine and said, smiling, "Hello again."

"Hello, to you. Come in. Skye's already here. And thank you for this," she said, taking the wine and closing the door behind him. "How'd it go with Danny?"

"Okay, I guess. I was hoping he'd open up a bit about his mother but maybe I'm expecting too much too soon. But I did tell him more about my mother and gave him an edited version of my falling-out with my father."

"Good for you. Did he say anything about the visit to Harbor House?"

"He said I must feel bad about my own mother not knowing me anymore."

Sam placed a hand on his forearm. "In spite of his often contrary manner, I think Danny is a sensitive boy. Like his father," she impulsively added.

Chase put his hand on hers. "Thanks, Sam."

The mood was broken by a voice behind them. "Coffee's ready," Skye said, "but perhaps you'd prefer wine?"

"I believe you two have already met," Sam said.

"Indeed we have," said Chase solemnly, his gaze fixed on Skye. "And coffee's fine with me."

Sam wondered if this meeting was a mistake. She was about to suggest opening the wine, after all, when Chase smiled and extended his right hand to Skye.

"At least now I know whom I'm speaking to," he said.

"Oh, I think you were pretty quick figuring that one out before," Skye said, shaking his hand.

Sam breathed an inward sigh of relief.

They settled into the living room with coffee and Skye got right to the point. "Sam's filled me in on what you discussed with her, Chase. I told her that unless new evidence or information comes to light, the case probably won't be reopened. So I'm not exactly sure what you two—or the three of us—can do."

While Sam appreciated her sister's frankness, she was annoyed at the negative slant she was giving. "Let's not rule out anything yet," she quickly said.

"Was there anyone else in the company besides this Nancy Wicks who suspected what was going on?"

Chase shook his head. "It was—and likely still is—basically a small business. There were only a handful of people in the office."

"So your uncle and cousins were the only ones really running the business." She thought for a moment. "It wouldn't hurt to talk to the Wicks woman."

"Wasn't that already done when the inquiry was going on?" Chase asked, reaching for one of the cookies on the plate that Sam had set on the coffee table.

To Sam's surprise, her sister blushed. "I didn't know about her." Then she added, "But I should have come back to question you."

"Yeah. Maybe it would have all come out right at the time, instead of thirteen years later."

There was no sound but the gentle crunch of cookie. Finally Sam could stand it no longer. "Look, there's nothing to be gained by imagining what might have been or should have been done back then. Let's work with what we know now." She looked at Chase. "Would you be able to find Nancy?"

"If she's still at the same address, yes."

"Then we'll start with her. Why don't you confirm her address and we can go see her tomorrow. And, Skye, maybe you could find out if there have been any other inquiries or suspicions about Trade Winds since."

"Presumably they'd have been cross-referenced with the old file," she said.

"Still, there might be something somewhere."

"Maybe."

Sam glanced sharply at her sister. She obviously wasn't pleased at the way things were moving along or simply didn't like being told what to do.

"There is one other matter," Chase said.

Both sisters looked at him.

"When I came home two years ago, I found out that my mother had sold her share of the company to my uncle. I know she didn't get what she ought to have and I argued with my uncle about it, but he basically told me the sale was final. I think my mother had already been diagnosed with Alzheimer's by then, so…"

"He took advantage of her," interjected Sam. "Wouldn't that make the sale invalid?"

Skye sighed. "I think Chase would have to hire a lawyer to look into the details. Unless he has definite proof of wrongdoing." She stood up. "I should go. Mom wants me to go shopping with her in the morning."

"Shopping?" Nina's dislike of shopping was legendary in the family.

"Yeah, go figure. I think there's a man in her life."

Sam didn't know if she was more shocked by this revelation than by the fact that Skye, who'd been home only a week, knew before she did. It also made her realize, sadly, how seldom she and her sister communicated.

She walked her to the door, where Skye leaned forward to whisper, "Don't forget what we talked about before Chase arrived. His part in this," she said when Sam frowned.

"And don't you forget you promised to do some checking around."

"Watch yourself," was all Skye said, closing the door behind her.

Seething, Sam headed into the kitchen for the bottle of wine. "Would you like a glass of wine?" she called out.

"Love to."

She spun around to find Chase standing in the doorway. "Heavens, you startled me. Here, you open it while I get the glasses." She handed him the corkscrew, reached for two goblets in the cupboard above the sink and hastened into the living room. She couldn't explain why she felt so nervous, but sensed it had a lot to do with her increasing change of mind when it came to Chase Sullivan.

JANICE CARTER   165

When he joined her, she was sitting in her chair, leafing through the file again. He sat on the couch. "Thank you," she said as he poured the wine. "Can you think of anything else we could do?"

"Hmm, yes, I can."

She raised her head. "I…uh…was talking about the case."

"Oh." His gaze didn't falter.

Sam knew her face was red, but sipped her wine, pretending she hadn't caught the nuance in his voice.

After a moment he said, "Sorry, I didn't mean that to come out like a bad line in an even worse movie. It's just that our conversations always have to do with Danny or my past. I was thinking on my way over here that I really know little about you. Certainly not as much as you seem to know about me."

She looked straight at him and said, "I agree with you about the first point, but as for knowing a lot about you, I hardly know more than…well, more than my sister."

He cocked his head, clearly puzzled.

"I mean," she went on, discomfited by his stare, "what I know about you are *facts*. Things other people know— or could find out. Your history."

"My history," he repeated softly. "Let's not go there tonight. Tell me about *your* history—especially with your sister." He reached for another cookie and settled back into the couch.

"Not much to tell." Sam shifted in her chair. "Identical twins raised by a single mother who is also a practising clinical psychologist."

"Divorced?"

"Yep. When we were two. My father couldn't take the impact of twins on his personal life."

"Do you have contact with him?"

"None at all. I think he made a halfhearted attempt at

maintaining contact for the first couple of years, but then he met someone else, started another family and so the story goes."

"Maybe it was better that way, being with only one parent, but someone whose love you never had any doubts about." He folded his arms across his chest, looking disarmingly like a psychologist.

Sam considered what he said. She'd never really looked at their abandonment by their father that way, but she saw that he was right. Nina had more than made up for a missing parent. "I suppose," she murmured, drinking more wine and wishing he'd fasten his eyes somewhere else.

"I gather you and your sister have a...well, I guess you could say a communication problem."

Sam's laugh was derisive. "I guess you could say for sure. We look alike, but we're very different."

He nodded. "That was my first impression when she came into my shop. Now I'm not so sure."

"How do you mean?"

"I noticed when we were talking tonight that you and she seem to have some kind of mental connection. I can't explain it. She'd say something and your body language signaled a reaction. Then you'd both look at each other at the same time. Am I making any sense?" He grinned suddenly, unfolding his arms and relaxing against the cushions. "Maybe it's a twin thing."

"I've been edgy around Skye lately, so perhaps that's what you're seeing."

"Edgy?"

"We had a falling-out some months ago," she said dismissively, hoping he'd drop the matter. But no such luck.

"What about? It's none of my business, but I'm curious." He leaned over to refill her wineglass, adding a bit more to his at the same time.

All of a sudden, Sam found herself wanting to tell him about it. "The story behind the story really goes back to high school," she said. "When we were in twelfth grade, I was dating a guy I didn't really like all that much, but at the time, having a date seemed to be more important than *who* you were dating. My sister and I had this rivalry about, say, who would snag the first date for the monthly school dance, that sort of thing. Anyway, Skye and I had an argument one day about dates and I'm not sure which one of us suggested the idea or maybe it hit us both at the same time—that mental thing we had going, as you said. So we decided that the next time he asked me out, we'd trade places and see if we could fool him."

"Ah, the old switcheroo trick," he said, raising an eyebrow.

"Yes, and Skye was always a good actor, which is why I think she's so good at undercover work. Anyway, the poor guy had no idea and was incredibly embarrassed when she finally told all. Especially after a rather heavy make-out session."

"Uh-oh."

"When she came home that night, we had a laugh about it, but I felt really guilty afterward and apologized to him the next day. He told me very bluntly what he thought of both of us and never asked either one of us out again. But the prank taught me something about respecting other people and I refused to use my twin-hood to play any more tricks again. Not even on our mother—because we'd done that as children. I made Skye promise never to pretend to be me and vice versa." Sam paused to take another sip of wine.

"So fast forward to last Christmas. I was engaged to be married to Todd—I'd been dating him for a while and I thought I loved him and he loved me. Skye was living in

D.C. then, as she still is. We were all at my mother's for dinner and I offered to do the dishes. Skye came into the kitchen as I was starting and said she'd take over, that I'd done a lot of the preparation so I should take a break. So I did. I joined my mother in the solarium—it's across the patio from the kitchen. Todd had gone outside to get something from the car."

"I think I'm getting the picture."

"It was like a scene in a French farce. Fiancé mistakes twin, kisses the wrong one."

"But it was a bit more than a simple kiss," he said quietly.

She sighed. "Yes. So much so that I couldn't forget about it—as my ex so diligently tried to persuade me to do."

After a moment, he asked, "And now?"

Sam smiled. "Now I don't even know what I saw in him."

He smiled back. "But you're still angry at Skye."

"I'm not sure. I thought I was, but maybe I'm more angry at myself. That she obviously saw something in Todd I missed. That worries me."

"I gather you haven't settled the matter with her, then." He finished the last of his wine and set the glass on the coffee table.

"No, though I want to. But we both seem to keep skirting around the whole thing. Or we argue about some trivial incident when…"

"What you really want to say are all the things you never said at Christmas."

She nodded. There was nothing more to say. After a few seconds, she quietly asked, "More wine?"

He looked at his watch. "Thanks, but I should get going. I've got an order to finish tomorrow and it's getting late."

She felt a rush of disappointment, hoping her story hadn't bored him or put him off completely. At the door, he paused and took hold of her hand.

"Personally I can't understand how any man could mistake you for your sister." He pulled her closer, lowered his head and kissed her.

His lips were soft, but demanded more than a chaste good-night kiss. Sam brought her arms up around his neck and held him against her, giving in to the warm, sweet rhythm of his body pressed into hers. When he pulled away, she sagged into him. He chuckled softly, steadying her with his hands.

"Thanks for the history, Sam...and for other things I hope to share with you in time. Good night." He closed the door behind him.

Sam felt stunned. Her life had just taken a sharp turn in a very unexpected direction. She ran her tongue along her lips, still tasting him. She wanted the sensation to last as long as possible.

CHAPTER TWELVE

SAM WAS AWAKENED by the buzz of the front door. She shot up, disoriented, and looked automatically at her clock-radio. Nine. In the morning. On Saturday. She groaned and fell back onto the pillow, but the caller persisted. She reached for the phone on her bedside table and connected to the person at the door.

A muffled voice answered her sharp hello. High-pitched but assertive. When Sam repeated her "Who is it," the caller shouted, "Danny!" She closed her eyes, wishing she was simply dreaming. She crawled out of bed, threw on a robe and waited, bleary-eyed.

"It's Saturday," she said as she flung open the door. "Aren't you supposed to be with Chase?"

He brushed past her, his bad mood hunkering on his shoulders like a raven in an Edgar Allen Poe story. Sam stared speechlessly as he swept through the living room and kitchen, pausing outside the bathroom. Although his eyes darted toward the open bedroom door, he held back, obviously reluctant to cross that particular barrier.

"Can I ask what the heck you're doing?" she snapped.

"Is he here?"

"Who?"

"Chase," he said, looking her straight in the face.

"And why would he be here?"

For the first time, Danny faltered. Glancing away, he

muttered, "He left a message at Minnie's to say he couldn't have me this weekend 'cause he had to finish an order or something."

Right. He'd mentioned that last night. "And?"

His shoulders rose up and down under the oversize hoodie. "I thought maybe he was here, that's all."

"But why would he be here?"

Danny's eyes widened, incredulous. "You two were really deep into it the other night when I stayed over. I thought...well...when I heard he was copping out on me, I thought maybe he was with you. *You* know."

Sam knew if she hadn't been fantasizing about that very *you know* for part of the night, she'd have been far angrier at the suggestion than she was. She closed the door and moved past him to the kitchen. "Have you had breakfast? Want some orange juice or something?"

"I'm not hungry and you can't just change the subject, okay?"

Sam spun around. "Listen, Danny. You wake me up on a Saturday morning—my sleep-in day—to accuse me of..." she sputtered, "whatever...."

"Whatever." He sneered. "Are you—"

"No, I am not. I know what you were going to ask and although it's absolutely none of your business and I can't believe I'm explaining myself to a *twelve-year-old boy,* I will say once and for all, no. Satisfied?"

He remained silent, but Sam noticed his stubborn chin relaxing a bit. He averted his face. "I was gonna say 'dating.'"

"Yeah, right," she muttered. Then she caught his eye and grinned. "Why do I feel like my mother just barged in on me?"

He might have smiled back, she figured, had she used any other word but *mother.* "I was serious about breakfast,

Danny. Let's have some juice first and then decide what we can cook up." She went on into the kitchen before he could stop her. By the time she carried two tumblers of juice into the living room, he was slumped, legs sprawled out in front of him, on the couch. He took the juice with a mumble that Sam guessed was a thank-you and she sat across from him in her chair.

She sipped her juice slowly, wondering what to say to him. Danny had definitely misinterpreted their quiet talk the other night in the kitchen while he slept—she thought—on the couch. And while her attitude toward Chase had changed drastically in the last week, she was only now beginning to realize that her feelings for him had changed, as well. A single kiss had certainly confirmed that. *But it was only a kiss.*

The memory of Skye's sheepish expression when Sam confronted her at Christmas rose in her mind. It was only a kiss, she'd said, with such dismissal Sam had wanted to strike her. *Funny how little I care about that now.*

"So let me get this right. You thought your father and I were dating and that maybe he'd spent the night here."

Danny couldn't meet her gaze. "Yeah," he muttered into his glass.

"Well, we're not and he didn't. Okay?"

He shrugged.

"Anyway," she went on, imagining there might be a future possibility of that very scenario if his kiss was anything to go by, "would it be so terrible if we were?"

Danny's head shot up, his eyes narrowed. "Not terrible for you but maybe for me."

"Why?"

"Oh, forget it. It doesn't matter, anyway, now that I know what's what."

"But it *does* matter because I can see you're upset about

it—or about something. Why don't you tell me what's bothering you?" She set her glass down on the table and leaned forward in her chair.

Rather than answer, he concentrated on finishing his juice. When he did, he seemed to drift off, lost in thought, as he ran his fingertip along the rim of the empty glass.

"Danny?" she prompted, softening her voice. "What is it?"

He uttered an impatient sigh and looked as if he'd rather be anywhere else. "Now I see how silly it is, but I was thinking, what if you and Chase…you know, liked each other and wanted to get together. And that would be nice, I guess, for you, if it did happen." He paused. "Even though it won't, 'cause you're not dating, anyway." He stressed the last few words.

Sam wished he'd get on with it, but didn't dare interrupt.

"But suppose it did happen. I know some kids whose parents split up and they have stepmothers and fathers and all that. My friend Jeff tells me things are okay for him now, but he still misses the way his family used to be." Danny raised his voice. "I know my mom is going to die. Nobody really talks about it, but I know, okay?" He shot her a defiant look.

It was all she could do not to get up and go over to him. In spite of his expression, he fairly screamed pain. She couldn't speak for a long moment. "We don't talk about it, Danny, because—like you—no one wants to think about it. Maybe people do that, hoping the reality is never going to happen. All of this—knowing someone who's dying— is all new to me, too."

He seemed to mull that over. "Yeah, I guess. But see, the point of looking for my father was so I'd have someone after Mom…and so I wouldn't have to go into a foster home. If my…if Chase meets someone and falls in love and gets married and has kids…well, he may not want me around anymore. I'm not a cute little kid and I have problems at school and things on my mind and all that kind of stuff."

Sam knew right away what he was getting at. "You're worried that your father may want to start a new life with someone and you won't fit into it. Your mother will be gone and you'll have no one," she said softly.

He looked up. His eyes were red. "Yeah," he whispered.

Sam fended off an overwhelming urge to cry. She took a deep breath and said, "Chase would never in a million years do that, Danny. And I'm not talking about just accepting responsibility for you. He wants to *know* you—as a person and as a son. You're both still in the process of finding out about each other. It takes time. But believe me, if Chase didn't care about you, he'd simply write a check and hand it to your mother. Why do you think he took you to Harbor House the other day to meet his mother?"

Danny flushed. "I wasn't very nice that day, not when we first got there. I didn't know why he dragged me to an old people's home. But then after I met Martha, I kinda figured it out."

"What did you figure out?"

Another shrug. "That he wanted me to know something about him and his childhood." He stopped for a minute. "It was weird how she thought I was him as a kid. Afterward I wondered if it made him feel bad."

"Maybe he felt sad for a few seconds, but then I think he felt really good about how nice you were to Martha. And how you didn't correct her about the confusion. I think he was very proud of you."

"Really?"

Sam nodded. She felt a lump in her throat at the hope

in his voice. "And there's another thing, Danny. You may have started out as my client—" she paused, smiling "—but you've ended up as a friend. Friends stick together, right?"

"Yeah," he whispered.

After a moment, Sam said, "I have an idea and you can say no if you like. How about coming with me over to my mom's place for the day? I'll introduce you to my twin and we can all hang out."

When Danny agreed, she smiled. "Here," she said, handing him the TV remote, "entertain yourself while I dress and call my mother."

On the drive to Nina's, Sam filled Danny in on a few basic particulars of her life.

"What's it like being a twin?" he asked. "Do you dress the same?"

Sam laughed. "Heavens no. I think our mother did that when we were babies, but she wanted us to develop our own personalities. We were always put in different classrooms at school, if possible, so we would focus on making our own friends and not rely on each other for companionship."

"That sounds like a good idea. Do you ever do stuff together?"

"We used to, when we were younger and still living at home. But we went to different colleges and now Skye—that's her name—lives and works in Washington, D.C."

"Yeah? Skye, that's a neat name."

"She always said she got the best name because she was born first. She's fifteen minutes older than me."

"Samantha's a nice name, too," Danny quickly said.

"She's an FBI agent."

"Cool!" Danny turned her way, his jaw dropping. "Does she have a gun and everything?"

"Oh, yes, though I've never seen it. She may not have

it here because she's on holidays." *Supposedly.* Sam wondered if Skye had made a decision yet about helping her and Chase get evidence against Trade Winds.

She found out soon enough. "He's cute," Skye whispered as Danny headed farther into the foyer to meet Nina. "So are we babysitting today or what? Mom said our shopping expedition was on hold."

Sam turned to face her sister. "I think Danny would be very offended by that suggestion, Skye. He's been looking after a terminally ill mother for the past six months."

"Sheesh, lighten up. But seriously, what's happening? I thought you and Chase were all hot to track down Nancy Wicks."

Sam pulled her by the arm to an alcove at the end of the hall. "Are you going to help us with this or not?"

"I don't know. The thing is, I'm in a bit of trouble over the Trade Winds thing."

"What do you mean?"

"I had a call from my section head this morning."

"This morning?"

"Well, it was noon his time but still Saturday."

"What about?"

"He had a call from the head of the field office here, who apparently had another call from some muckety-muck in the state government who just happened to be an old buddy of…"

"Bryant Sullivan?"

"You guessed it. Anyway, Sullivan has accused me of harassment and since the case hasn't been officially opened, I was warned off."

"How?"

"Keep away from the place and the people or risk suspension."

"Oh, Skye. That's serious."

She looked away. "Especially since it would be my second suspension."

"Your second! When was the other time?"

"Just before Christmas. Another reason for my bad behavior."

Sam narrowed her eyes. "I hope you're not trying to justify what you did."

"No, I'm not," Skye said angrily, turning toward her. "I'm only saying it was just one more problem I was dealing with at the time. Can we drop it now? Mom's headed our way."

"I asked Danny if he'd like us to take him sightseeing," Nina said as she came up to them. "He would. Can you believe he's never been to Chinatown or up the Space Needle? So is that okay by you, Sam?"

"Sounds great," Sam said.

"Wait a minute, Sam," Skye said. "You and I were planning a little expedition, weren't we?"

"Shopping?" Nina asked.

"Sort of. Just checking out something," Skye said.

Sam gnawed on her lip. She knew if she turned Skye down, her sister might not give her a second chance. "Do you mind taking Danny on your own, Mom?"

"Not at all, but you'd better speak to Danny, Sam, because he thinks you're spending time with him today." She walked off to join Danny, who was wandering through the living room.

"What kind of expedition are you talking about?" Sam asked Skye.

"Going to see Nancy Wicks."

"But I did tell Danny we'd do something together."

"Come here." Skye pulled Sam by the arm to the entrance to the living room. Sam could see Danny and Nina deep in conversation in the solarium at the end of the room. "I think Nina's got you covered for part of the day, at least."

"What about that suspension thing?"

"I'll stay in the background. Besides, this Nancy doesn't know me at all. We don't even have to *mention* the FBI."

"You mean, *I* should ask the questions?"

"Don't sound so horrified. We'll talk about what to ask on the way."

"I don't even know where she lives."

Skye rolled her eyes. "Really, Sam, you make a lousy P.I. She's in the phone book."

"We have to see if Chase can come."

"Why? We can do this on our own."

"But he knows Nancy. And this concerns him most of all. He has to be there. Why the look? Do you have a problem with him coming?"

Skye turned away, heading for her bedroom. "No, just that I'll feel like a third wheel or something."

"What? Tell me you don't mean what I think you do." She marched after her sister.

Skye stopped and turned away. "You know exactly what I mean. I was only with the two of you last night for an hour, tops, and it was like dodging blanks on a maneuvers course."

"Oh, come on."

"The looks, Sam. The checking each other out. Whatever you want to call it. I'm surprised our hair wasn't standing on end with all the electricity zinging around the room."

Sam dropped her hand from Skye's arm. "If I seemed to be looking at Chase a lot, it was because I wanted to see his reaction to what you were saying about the fraud scheme and all that."

Skye smirked. "Please, Sam, that's real lame. If you haven't figured out yet that you're attracted to the man, there's not much I can do for you. Except stay out of it."

"See, that comment is what bugs me. What do you mean by it?"

"Been there, done that. I'm not going to be blamed for any more of your failed relationships."

It wasn't anger that choked Sam's reply, but pain. Pain at the realization that she and Skye had drifted so far apart that her twin could believe, much less utter, such a cruel remark. She stood still, taking slow, calming breaths to fend off a rebuttal that would only take them both down a path Sam knew she dared not go.

Lowering her voice, she said, "I'm not going to respond to that now, Skye, but we will go back to this, trust me." She started toward the solarium to tell Danny about the change in plans, then stopped and turned around. "Maybe you've given up on our relationship, but I haven't." Inwardly shaking, she spun on her heel before Skye could say another word.

Danny was graceful about the change in plans. "Will you be seeing Chase? I thought he was busy this weekend."

Sam hesitated. It wasn't her place to inform Danny about what was happening with his father and Trade Winds. On the other hand, she didn't want him to think she'd lied when she denied being romantically involved with Chase. "Yes, he does have work to do, but we have some business to discuss that's very important and he may decide to meet with us, after all. I know he'll explain it all to you at some point. I can tell you it's not about you or your mother, but about Chase and…uh…a legal matter Skye and I are helping him with. I'm sorry if that seems vague, but for now…"

Danny's dark eyes bored into hers, and Sam sensed he knew more than he was letting on. "Sure. If you're talking to him, can you tell him my mother's feeling much better, but she'd like to see him again—soon?"

His message resonated. While she and Skye were carrying on with their petty arguing and plotting with Chase to rectify the past, Emily and Danny were clinging to their last times together. Sam placed a hand on Danny's shoulder, giving it a squeeze. "I will, Danny, and tell your mom I'll be in to see her, too, as soon as possible." Impulsively she bent down to give him a quick kiss on the top of his head. "Bye then, see you later."

On her way to the kitchen to call Chase, she met Nina, carrying a tray of muffins and juice. "I talked to Danny, Mom, and he's okay with my going off with Skye."

"What's going on, Sam?"

"Mom, I'll tell you all about it soon, but not now. It's something to do with Chase and his family's business."

"You know that Danny is very fragile right now." Nina's stern face suggested nothing else mattered.

Sam pursed her lips. "I do, Mom. And the matter that we're trying to resolve will actually benefit Danny someday. So even though it may seem as if we're not thinking of him, we are."

"Of course, dear, I wasn't suggesting otherwise. I'm simply reminding you that he needs a lot of support. After we finish our sightseeing, I plan to go with him to the hospital and meet Emily."

Sam recalled her mother's reaction to the Benson-family plight when she'd first told her about Danny's office visit. How she'd advised her not to get emotionally entangled. "Thanks, Mom," she said, thinking how many things had changed since that fateful day. She kissed her mother's cheek. "I'll give you a call later."

Skye was nowhere to be seen, so Sam went on to the kitchen to call Chase. He picked up right away.

"I was wondering when you'd call," he said. "I've rearranged my work plans so I can be free to go see Nancy Wicks. Still up for it?"

Sam marveled how a voice that signalled trouble mere

days ago could elicit such pleasure now. "Yes, but there's a small glitch. I'm here at my mother's with Danny, but he's going to spend the day with her."

She heard a muffled curse. "What's he doing there? I left a message at Minnie's before I came over to your place last night that I'd meet him at the hospital on Sunday."

Reluctant to clarify the real reason for Danny's impromptu visit, Sam said, "He just showed up at my place this morning. I think he needed some company. Anyway, I've been wanting to introduce him to Mom, so this works out okay. Why don't you give me Nancy's address and I'll meet you there."

"Sure. I'm already in the city so I can be there in about half an hour."

After jotting down the address, Sam disconnected and went looking for Skye.

She was in her old bedroom, working on her laptop. The room served as a den now, with a pull-out couch, but remnants of high-school days could still be seen. Yearbooks were lined up sequentially on the built-in shelves and, in one corner, a framed poster of the senior-year musical that both of them had performed in.

"I called Chase and we're meeting at Nancy Wicks's place. Are you coming?" When Skye swung her chair around to face her, Sam tried not to show surprise at the redness in her sister's eyes. She couldn't remember the last time she'd seen Skye cry, and she wondered if the argument they'd just had was the cause. Although she still needed to tell Skye about her anger and sense of betrayal over the Todd business, she felt bad. "We'll manage on our own if you'd rather not come."

"I'll come. Last night, you asked me to find out if there have been any further inquiries about Trade Winds since the last investigation, but since I'm forbidden access to the files now, I won't be able to do that. Maybe Nancy can add something to what we've got." She paused to shut down the computer. "Is that okay with you?"

Sam felt a rush of warmth for her sister. "Of course it is. I'll wait for you at the front door."

When Skye joined her a few minutes later, Sam noticed that she'd washed her face and applied a touch of make-up. As Skye walked out the door, Sam patted her lightly in the center of her back—a reassuring touch they'd often used on each other as children. *When all this is over,* she thought, *I'm going to do whatever it takes to get my sister back.*

CHAPTER THIRTEEN

CHASE WAS SURPRISED to see both sisters climb out of Sam's car when he pulled up in front of Nancy's place. He watched them walking toward the pickup, thinking that, in spite of the difference in their clothing styles, it was damn difficult to tell them apart. He knew that Skye had slightly deeper lines in her forehead, maybe from frowning at criminals the past few years, and Sam's voice was gentler than her twin's. But those subtleties aside, he understood how easily they could fool a person. Like the high-school romance Sam told him about last night.

He smiled, thinking of the goodbye kiss for the umpteenth time since leaving her place. It had been impulsive and, initially, meant as a sign that he appreciated her confidence. But as soon as his lips touched hers, he knew it was no platonic gesture. He hadn't experienced such desire in a long time. Far more than merely sexual, there was also warmth and comfort in the kiss, as if it had been the most natural thing in the world to do. As if he'd been kissing Samantha Sorrenti for years. When he woke up, her face was the first thing he saw in his mind's eye and he could still taste her lips.

He got out of the truck and met them on the sidewalk. "I called Nancy after I spoke to you, Sam, to give her a heads-up. She sounded mystified when I mentioned we wanted to talk to her about Trade Winds, but I reassured her I wasn't here representing my uncle."

"Why would she think that?"

"I don't think she ever found out what happened after I returned to Seattle." He looked at the wood-frame bungalow before them and headed for the front door. "I thought Skye was doing some other fact-finding today," Chase said in a low voice as Sam caught up to him. Skye was a few feet behind her.

She turned toward him, so close he could have leaned in an inch more and touched her skin with his lips. The thought made him feel almost light-headed.

"Skye's been warned off the case." She glanced back at Skye. "I'll fill you in later," she whispered.

Warned off the case. He had a gut feeling that Bryant was responsible for that, knowing his uncle had connections in local and state government. The futility of what they were attempting swept through him. His uncle had money and contacts, while he had a few scraps of paper that didn't prove anything.

He stopped on the doorstep. "Is there any point in going through with this?"

"It's worth a shot," she answered immediately. "For Danny."

He wanted to kiss her on the spot, but rang the doorbell instead.

When the door opened, he was transported back thirteen years. Nancy Wicks hadn't changed a bit. Tiny as a sparrow and sporting a huge smile, she cried, "Chase!"

He bent at the waist to receive her hug. "Hi, Nancy, it's good to see you again. Let me introduce you to Samantha Sorrenti and her sister, Skye," he said, gesturing first to Sam at his side and then to Skye, coming up behind them onto the porch.

"Whoa! I haven't even had my daily glass of wine and already I'm seeing double."

"I see you've still got your sense of humor," Chase said as he and the twins followed Nancy into the front hall.

"It's certainly improved since I left the company. Come into the den. Tom's made coffee. Everybody want a cup?"

Chase heard either Sam or Skye—which, he couldn't be sure—murmur assent as he trailed after Nancy down the hall. Her wiry, steel-gray hair bobbed around her head with each step. She'd always walked with such bouncing exuberance, ready for anything and everything. No employer in his right mind would have let Nancy Wicks go. At least, no one but Bryant Sullivan. They entered a small den where a tall, white-haired man carrying a tray of coffee mugs met them. "Just put it on the table, Tom," Nancy said, and turning to them, introduced her husband.

After a few minutes of polite conversation, sipping hot coffee and complimenting Nancy on her homemade oatmeal cookies, Chase got right to the point. "Nancy, we came to talk to you about what happened at the company thirteen years ago."

Nancy's smile disappeared. "Has Bryant sent you?"

"No, no, as I told you on the phone, I'm not here representing him."

"I heard via the grapevine that you resigned soon after I left," she said.

"Actually I was fired, but I would have quit anyway."

"Was it about those companies?"

Chase locked eyes with Sam over Nancy's head. "Yes."

"I've been waiting years for someone to ask me about those companies," Nancy said. "I heard there was an investigation, but no one came to talk to me."

"Why didn't you call the FBI yourself, then?" Skye asked.

Nancy looked across the room at Tom. There was an awkward silence until Tom said, "Actually, I called the FBI—twice."

Chase glanced from Nancy to Tom. "I don't understand," he said.

"Nancy was stressed out over this thing," Tom said. "She was convinced there was something underhanded going on, but when she tried to get answers from her boss, he just put her off. She talked to you about it, Chase, but in the meantime I couldn't stand seeing her come home every night worried sick that she was involved in something illegal. So I decided to stir things up a bit."

"It was *you!*" Chase was stunned, thinking back to the day he'd returned from the trade show and his father's accusation of betraying the company and the family.

"Maybe I caused some trouble for your family?" Tom asked hesitantly.

Like maybe blasted it apart. But the past was long gone, Chase reminded himself, and the family held together by strings, anyway.

"Nancy—and Tom—Chase hasn't mentioned yet that my sister, Skye, was the FBI agent who went to the company to make inquiries after…uh…your anonymous phone call," Sam put in, saving Chase from having to respond to Tom's revelation.

Nancy's jaw dropped. "No kidding."

"We came to find out exactly what your suspicions were before your husband made his phone call and what evidence you saw to confirm those suspicions," Skye put in.

"Well," said Nancy, drawing her five-foot frame up straight in her chair, "you may recall my talking to you about a couple of companies, Chase. We'd hired them to fill some government contracts and I had a question about one of the invoices. Contacting the company was just like spinning wheels. Going in circles. I'd get a voice mail to tell me to call another number and that one would be out of service. That kind of thing. I talked to you about it,

Chase, before I went in to see your uncle. He was a gruff man and I avoided him as much as possible. Anyway, you'd only been in the department a few weeks and didn't know much." She grinned mischievously. "Window dressing, the girls in Shipping called Chase," she said to Sam and Skye.

Chase saw the amusement in Sam's eyes and felt himself redden.

Nancy went on. "When I did get up my nerve to talk to Mr. Bryant, he didn't seem concerned at all. Basically told me his sons had given the jobs to those companies and they would look into the matter. Not long after that, I think you went and talked to him, Chase, because we couldn't track down some numbered company. Everything started moving very quickly after that. Tom here called the FBI—and I want to say right now that I had nothing to do with that." She glared at her husband.

"She didn't," asserted Tom.

"Then Chase was sent off to that trade show and the very next day, Mr. Bryant told me my job was being made redundant. He said Chase was going to share my work with his cousins and…well…that was the end of more than ten years with Trade Winds. I figured out what was happening, but had nothing to hold against them but suspicions. And we didn't have the money to hire a lawyer to appeal my dismissal." She stopped, her eyes glistening.

Tom reached over to pat her hand.

"But to Bryant's credit," she added, as if not wanting to offend Chase about his relatives, "he was very kind about my severance package. It was a nice one."

Chase pursed his lips. Kindness had definitely not been his uncle's motive and he bet Nancy knew that, too.

Sam pulled the folder out of her large shoulder bag. "Skye managed to get a copy of her old file. Can you take a look at this and see if you recognize or recall any of the companies mentioned?" She handed the folder to Nancy, who sifted through them carefully.

"This one," she said, holding up a slip of paper. "H. J. Weiner and Company. It was the first one, I think, that I couldn't trace. See the invoice? They billed us nineteen thousand dollars for consultation. I never did find out what *kind* of consulting and why it should have cost us so much. Mr. Bryant gave me the order to pay it and I did. But I wasn't happy about it." She folded her arms across her chest indignantly.

Chase realized right then that they'd gotten all their answers. "Is there anything else you can tell us, Nancy?" he asked.

She shook her head. "No, I'm sorry. If I'd known what was going to happen, I'd have photocopied some things, or gone to the FBI myself. But it all came so quickly. They gave me a check and one of the boys—Terence, I think—watched me like a hawk while I cleared out my desk. That really ticked me off. As if I was the one who'd been stealing from the company, instead of the person trying to save them money."

Chase looked across at Sam, raising his eyebrow. She got the message and rose to her feet. "Nancy," she said, "thank you so much for meeting with us."

"I don't think I told you anything you didn't already know."

"It was important to confirm our suspicions, Nance," Chase said.

"You *are* going to look into this, then, are you?"

"Definitely," Chase said. He bent his head to kiss Nancy on the cheek. "It was good to see you again."

"Don't stay away so long this time," she said, poking him in the chest. "Come back and fill us in on everything. I want the whole story next time."

Chase smiled. "For sure, Nance."

Moments later, standing on the sidewalk with Sam and Skye, he asked, "What now?"

Sam was still looking back at the Wickses house. Finally she turned around and the flash of uncertainty in her face made him want to pull her to him. The desire to toss the whole business aside had never been stronger.

"Well…" she began, looking from him to Skye. "I think we can't do too much more until we find out if one of the companies is fake. And if so, then we have to prove somehow that Trade Winds just made up that company. Have I got it right?" She turned to Skye.

"I have a friend who might be able to help me track down the Weiner company."

"Can you do it without getting yourself into more trouble?" Sam asked.

"Keep your fingers crossed. How about I borrow your car, Sam, and you can go back with Chase?"

Chase glanced away, not wanting either of them to see the eagerness in his face at the proposal. He waited anxiously until he heard Sam say, "Um, sure, if Chase doesn't mind."

Keeping his voice as neutral as possible, Chase replied, "No, not at all."

"Okay, then, give me your keys, Sam," said Skye, "and I'll phone you if I find out anything."

Chase watched her climb in the car and start up the engine. The car made a fast three-point turn and as it zipped past them, he could have sworn he saw Skye sporting a huge grin.

He looked at Sam and said, "I don't know about you, but I haven't had any lunch. Are you interested? I know a great little place near the market." Her face lit up with pleasure, and he knew—for now—the past was history. All that mattered was exploring this new and exciting development in his personal present.

LUNCH, though every bit as delicious as Chase had promised, was merely a backdrop to the far more enjoyable pleasure of tracking every movement of his long fingers or his lips as he talked quietly and earnestly about his life on Bainbridge. The entire hour was a full sensory production, excluding the actual eating part, and Sam could have sat hours longer, taking in even more of Chase Sullivan. But unfortunately, the waiter had other plans and brought them their bill.

After Chase insisted on paying and sent the waiter away, he said, "After your call I contacted my client and got a couple of days' grace on that rush job. Since we have some free time, would you like to come back to the island with me for a bit—see my carvings?" His grin was teasing.

"How could I refuse?" Then Sam remembered Danny. "There might be a tiny problem. I'm not sure how Danny's going to take the news that I'm with you."

Chase frowned. "What's up with Danny?"

Sam quickly filled him in on Danny's morning visit, too embarrassed to look at him when she got to the part where Danny had suspected Chase might be in her bedroom.

"What?"

Sam held up a hand. "It's okay, Chase, really. I had a talk with him. The whole scene was driven by anxiety about possibly being rejected by you. Someday."

He was shaking his head in disbelief. "Haven't I proved myself yet? What more do I have to do to persuade him that I accept him as my son—he *is* my son—and that I won't shirk that obligation?"

Sam waited a moment before saying, "I don't think he wants to be merely an 'obligation' to you."

A stain of red crept up his neck. "You know I didn't mean that to sound so cold. It's just that mentally, I know he's my son and I have no problem accepting that. But emotionally…" He looked down at the table.

Sam placed her hand on his forearm. "Chase, no one expects you to suddenly love Danny as a father just yet. That will come. Just keep on doing what you're doing. Connect with him as an adult and eventually you'll both fall into the roles." She sighed.

He raked a hand through his hair. "You're right. Relaxing and letting things just happen is the best strategy. But I'm curious—what precipitated his impromptu visit?"

"Uh, well…it seems he was paying more attention to us the other night than we thought. He obviously misconstrued our hushed tones as we talked about Trade Winds and all that."

Sam didn't have to fill in the blanks for him. She saw that he guessed right away what Danny imagined they were talking about.

The waiter returned with the change and as soon as he left, Chase said, "Come on. I think we could both use a break from Trade Winds and—hell—even from Danny. How about it? Let's get impulsive."

"Why not?" She grinned.

"Okay, let's go to the island." He ushered her out of the restaurant and when they could walk side by side, he casually clasped her hand in his, a move so natural Sam felt as though she'd been linking hands with him forever.

The truck was parked in a lot near the market and as they reached it, Sam decided to make her phone call right away. Chase stood aside while she pressed the speed-dial button for her mother's, but Sam couldn't take her eyes off him. He caught her looking and she flushed, grateful to have the excuse to turn away as her mother answered.

"Mom, it's me, Sam. I just called to say that I'm going to be a bit later than I thought. Is Danny still with you? Or did you take him to Minnie's?"

"Yes, he's still with me. We've just come back from the hospital and I've been waiting for your call. I have an engagement this evening, Sam."

"Oh, sorry, Mom. I should have thought to ask before we left. Um, is it something flexible or…?"

"A dinner date, actually. With Bill Carter."

Sam digested that. Bill Carter was the family lawyer. And perhaps the mystery man Skye had alluded to? "Oh…well…would you be able to take Danny back to Minnie's place for the night? He can give you directions." She paused, took a deep breath and added, "Chase has invited me back to his place for a bit." There was a long silence. "Mom?"

"Yes, dear. I'm just processing that. So what shall I tell Danny?"

"The truth, Mom. I'm not asking you to make excuses for me."

"Is something going on I should know about, Sam? I mean, I don't want to keep things from Danny and at the same time I don't want to seem completely ignorant about my children's lives."

Sam had to smile. It was so typical of Nina that nothing could be unfettered by questions. "He and I need to talk over some things, Mom. About the possible legal trouble Chase might be in."

Another pause, followed by, "Ah, yes. The legal trouble."

Sam ignored the irony in her mother's voice. "Do you think I should speak to Danny myself?"

"No, no, that's all right. We had a little chat this afternoon about his visit to your place and the feelings that prompted it. He's a pretty amazing young fellow. And his mother is remarkable. I can see why you were compelled to stay with them, Samantha, in spite of the personal commitment involved."

Sam felt a rush of affection for her mother. "Could you tell Danny that Chase will call him in the morning?"

"In the *morning?*"

She saw right away what her mother was hinting at. "He plans to go to the hospital and I'll probably join him there."

When her mother responded, there was a hint of disapproval in her voice. "All right, Samantha."

"Oh, and is Skye at home? She has my car."

"She's here, but I haven't seen her for hours. She's been holed up in her room working on her computer. Do you want to speak to her?"

"No, it's okay." She hoped Skye was busy researching information on Trade Winds.

"Goodbye, then."

As Nina rang off, Sam thought about how quickly her mother had always been to come to their aid when they were teenagers. Not quite *no* questions asked, but few. And she was beginning to realize that perhaps the self-centeredness of her youth had continued on into adulthood. Why hadn't she considered that her mother might be seeing someone? In spite of her surprise at the news, she was happy for Nina. Bill Carter was not only a longtime family friend, but a warm and wonderful man. She tucked her cell phone back into her purse and turned to join Chase, standing by the truck.

"Everything okay with Danny?"

"Sounds like it. My mother's going to drive him to Minnie's."

"That's really great of her."

"Yes, it is. I think we don't really appreciate our parents until we're adults, do we?"

His face sobered. "I suppose." He lapsed into silence.

For a moment Sam thought she'd broken the spell between them but suddenly he brightened and said, "Let's talk about families on the way to Bainbridge."

"You've only heard the very tip of that gigantic iceberg from me."

"I'm all ears," he said quietly, opening the truck passenger door and, cupping a hand firmly around her elbow, helping her up into the cab.

The truck moved slowly through traffic around the market. "Saturday's the worst day," muttered Chase. "I should have known."

"The lunch was worth it," put in Sam.

He turned to her. "I hope so."

Sam wasn't certain if he was referring to food or company, though his expression suggested the latter. Personally she didn't mind sitting at a standstill in the cramped cab of a pickup if Chase was the man behind the wheel.

Five minutes later, Chase gave up. "I'll cut off at the next intersection. I know a shortcut to the ferry through some side streets. It takes us near the Trade Winds office. Are you interested in seeing it?" He shifted his attention from the traffic to Sam again.

"Yes, I am." She thought back to what Skye had told her about the history of the family-run company. "When was the last time you saw the place?"

"Two years ago, when I came back to Seattle from Alaska. My uncle and I had a *business* meeting." He snorted at the word. "So he called it. But it was basically a settlement deal. Stay far and clear of Trade Winds, drop any claim to it and your mother spends the rest of her life in comfort at Harbor House."

"The other night you said your mother had sold her share of the company to him."

"That's right. Bryant's lawyer showed me the paperwork and wasn't very subtle about informing me I'd have no chance of getting it back."

"Even if you could prove Bryant coerced an Alzheimer's patient?"

"Proving things like that cost money, Sam."

And that was that. Sam mulled over his predicament, while Chase finally managed to make his turnoff and wind through back streets toward the ferry docks. The truck crested a hill and Sam could see the harbor a few blocks below.

"This area was once solidly commercial," Chase said. "When Trade Winds was established as a shipping company, the port and dockyards were much closer. My father once told me the neighbourhood was alive with merchant marines, dockworkers, tradespeople and, of course, the taverns and boardinghouses associated with all that. Now it's mainly residential, with some office buildings." The street was lined with stately homes, some of which had been turned into apartment units and offices, with a handful of nondescript two- and three-story buildings scattered amongst them.

"It's a bit farther along," he said, slowing the truck down.

Sam stared out her window, trying to imagine what the street might have looked like in the late 1800s when Chase's ancestors set up business. Some of her own family had come to America from Italy a little more than sixty years ago, just before her mother was born.

The truck coasted into an empty parking space and Chase shifted into Park. "There it is," he said, pointing to a large, three-story stone edifice that fit in perfectly with its palatial neighbors. Except for a brass plate next to the door, fronted by a set of stone steps and wrought iron handrail, there was no indication that it was a commercial building.

"It's quite beautiful," said Sam, adding, "in a Gothic sort of way."

"Yeah, well, that was the style way back then. In the beginning, my great- grandparents lived upstairs, but later the family moved to Magnolia and changed this place into offices. When I was really little, my father sometimes brought me here on a Saturday morning. I got to explore the nooks and crannies—and there are a lot of them— while he had meetings or made phone calls."

He sounded so wistful that Sam turned her head. "So there were some good memories?" she asked softly.

His eyes met hers. "Some," he said. "A lot changed when I hit my teens. By then, my father had changed, too."

"How?"

He shrugged, looking uncomfortable. "Living the high life. Clubs. Drinking. Women."

"It must have been…difficult," she said, aware of the understatement but at a loss for another word.

"Very diplomatic, Sam. Frankly it was hell. Especially for Mother. But I got to leave." He stared blankly beyond her at the building.

Sam wanted to reach out to him, but he was miles away, lost in the past. Suddenly his expression altered into one of pure hatred. Sam turned to see a man in a business suit standing in the now-opened front door of Trade Winds.

Not as tall as Chase, but large-framed, he seemed to be talking to someone inside. Suddenly he pivoted and looked straight at them.

Chase swore.

"What is it?"

"My cousin Howard. He's…well…let's just say he's

not a nice person. I'm kind of breaking the agreement with my uncle by being here."

"We're just looking at the place," Sam said, staring at the man.

Howard moved slowly down the steps, speeding up as he seemed to recognize who was parked there.

"Let's get out of here," muttered Chase as he shifted into Drive and cranked the steering wheel.

The truck screeched out into the driving lane and Sam could see Howard lumbering to the curb, waving a fist at them, shouting something.

"He looks pretty ticked off."

Chase didn't reply. In profile, Sam thought he looked just as furious. More than that, she thought with a shiver, he looked dangerous.

The truck sped down the street and squealed to a stop at the first intersection. Chase turned to her, a bleak expression in his eyes. "This is going to sound lame, but do you mind if we blow off the trip to Bainbridge? I…" He gave up, looking away.

Sam thought she understood what was going on inside his head, but wasn't certain. All she did know was that the mood had shifted and a trip anywhere now was one headed for disaster. "Of course I don't mind. It's probably better that I go home, anyway. Do you mind dropping me off at the nearest transit stop?"

"Don't be silly. I'm taking you to your place."

There was little conversation after that. He drove slowly, as if in a trance. Sam couldn't figure out if he was replaying what had just happened or if he was trying to calm himself. Perhaps a bit of both, she decided.

By the time he pulled up in front of her duplex, she was relieved that the day had made an abrupt turnaround. Maybe things were moving too quickly between her and

Chase. Maybe there was still an awful lot more to learn about him.

"Thanks for lunch," she said, smiling. She started to open the door when he grasped her by the shoulder and pulled her to him.

"I'm sorry," he whispered in her ear. "I'll make it up to you. There'll be even more carvings to see the next time."

She giggled. "Don't be—" Silly, she was going to say. But the word was stifled by his lips landing on hers, his hands coming up to cup her head, holding it gently but firmly in place. No chance of escape. Not that she wanted one. Kissing him was like diving into a whirlpool, a breathless submerging. Salty lips and heat, her tongue tangling with his. Sun glittering ripples behind closed lids and wave on wave of pure pleasure cascading through her body.

His hands slipped down and under her sweater and she heard someone gasp—was it him or her?—as he touched bare skin. She pressed into him, but he suddenly tore his mouth from hers, gasping for air. Sam held on as long as possible, gradually drifting away from the kiss and his arms.

She sagged against the door, hoping her grin didn't look too hungry. "Wow," she murmured when speech returned.

"Wow," he echoed. He reached over to tug her sweater back into place, then clasped her hand in his.

"Funny how things have changed," she said.

"Funny and wonderful." His eyes bore into hers. "We're going to continue this," he promised, "as soon as possible."

"Yes," she whispered. Reluctantly, she slipped her hand out of his and opened the door.

"I'll call you later," he said as she stepped down onto the sidewalk.

He started up the engine and she stood for a long moment, watching the truck move away and down the street. Finally she turned to head inside and as she did so, noticed a car creeping past the duplex, its driver looking her way. Sam squinted into the late-afternoon sun, trying unsuccessfully to see who was so interested in her building. *Or her.*

CHAPTER FOURTEEN

CHASE SET HIS CHISEL down on the worktable and went to answer the phone. He was hoping it might be Sam, changing her mind about coming to dinner. When he'd called to invite her late last night, he'd heard the hesitation in her voice and wondered if she was concerned about how the dinner might end, or if Danny might find out about it. But he'd decided he was being paranoid and that she might simply have a lot of work to catch up on, as she'd explained. He was in the same position and could relate.

It wasn't Sam. "Oh, hello, Mrs. MacDonald. Has something come up with my mother?" He felt anxiety rise inside him. Harbor House had only called him once in the two years he'd been back, and that was after his mother had locked herself in a bathroom.

"Not exactly, Chase. And I'm sorry to bother you on a Sunday morning, but the phone call was most unusual so I thought I'd better. At least, before I talked to Mr. Klein about it."

Chase frowned. Klein was the manager of Harbor House. "That's quite all right," he said as patiently as he could.

"Your uncle, Mr. Sullivan, phoned to say that from the first of next month he'd no longer be responsible for your mother's account. He said you'd be paying it. I thought I'd better confirm with you before talking to Mr. Klein and changing the paperwork."

Her message bounced around meaninglessly in his head. "Sorry, but when did my uncle call to tell you this?"

"Just an hour ago."

Chase tried to focus over the hammering at his temple. He closed his eyes and suddenly saw his cousin outside the company yesterday afternoon, staring angrily at the pickup truck. Howard. "Um, could you hold off on the paperwork for me, Mrs. MacDonald? To tell you the truth, my uncle hasn't contacted me about this yet."

There was a brief silence on the other end. "Oh, dear. I hope everything's okay. I assumed you knew."

"If you could give me some time—maybe till tomorrow?—I can settle this misunderstanding."

"Certainly, Chase. Give me a call when you have. The changeover doesn't happen for another week."

Chase hung up, passing a trembling hand across his face. Bryant was definitely playing hardball. He had no doubt that Howard went running to his father about the visit, as innocuous as it was. Never had he dreamed his uncle could be this petty and mean. Yet he ought to have known, having been witness to such acts before. But he wasn't going to let them get away with any more intimidation.

He tore off his canvas work apron, searched quickly for his keys and headed out. The worst part was waiting for the ferry. The half-hour ride was interminable, but at least afforded him the chance to think about what he'd say. He already knew what he wanted to do, but breaking the law was a last resort. And he tried not breaking any on the drive into the hills up to Magnolia where Bryant still lived, a mere eight blocks away from Chase's childhood home.

Fortunately the gate was open. Chase doubted he'd have been able to wait for someone to let him in. He wheeled the pickup around the circle, braking hard right at the front door. He banged on the steel-enforced panel with his fist and stuck his left index finger in the fancy door buzzer at the same time.

The door swung open while Chase's fist was raised, about to come down on the panel one more time. A matronly woman, no doubt a housekeeper, stood in the doorway, a look of fearful apprehension in her face.

"May I help you?" she asked, the words almost choking her.

Chase dropped his arm. "Yes. You can tell my uncle Bryant that his nephew, Chase, is here and wants to see him. Immediately."

"Your uncle isn't well today. He's resting. Perhaps if you came…"

Chase brushed past the woman. He hadn't been in the house for several years, but it hadn't changed much and he remembered the basic layout. Standing in the center of the gleaming foyer, he debated where to begin his search for Bryant.

She saved him the trouble. "He's in the solarium, off the den and to the right of the kitchen."

"I know where it is," Chase said, and spun around, leaving the woman speechless before the still-open front door. The house was huge and Chase doubted his cousins lived at home. Bryant's last wife had died a few years ago and, except for a couple of staff, he was all alone in the mausoleum.

In spite of the size of the place, it didn't take him long to find the solarium. His uncle was sitting in an armchair, his legs up on a footstool and covered with a blanket, reading a newspaper. His head shot up, shock in his face as he saw Chase.

"You know why I'm here," said Chase, standing in front of his uncle, hands on his hips.

"How dare you storm into my house like this?" Bryant blustered. "Get out now, before I call the police."

"Maybe that's a good idea, Bryant. Go ahead. While I'm at the station, explaining away my surprise visit to my dear uncle, I'll drop a few hints about Trade Winds."

"I doubt that, boy. I doubt that very much," said Bryant. "We had an agreement and you broke it."

"By parking in front of the company building for thirty seconds?"

Bryant frowned. "You know what I'm talking about. I refuse to discuss the matter further. I'll give you two minutes to clear out." He raised the newspaper and began to read again.

But Chase saw the paper shaking in the old man's hands and, for the first time, realized that fear had changed sides. It didn't make him feel any better, but it did make him determined to stay. "I don't know how you can sit there, knowing what you're doing to my mother. Knowing what you've done to my family, you and your offspring."

The paper dropped onto his lap. Bryant's eyes flashed. "You mean, what *you* did to your family. You shattered your father's trust and love when you made that call to the FBI."

"For the record—*again*—I did not make that call. Besides, the whole scene thirteen years ago was a set-up concocted by you and your sons. You know that. So please have the decency to drop the act."

"*You* have the decency to think about your mother for a change. If you were so concerned about her welfare, why did you break your promise? You knew what would happen."

"I didn't break any promise and you know it. Just tell me this—how long did you and my father carry out your scam? For all the years you both ran the company or just when you started getting those government contracts?"

"Your name was on those invoices," retorted his uncle.

"Not all of them," said Chase. "It won't take much to reopen the case."

"My friends have taken care of that," he said, dismissing Chase's implied threat with barely a sniff.

"Friends can be embarrassed by bad publicity."

Bryant retrieved the newspaper, but this time, didn't even pretend to read it. Instead he lapsed into silence, staring off into space.

"You didn't answer my question," pressed Chase. "When did you and my father cook up the fraud scheme?"

A peculiar expression flitted across Bryant's face. Chase puzzled at it for a few seconds until a tiny lightbulb illuminated in his mind. "My father didn't know about it, did he?"

The paper fluttered to the floor. His uncle looked up at him, suddenly a vulnerable and very old man.

"That's why our fight was so horrendous," said Chase, seeing the scene in his mind. "His mistake was to believe you, rather than his own son. Because you were his only sibling. His business partner. Supposedly his best friend. How much easier to believe you than his rebellious son."

Bryant's chin trembled. "Get out now or I *will* call the police."

"You're contemptible. I don't know how you can look yourself in the mirror. You screwed your own brother and now you're doing the same to his sick and defenseless wife. You disgust me." Chase turned and strode to the door.

"*You* can look after your mother now," cried his uncle. "Time to be a man, instead of a boy running from your problems. You should've thought of the consequences before you teamed up with that woman." His laugh pitched.

Chase didn't trust himself to look back. He made his way to the front door in a daze, thoughts and emotions fighting to trip him up any second. There was no sign of the housekeeper. A good thing. The poor woman had been frightened *before*. He shoved the door with the flat of his hand and stood on the threshold, blinded by the sun.

"What the…?"

Chase watched as his cousin closed his car door and headed his way. Terence, not Howard. Probably another good thing. Chase kept right on going toward his pickup.

"What are you doing here?" Terence asked, frowning.

Chase opened the truck door and climbed inside. Starting the engine, he saw Terence moving closer toward him. So tempting, Chase thought. A slight swerve of the steering wheel. He killed the image. Reversed away from his cousin, spun around and shot down the circular driveway to the main road. He didn't stop shaking until he reached the closest Starbucks.

It wasn't until later, on his way to the hospital to see Emily, that he recalled part of Bryant's rant as he was leaving. *Teamed up with that woman.* What woman? He'd been with Sam, but how would they know…? Uh-oh. They thought she was Skye. And that explained the extreme reaction. Howard told Bryant he'd been with the FBI agent.

SAM STOPPED outside Emily's door. She felt guilty about not coming sooner. She hadn't seen her since the day Danny stormed out. How long ago was that? Only days, but it felt like weeks, so much had happened. Such as, *I think I'm in love with your son's father.* How awkward was that? Sam exhaled, then took a quick deep breath and gently pushed open the door.

Emily was propped up on pillows, staring listlessly at the muted television suspended from the ceiling in the corner opposite the bed. She half-turned her head at Sam's approach and gave a wan smile.

"You're the very person I wanted to see," she said in a voice so low Sam had to strain to hear.

Sam smiled back and perched on the bedside chair. She patted the back of Emily's hand, resting at her side. "How are you today?"

"Not too good," Emily said. "Slight fever. I met your mother yesterday," she went on, changing the subject. "She's a wonderful woman. You're very lucky."

Sam nodded. "I am."

"She was so great with Danny. I could tell right away how much he liked her."

"Yes, she's good with kids." Sam heard herself say what she'd never have admitted in her adolescence. But it was true, she realized. She'd just never seen it.

"And Danny agreed to meet the counselor your mother recommended." Emily closed her eyes.

Sam watched her chest rise and fall beneath the cover. The time between each breath seemed long. There was a fine sheen of perspiration in her face and her skin color had a yellowish tint. Sam felt a surge of apprehension. Emily's condition was rapidly deteriorating.

Her eyes flicked open and she looked up at Sam as if she were seeing her for the first time that day. Then she must have remembered, because her expression shifted and she frowned. "Sorry. Sometimes the fatigue just takes over. I wanted to see you, Sam, because I have a favor to ask."

"If it's about Danny, not to worry," Sam quickly said. "I will most definitely stay in his life."

"Yes, please. It means so much to me…knowing he'll have a woman's influence. And I know Chase is going to take him in. He's been talking to Minnie and Danny about it." She paused again, taking slow breaths.

"Chase told me they'd arranged for Danny to spend

weekdays with Minnie until the end of the school term," Sam said. "Then he'll move permanently to Bainbridge, with Chase."

Emily nodded. She started to speak, but had to stop.

"Not to worry, Emily. All of us are going to take very good care of your son."

Tears welled up in Emily's eyes and spilled over. Sam took a tissue and dabbed them gently, trying desperately not to cry herself.

After a long moment, Emily said, "I'm hoping for something more for him, Sam. Something he's never really had."

Puzzled, Sam asked, "What?"

"A family, Sam. That's what I want for my boy. A family of his very own."

"We'll do the best we can there. Danny will be a part of my family, now, too."

Emily's head rolled slightly from side to side. "Not what I mean," she whispered.

Sam leaned closer to the bed to hear. "What do you mean?"

"I may be dying, but my eyesight and intuition are in full working order." Emily smiled weakly. "When Chase mentions your name, or you say his...I can hear it in your voices. See it in your faces." Her chest pumped slowly from the labor of such a long speech.

Sam felt her face heat up. She knew what Emily was hinting at but didn't know how to respond. *Yes, I think I'm in love with him. But it's all happened so fast and I'm not positive he feels the same or if it's all just physical lust. And heaven knows where any of this is going to go....*

"Uh...you're right, Emily. I have changed my mind about Chase—drastically." She smiled. "But I simply don't know how it's all going to end."

"Just…let it happen," murmured Emily. "Don't fight it. You two were made for each other." She stopped and closed her eyes.

Sam watched Emily drift off. When she realized she was sleeping this time, she stood up, leaned over to Emily and whispered, "Whatever happens, I will make some kind of family for Danny." She kissed Emily on the forehead and quietly left the room.

Outside in the hallway, she sagged against the wall and searched in her purse for a tissue. A nurse came by and stopped to ask if everything was all right.

"I'm fine, thanks. I've just been in to see Emily Benson. She's not doing well."

The nurse shook her head. "Are you family?"

"Kind of."

"Well, I'm not permitted to talk about her condition unless you are, but we're calling in family today."

Sam nodded mutely, understanding the subtext of that statement. The nurse patted her on the arm and walked on. Sam dug blindly into her purse for her phone and called Chase. He didn't pick up, so she left a message to say she was at the hospital, but leaving for home. Could he call her when he arrived at the hospital? Last night they'd planned to meet there, but Sam didn't think she had the emotional stamina to stay longer. Besides, the nurse had said *family* and right now, that meant Danny and Chase. She took the elevator down and headed for the transit stop to take the bus home. Skye still had her car. It was typical of Skye to assume Sam would manage in the meantime. Sam mentally scolded her twin while waiting for the bus. When it finally came, disgorging many hospital visitors, Sam decided to go to her mother's, instead.

The bus ride was interminable, with at least three route changes. By the time she got off at the stop two blocks from her mother's, Sam was ready to have it out with her sister.

"She's not here," Nina said, seconds after Sam walked in the door. "But she left a note for you, in case you called or came by."

"Why did she take my car? Couldn't she have taken yours?"

Nina gave her a sharp look. "I've no idea, dear. I thought you knew all about it."

Sam slumped onto the couch in the living room. "I expected her to drop it by last night or even this morning. I had to take the bus to the hospital."

"I hope that's not a whine in your voice," Nina teased.

In spite of her frustration, Sam had to grin. "Sorry. I think it was. It's just that Emily's not doing well at all—a nurse told me the hospital has called her family. That sounds serious, doesn't it?"

Nina sat on the edge of the couch next to her. "I'm afraid it does, dear. If you want to go back to the hospital, you're welcome to use my car."

"Thanks, Mom, but the nurse emphasized the *family* part. Besides, I think it's better for Chase and Danny to have time alone with Emily."

Nina took Sam's hand. "Emily and Danny are very lucky to have you for a friend, Samantha." She paused a moment, then stood up. "I'll get that note."

Sam headed for the kitchen and a glass of water. Standing at the sink, she glanced to her right, into the solarium across the patio. She saw herself sitting in the armchair there, facing the kitchen sink—and Skye. How insignificant that whole incident seemed now. And how many light-years away from Todd was the man she'd now come to love. She set the empty glass onto the counter and turned at her mother's entrance.

"Here you go, dear."

Sam took the note and sat at the table, while Nina continued emptying the dishwasher.

Hi, Sam.

Sorry about the car. You're probably ready to throttle me! I have an errand and will pop by your place later this afternoon. I spent most of yesterday searching listings of government contracts on the Internet and making phone calls. I managed to come up with an interesting piece of information. A numbered company that's received two recent orders from Trade Winds (for contracts for supplies to the Defense Department) turns out to be owned by H. J. Weiner and Company. Sound familiar? Anyway, a buddy of mine has just let me know that Weiner and Company is registered under the name Terence Bryant Sullivan. No kidding. The old circle game. We got them, sis. Now to gather what we've got and persuade someone at the field office to check it out. Got my fingers crossed. See ya later.

Sam felt excitement rising inside. All nasty thoughts of Skye vanished. Her sister had really come through. "Mom," she said, raising her head, "I'm going home now. Skye said she'd drop the car around later today."

"Shall I give you a lift, dear?"

Sam hesitated, tempted to say yes. But at the moment she didn't feel like exposing herself to Nina's inevitable questioning about Chase. Her feelings for the man were too new, something she wanted to hold tightly to her chest—for now. Her mother must have inferred the truth, because as Sam walked to the door, she said, "We'll catch up later."

"Okay, Mom. And I may have some questions for you, too." She grinned teasingly. "About Bill Carter."

Nina smiled. "I guess we both have some catching up to do."

"Yep," Sam said, and gave her a quick goodbye hug. The hike to the bus stop was interrupted by her cell phone. Chase. A delicious warmth flowed through her at the sound of his voice.

"Hi, there," he said. "Got your message. Where are you now?"

"Heading home on the bus. Skye still has my car." She paused a beat, almost afraid to ask. "How's Emily?"

"They think she's got pneumonia. Doing some tests."

Sam closed her eyes. Pneumonia. She doubted Emily would have the strength to battle this last assault on her poor body. When Sam could speak, her voice was husky. "Where's Danny?"

"Still at Minnie's. I'm going to go pick him up right now."

She hesitated, wondering if this was the time. Still, he needed to know. "I have some news, too."

"What?"

Sam gave him the gist of Skye's note. He didn't respond for a moment.

"This is big, Sam," he finally said. He told her about the visit to Bryant and the phone call that had precipitated it.

"That's awful," Sam said. "What will you do?"

"Well, given what you've just told me, I think I've got a huge bargaining chip."

"But you're going to let the authorities handle it, right? I mean, we have to call in the FBI now."

Another pause. "I suppose. But it'll mean the end of the company—my family's business."

"Chase, it hasn't been your family business for thirteen years."

"Yeah, I guess you're right. Funny, I just never thought this whole thing would be resolved. I was resigned to carrying it with me the rest of my life."

Sam wished she was with him, to wrap her arms around him. "Some of it always will be with you," she said, lowering her voice.

"Right. Sam, I..."

Static buzzed the signal and she couldn't hear the rest of what he said. "Say again?"

"I said I thought about you all night."

Sam shivered. She glanced quickly at the two other people waiting at the bus stop, then moved farther away. "Me, too," she whispered.

"Can't hear you, Sam. You're breaking up."

"Me, too!"

"Ah. Good. Listen, I got a call coming in. I'll get back to you."

Sam closed up her phone, thinking the day was going to be a long one. The bus arrived and she stepped on. But surprisingly, the trip home wasn't too bad because she spent the forty-five minutes with thoughts of Chase's promise to continue the kiss begun yesterday, alternating with worry about Emily and Danny.

The first thing she spotted as she rounded the corner to her duplex was her car parked in the No Parking zone. She smiled, thinking Skye might at least have placed a sign in the windshield. Officer on duty or some such thing. Sam bent down to check inside as she drew near, noting that her sister had also not locked the car.

Impulsively she withdrew her cell phone from her purse. She'd get her to come outside and move the car herself. That is, if she was up in the apartment. Sam leaned against the passenger door and looked up at her apartment window. The phone rang and instantly, another chime joined in. Sam frowned. She jumped away from the car and looked around. The muted but distinct peal of Skye's cell phone was coming from inside the car. Sam opened the passenger door.

Skye's black leather handbag was lying on the floor.

CHAPTER FIFTEEN

CHASE SWITCHED off his phone and leaned against the wall of the hospital waiting room. Minnie's call was disturbing, to say the least. Danny had left her apartment while she'd been at church. Chase told her to have Danny call if he came back. He checked the time on his phone again. It was almost three o'clock. Where the heck was he?

He debated calling Sam again but guessed she was still making her way home. Besides, it was his problem, not hers. He began to pace, trying to figure out where the boy might be. Anger surged in him. Danny's timing couldn't be worse. Minnie had insisted he'd been fine when he went to bed last night, so whatever prompted this disappearance occurred in the night or early morning. And he couldn't call any of Danny's friends because, except for a single reference to someone named Jeff, he had no idea who they were. A sense of inadequacy about how he was handling the job of parenthood rolled over him.

He wished he could ask Emily if she had some idea of where he'd be, but she was sleeping. Besides, she couldn't afford to expend any energy in worry over Danny. Deciding to wait a bit longer before driving out to Minnie's he headed down to the cafeteria for another coffee. As he stepped off the elevator, he bumped into a tall, white-haired man in a lab coat. Emily's doctor.

"Ah, Mr....uh..."

"Sullivan."

"Yes, I was hoping you'd arrived. I want to have a word with you about your wife."

Chase didn't bother correcting the mistake. He followed the doctor to one of the few vacant tables in the cafeteria. When they were settled, Chase had to lean forward to hear the man over the hubbub of people's voices, clinking dishes and cutlery.

"Emily's prognosis isn't good and that's why we called you. I need to inform you that we have a DNR on her file."

"A what?"

"A 'do not resuscitate' instruction. Emily signed it when she was admitted to the palliative ward. It basically means that we don't take any heroic measures. If she goes into cardiac arrest, say, we don't try to revive her."

Chase turned away for a second, gazing blankly at a weary-looking couple at the table next to theirs. "I see," he finally said.

"The thing is, I'm worried about your son. He was in a highly agitated state the last time he saw his mother. I don't want him to be alone with her."

Chase nodded. He couldn't speak over the lump in his throat.

The doctor stood up and patted him reassuringly on the shoulder. "We'll make sure Emily doesn't suffer."

He didn't see the doctor leave. The room swam in a watery haze. Chase blinked, wiped his eyes and forced himself to his feet. He needed a quiet corner to think.

SAM RAN UP the stairs, taking them two at a time. Hopefully Skye was there, totally ignorant of the fact that she'd left her purse in an unlocked car in a No Parking zone. But the apartment door was locked. She fumbled for her keys, then let herself in.

"Skye? Skye?" Sam wandered from room to room, but the silent apartment offered up no clues. Tossing Skye's purse onto the couch, Sam immediately called her mother. The line was busy. She left a terse message asking Nina to call her right back. Impulsively, she tried Chase, but the line was busy.

Frustrated, she pocketed her phone and began pacing. Knowing her sister, she'd probably decided to dash to the corner convenience for a soda or something. Sam ran to the purse and rummaged in it. Skye's wallet was still there. Okay. No impromptu shopping. The car keys were also in the purse, suggesting Skye had been on her way out of the car when something—or someone—stopped her. Perhaps she'd been accosted by one of the other tenants and was chatting merrily away while her twin sister was freaking out.

Sam picked up her phone and called the tenant in the ground-floor unit. No answer. Skye obviously wasn't in the building. So where was she? When she tried Chase's number again, she got his voice mail.

"Can you call me as soon as possible? Skye seems to have disappeared."

Sam rang off and headed for the kitchen and a glass of cold water. She needed to calm down and consider where Skye might have gone. *Without her purse and phone.*

Wherever Skye was, Sam was dead certain she hadn't gone willingly.

SHE TRIED not to give in to the panic, so focused on anger instead. Anger that she'd so foolishly ignored the man getting out of the car parked behind her. Not that she'd had any reason to be suspicious of him. Even her realization that he was moving swiftly toward her hadn't sounded any alarms because she knew she'd parked Sam's car in a No Parking zone. She'd gotten out of the car and had been bent over, reaching for her purse on the passenger seat when he suddenly came at her from behind.

The hard pressure of a gun's barrel against her lower back was a sensation she'd experienced only once before and had hoped never to experience again. He'd grabbed her by the collar of her jacket, pulling her against him and the gun. She'd turned her head, looking for someone on the street to help her. But, impossibly on a Sunday afternoon, there hadn't been a single person around.

When he'd marched her toward his car and she'd seen that the trunk was already popped open, her stomach heaved. By then she'd recognized him. Everything fast-forwarded. The push into the trunk, so swift she had no chance to fight back. He was big and strong. Silent, too.

Does he know about Sam?

Skye guessed they drove about fifteen minutes. He drove fast around curves and she had to cling to the spare-tire unit to keep from being tossed around. The car braked sharply and she was thrown hard against the metal plate holding the tire in place. The blow to her head brought tears, but she welcomed the pain. It sharpened her senses and her anger. As soon as she heard the trunk latch unlock, she braced herself to leap out at him.

But he was quicker than he looked and perhaps smarter, too. The trunk flew up and just as Skye was about to uncoil and spring up, a fist punched her right in the solar plexus. She fell back into the trunk, gasping to catch her breath. When he swiped a piece of duct tape across her mouth, panic overwhelmed her. Whatever his plan for her had been, Skye knew she was in serious trouble. He rolled her roughly onto her side, jerking her arms out from under her and to her back, squeezed both wrists together with one of his hands and then wound a long swath of duct tape round and round them. She lay helplessly in the hollow of the trunk, staring up at him as she tried to control her breathing. The smile on his face was chilling.

"I just want you to know that I personally have had it with you people," he said. "Pop's in intensive care right now because my jerk of a cousin started butting his nose into things. And I can't really tell you how long you're gonna be around here—Terry and I have to make some plans. So before I drag you outa there, I want to warn you that if you do anything to attract attention, your stay will most definitely be cut very short. Understand what I'm saying?"

She nodded.

"Okay, so I'm gonna pull you out and we're going to walk into the house as quickly as we can." He took one last look around him before reaching down to grab her under one arm and pulled.

Skye winced as her legs scraped over the edge of the trunk. Her knees gave slightly as she put her full weight onto them, but he wrapped one arm around her waist and half-dragged, half-walked her to a closed door. She knew where they were. The Trade Winds building that had once been the family mansion. She certainly hadn't imagined a few days ago that she'd be back so soon, and under such circumstances. The thought might have made her laugh, had the duct tape not been so tight over her lips.

He unlocked the door, holding her against him with his other arm. When it swung open to reveal a dark staircase leading into a basement, she braced her heels against the landing step, refusing to move. He shouted at her and a door leading from the landing to the ground floor suddenly opened. A man stood in the frame, his jaw gaping. Must be Terry.

"Howard, what the hell…"

"Help me get her down into the wine cellar."

"Are you crazy? Do you know what you've done? Do you think this is going to help Pop?"

"It's going to make me feel better," Howard said, his face reddening.

Terence backed up. "You're on your own, then. I'm not getting involved."

"Yeah? We'll see about that." Howard jerked her away from the landing and took two steps at a time down into the basement, pulling her behind him.

She had no choice but to comply, knowing that if she resisted, he'd simply throw her down. And breaking a bone would mean the end of any chance to get away. She couldn't see over his wide back and shoulders, but heard him breathing heavily as he worked at some door mechanism. Then he turned abruptly and pushed her forward into a small, unlit room. Or closet, more like it, she thought, just before she landed with a thud on the concrete floor.

As he closed the door behind her, he shouted, "You shoulda stayed out of it. It's all your fault—and my cousin's."

Skye tucked her legs up beneath her and maneuvered herself into a sitting position. If he'd been foolish enough to bind her wrists in front of her, she could have started working away at the tape on her mouth. She heard his heavy footsteps lumbering up to the ground floor. Doors slammed and voices raised. *Guess they're arguing about me.* Skye breathed deeply through her nose, forcing herself to be calm. Giving in to panic would achieve nothing. She lowered her forehead onto her knees and tried to think. Tried to zero in on some kind of twin telepathy to summon her sister.

Would Sam figure it out? And in time to save her? Those were two questions she decided to tuck away. The answers were just too much to consider at the moment.

NOT KNOWING where to begin looking for Danny, Chase called Nina Sorrenti. She'd been with Danny yesterday and could maybe shed some light on where he might have gone. The fact that she was listed in the directory was a bonus. Of course, he could have gotten her number from Sam, but he was reluctant to drag her into this. And Nina was every bit as gracious as he'd hoped she'd be.

First he apologized for calling her without a formal introduction.

"That's quite all right," she said. "I feel as though I know you, anyway."

That gave him pause, wondering whether she'd garnered information about him from Sam, Danny or Skye. "Danny seems to have taken off," he said, giving her a summary of Minnie's phone call and the need for Danny to get to the hospital.

"Oh? Samantha told me that Emily wasn't doing well."

"She has pneumonia."

After a few seconds, Nina murmured, "Oh, dear." Her tone said it all.

"I don't have any idea where to start looking for him and was wondering if you could give me any suggestions."

"Hmm. Let me think." The line was silent for so long Chase wondered if he'd lost the connection. Finally she said, "Yesterday when we were out sightseeing, we went to the Space Needle, which he loved, and afterward I drove through Queen Anne for an even better view of the skyline. He loved it and said his mother would have loved it, too. I regretted not having a camera, but told him I'd take him back as soon as possible to get a photo of the view for his mother."

"So whereabouts in Queen Anne were you?" Chase tried to hide his impatience. The neighborhood she was referring to was huge.

"There's an overlook at Kerry Park where we stopped to see the bay and city."

Chase swore under his breath. Kerry Park was a long way from Minnie's place. Still, Danny had no qualms about traveling around the city. "Okay, that's a start. I'll check it out."

"Is there anything else I can do?"

He thought for a moment. "Danny's going to need some professional help, Ms. Sorrenti. I know you've been facilitating that and I appreciate it. Emily talked to you about it yesterday, I believe?"

"Yes, a bit. But I could see she wasn't having a good day. Please feel free to call me anytime. And please, it's Nina."

"Thanks. I will…Nina."

After tucking his phone back into his jeans pocket, Chase went to the nurses' station on Emily's floor, leaving his phone number and a request to call him should Danny arrive at the hospital. He called Sam, but her line was busy and, rather than complicate things more, decided not to leave a message. He had a rough idea where Kerry Park was. He just hoped Danny was still there, if indeed that was where he'd gone.

THE MORE SAM LOOKED at the evidence, the more convinced she was that something bad had happened to Skye. She finally got through to her mother, who told her Chase had called about Danny's whereabouts.

"Have you caught up with your sister yet?" asked Nina.

Sam opted for a white lie. "No, I haven't, but I'm sure she'll show up."

"She left here ages ago. Let me know when she does. I want to find out if she'll be home for dinner."

Sam was torn between laughter and tears. She knew

Nina would want to know what was going on, but she didn't want to frighten her mother just yet, at least not until she'd contacted Chase. "I'll call you soon," she promised, and hung up.

By the time she reached Chase, she was on her way to her car. She quickly filled him in.

"Chase? Are you still there? Did you get what I just said?"

"Yes, Sam. Listen, I'm on my way to Kerry Park. Your mother said he really liked the place, and so I'm thinking he might have returned there. Now, about Skye. Are you positive she simply hasn't taken off on her own?"

"Without her purse or wallet? Her cell phone?" Sam heard her voice rising with each word.

"No, I guess not. This doesn't look good. But there's something I should tell you. Yesterday, when we stopped in front of Trade Winds and my cousin Howard saw us? I thought he was reacting to my being there, but this morning I learned it was you he was angry about."

"Me?"

"Not you, but Skye. He saw you and thought he was seeing your sister. He figured I was in cahoots with the FBI and freaked out."

"Oh." Her mind raced, sorting out the implications of what Chase was telling her. She'd reached her car and climbed inside. She ducked her head, searching the floor for any clue to Skye's disappearance. Nothing. This wasn't a fairy tale, she told herself. No trail of bread crumbs to follow.

"You still there?" Chase asked.

"Yep. Just getting into my car. Listen, I thought of something. After you brought me home yesterday, when we were out front...uh...well...saying goodbye?"

"I vaguely recall that," he teased.

"Right. Anyway, when you left, another car crawled past as I was standing on the sidewalk. The sun was in my eyes, but I could tell the driver was looking my way. As if he was checking out my building—or me. Do you suppose it could have been Howard? Maybe he followed us."

"Maybe." Chase paused. "Probably. This is really not looking good. Call the police."

"Skye's an adult—don't they make you wait twenty-four hours or something for missing adults?"

"There are extenuating circumstances. Her purse and things were left behind, you said."

"I'm betting one of your cousins has taken her. You said they were ticked off—maybe seeing us together was the last straw. Maybe they found out we've got information about those companies."

"I can't believe one of them would be crazy enough to kidnap an FBI agent."

"Say they did. Where would they take her?"

"I've no idea. Anywhere."

"But if it was an impulsive act, maybe they'd want to just keep her somewhere till they decided what to do with her."

There was a moment of silence. "Maybe you should have been the FBI agent, rather than your sister."

"Ha, ha. Think, Chase."

"Okay. Supposing you're right. Maybe the best option would be the Trade Winds building."

"Okay, I'm going there."

"No, wait. Not by yourself. As soon as I get to Kerry Park and hopefully find Danny, I'll call you back and we can sort this out together. Don't do anything till I call you. Promise?"

Sam hesitated. She hated to jeopardize this budding relationship with a lie, but her sister might need her. "Uh, sure. Okay. Call me when you find Danny."

As soon as they disconnected, she started to press 9-1-1, but then stopped. Trade Winds wasn't that far away. She'd check it out first, then call the police.

CHASE REACHED the Kerry Park overlook ten minutes after talking to Sam. His palms were sweating and his heart racing. He had a feeling she wasn't going to heed his advice and that scared him. He'd always considered his cousins liars and fraud artists, rather than major criminals. But he knew from experience that Howard had a mean streak and little impulse control. What Sam had suggested was a more likely scenario than Chase wanted to admit. Especially after his visit to Bryant.

He parked the truck on a side street and walked briskly through small knots of people taking photos or simply looking at the view. There were quite a few tourists and locals at the site. It was a Sunday in mid-May and a clear, sunny day. Mount Rainier thrust above the city.

Chase strode along the fence barrier, eyes scanning from left to right. Then he doubled back. This time he stopped to look out and below, noticing a set of stairs leading down the slope to a playground and tennis courts. He squinted, searching amongst the scattered people for someone who might be Danny. Just when he was considering using one of the telescopes, a familiar shape moved into his line of vision.

He took the steps two at a time, brushing rudely past people, ignoring their protests as he kept his eyes fixed on Danny. The boy had moved to a bench and was watching some children playing on the climbing apparatus in the playground.

Breathless, Chase could barely speak when he reached the bench. Danny turned, but hardly seemed surprised to find him there. Chase sat down on the bench and waited until he'd caught his breath.

"I was worried about you, Danny."

"Oh, yeah?"

"No one knew where you were."

Danny frowned. "How'd you find me, then?"

"I called Nina Sorrenti. She told me how much you liked it."

"She's pretty nice."

"Yes." He craned his head, noticing the camera on the other side of Danny. "You wanted to take some photos for your mother."

Danny just nodded.

"It's a good day for picture-taking. I haven't seen Rainier that clearly in a while."

Another nod.

Chase grit his teeth. He was desperate to call Sam back, but knew he couldn't rush Danny. He thought about telling him what was happening, but decided the kid had enough on his mind. "Get many pictures?" he asked.

"Enough."

"Shall we go show them to your mother?"

Danny's head swiveled. "Now?"

"Why not?"

He shrugged. "No reason. Thought maybe you'd be angry."

"I wasn't angry, Danny. I was scared."

Danny searched his face. "You don't look scared."

"Adults are good at hiding their feelings."

"Yeah. I've learned that." He stopped for a minute. "Yesterday, Nina and I talked about my mother and some other stuff. Nina gave me permission to call her that," he quickly explained.

Chase tried not to smile. "So do you think you might be interested in talking to one of her colleagues?"

"I think so," Danny said. He looked back at a group of

children chasing some others, laughing. Suddenly he got to his feet. "Maybe we should go now."

Chase followed him up the stairs, one hand resting lightly on his shoulder. When they got to the top, Danny said, "One more picture, okay?"

"Sure. How about I take one of you with the Space Needle behind you?"

"Okay. Did you know Mom and I never went up there? Yesterday was my first time."

Chase pretended to be setting up the camera. He wished, suddenly, he'd been around before, when Danny was younger. He fought tears. *Well, you're here now. And here to stay.* When he could safely raise his head, he smiled at Danny, who was leaning against the fence. "Move a bit to your left," he said.

As he raised the camera, a woman beside him said, "Would you like me to take a picture of you and your son together?"

Chase glanced at Danny. Their eyes locked. "Yes, we'd love that," he said. He walked over and stood beside Danny, draping one arm loosely across his son's shoulders.

SAM NOTICED a small side street about half a block from the Trade Winds building and turned onto it. She guessed there might be parking behind the buildings and she was right. An alley led off to her left, running parallel to the main street. When she got out of the car, she stood for a moment, planning her next move. The predominantly residential area was quiet, with few people around. It was almost five. She checked her phone again but no messages. Had Chase not found Danny yet?

She put that worry aside for the moment and focused on her missing twin. Now that she was here, she might as well check the place out. She stowed her purse under the driver's seat and locked up. Set her phone on vibrating mode and tucked it into her shirt pocket. Took a deep breath and walked into the alley. Most of the houses were enclosed by tall fences, but at the rear of the Trade Winds building was a small parking area. Sidling along the fence, she reached the place where the fence ended and the parking began. She stopped short of it, protected by the neighboring fence, to see if anyone was around. So far so good. Then she poked her head out for a quick peek.

Two cars were parked at strange angles in the small space. Behind one of the cars was a windowless door. Sam froze. Her phone was vibrating in her pocket. Keeping her eye on the door, she flipped open the phone. It was Chase.

"I've found Danny," he said, his voice low.

"Speak up," she hissed.

"Can't. He's too close. Wait."

Static, followed by Chase, a bit louder now. "It's okay. He's gone to look at some flashy sport car parked near us. I'm taking him back to the hospital, but I can't just leave him there. He's bound to be upset when I tell him Emily has pneumonia."

"Call my mother. She'll meet him at the hospital and take him home for a sleepover, if necessary." She waited. "Did you hear me?"

"Yes. Okay. I hate to do it, but it's the best option right now. I'll come by your place right after."

"Uh…well…don't do that."

"What? Why not? Where are you?"

"Um…at Trade Winds. In the little parking lot behind the building." She heard him swear.

"Look, go wait by your car," he said. "In fact, get inside it and lock the door. I'll get there as quickly as I can. We'll figure out our next step then."

"Uh-huh. Say, remember telling me how you used to

play here when you were little? You said you explored all the nooks and crannies?"

"Yeah. Why?"

"Where were some of them? Think you could still find them?"

"For sure. But wait for me, okay? Promise?"

"I'll do my best," she said, and disconnected before he could say another word.

She put her phone back in her pocket. Checking the rear door once more, she took a deep breath and crept across the parking space.

Heat emanated faintly from the first car she passed, but the car closest to the door was cool. When she reached the windowless-door, she saw that the latch was resting lightly on top of the frame. Someone had been in a big hurry. Sam splayed her fingers on the edge of the door and gently tugged.

Somewhere in the building two men were arguing, loudly and fiercely. She pulled the door open wide enough to squeeze through onto a small landing. A set of stairs at her right led to the ground floor and another, down to a basement. The voices were definitely up, so Sam took the other route.

She made sure the door was left in the same position as she'd found it, in case she needed a fast exit. The stairs descended into darkness, but there was enough light from the small gap in the door to orient herself. She waited at the bottom for her eyes to adjust. There was a long, narrow hall with closed doors off each side. She moved slowly ahead, her fingertips running along what felt like a wood-paneled wall at her right. If there was a light switch, she didn't find it. Reaching the first door, she turned the handle. Locked. Likewise for the second and third. Sam stopped at the end of the hall.

The voices above were muted by the thick basement walls and ceiling. She dreaded the possibility of having to go up there, but she would if necessary. Skye was in the building somewhere. She could feel it.

Her cell phone vibrated again. She flipped it open and whispered a hello as loudly as she dared.

"Sam? Where are you? Why are you whispering? No, no. Please don't tell me…"

"Yes, I am," she hissed. "I'm in the basement. I can hear men's voices upstairs. They seem to be arguing."

"How many cars in the parking lot?"

"Two. One got there just before me, I think."

"I've left the hospital and your mother is there with Danny. Why don't you go back out and wait for me at your car? I can get to you in about fifteen minutes."

"All the doors in the basement are locked. Is there another way in or out of here?"

"Where exactly are you?"

"At the end of this corridor. It's a dead end." She heard a muffled exclamation. "Chase?"

"It's not a dead end. There's a secret panel in the wall—not sure if it's to the left or right. I found it when I was a kid. Face the wall dead center and press your fingertips against it, up high. Try left and right. There'll be a click and the panel will open. Small room behind. It was a storage room for booze during Prohibition."

"Okay. I'll call you back."

"Wait—"

Sam disconnected before he could tell her again to leave. *Sorry, Chase, I've got to do this.* She reached up and ran her fingers along the wall to her right, pressing lightly in a line. Back and forth and again. The voices upstairs seemed to be lower now, with longer pauses. That worried Sam. As long as she could hear arguing, she knew where they were. She decided to try the left side, but had no success there, either.

Her underarms were damp with perspiration and her pulse pounded in her ears. Chase must have got it wrong somehow. She went back over his instructions. *Found it when he was a kid. When he was much shorter. High then, lower now.* Starting at shoulder height, she repeated the process, reading the wall with her fingertips. And by the time she had scrolled down to just above her waist, she felt a slight give.

She stopped, wiping her forehead with the back of her hand. This had to be the place, but the panel wasn't swinging open the way secret doors did in the movies. She pressed harder. The wall here was definitely spongey and as she moved along, it began to give slightly. When she was almost at the center starting point, a small section of the wall shifted left and under the exterior panel. *Aha. A sliding door, not a swinging one.* Footsteps thundered from above her head, seeming to move in her direction. She had to hide.

There was just enough light at the entrance to expose notched shelving on both sides of a narrow room. Wine racks? she wondered. More shouting from upstairs. Heart racing, she set one foot into the dark interior. Just as she turned to close the sliding door behind her, she heard a faint humming sound. Unable to see even her hand, she inched forward in the dark until her right foot stubbed against something soft. She bent down, feeling with her hands. Finding cloth. She ran her fingers up the fabric to smooth, warm skin. Hair. Her stomach lurched and she bit down hard on her lower lip so as not to cry out.

"Skye?" she whispered.

CHAPTER SIXTEEN

SAM FELL to her knees, fingers scrabbling at the tape across Skye's mouth. She made low shushing sounds as Skye struggled to communicate, digging her nails under the tape and pulling it down inch by inch. First one side, then the other. She felt her sister flinch once, and realized she'd either scratched her or the tape had caught some hair. Small injuries, she told herself, as she worked away at the binding. The instant the tape came way enough for Skye to talk, Sam clapped a hand on her mouth.

"Let's get out of here." She paused, almost afraid to ask. "Did he hurt you?"

"No. Just my pride. So stupid," Skye whispered back. "He was at your place, waiting for me. I got out of the car and he came up behind me with a gun. Made me get into the trunk of his car. In broad daylight. No one around." She stopped, catching her breath.

"It's okay, Skye. Relax."

"He taped my hands, too." She gave an awkward half-turn, showing Sam her bound wrists.

Sam muttered an expletive. She tried to dig her finger-nails underneath, but there was no gap between skin and tape. "I can't find the join!" she cried. "It's too tight."

"Never mind," Skye snarled impatiently. "Let's just get out of here."

Sam placed her hands under Skye's armpits and pulled

her sister up. Gasping, she leaned against the wine racks with Skye swaying into her. They crab-walked between the wine racks to the panel door. The voices upstairs were louder now, shouting. A door slammed and heavy footsteps reverberated through to the basement. Sam, her arm around Skye, froze.

"Did you call the police?" Skye asked.

"Not yet."

"Call them."

Sam recognized that tone. Skye was rallying. She dug out her cell phone and pressed 9-1-1. As soon as Sam gave the address, the dispatcher informed her there'd been a call about a burglary on the premises.

"Burglary? No, there's no—"

"Give me the phone," said Skye, raising her taped hands. Sam placed the phone at her sister's ear.

"This is Agent Skye Sorrenti speaking. We have a possible hostage situation with an abduction of an FBI agent. Two suspects, one armed. Approach with caution. Rear entrance." She gave her badge number and jerked her head, indicating for Sam to take away the phone. "Let's go."

They scurried along the dark corridor, but as they reached the bottom of the cellar stairs, someone thundered down the steps to the landing above. Sam pulled Skye into the stairwell. The back door slammed shut and silence fell over the entire building. Except for their ragged breathing. After a painfully long moment, Skye whispered, "We have to go now. Me first."

"No. Your hands are tied. Me first."

"No, I can use my feet."

"Yeah, just like you did when he got you."

"Are you going to rub that in for the rest of my life?"

"Maybe. If I have to."

Skye drew her head back to look Sam in the face. "You're serious."

"Yep."

They both grinned at the same time. Sam teared up. They were still in danger, but she had her sister.

"So much for the big FBI agent," Skye murmured.

"You said it, not me."

Skye nodded.

"Let's go," said Sam, heading for the bottom step.

"Wait. About last Christmas."

"Geezus, Skye. *Now?*"

"It had nothing to do with taking Todd away from you or that competition thing. I had this gut feeling about him, that he wasn't good enough for you. I tried to tell you before, but I thought you wouldn't believe me. Whenever I was alone with him, he was always making these suggestive remarks. Finding excuses to brush against me. I should have just come out and told you, but—"

Sam placed two fingers on her sister's lips. "Shh. It's ancient history. You did me a big favor." She paused, adding, "Just keep your mitts off the one I have now."

"You don't have to worry about that one, Sam."

Sam kissed her sister on the cheek. "Me first," she said, and led the way up the stairs to the landing.

The rear door was fully closed. Sam swore under her breath. She heard Skye coming up behind her, and as she turned to tell her to wait, a man's voice sounded from her right. She spun around. Howard was standing in the doorway at the top of the other set of steps. The gun in his right hand wavered slightly as he looked from Sam to Skye and back to Sam.

"Son of a bitch," he muttered. "There's two of you."

CHASE WANTED to throw his cell phone out the window in frustration. Traffic was typical for a balmy Sunday afternoon. Tourists, shoppers and gawkers. He wove the pickup in and out of lanes, feeling and hearing the outrage behind him as he cut drivers off and braked hard for the occasional jaywalker. He had one goal—to get to Sam as quickly as possible.

He couldn't pinpoint the day or the moment when Samantha Sorrenti ceased to be an adversary and became a friend. Well, not exactly a friend, he qualified, because what he'd been feeling for her the past few days had little to do with friendship. He wasn't certain he could call it love yet, though it was far more than physical desire. He simply wanted to be with her. To see her green-flecked eyes light up or the tiny crease of worry between those eyes when she spoke about Emily or Danny. The soft sibilance as she whispered his name. Her full, sweet lips and… He groaned. *Focus,* he told himself. *Drive.*

At the intersection before Trade Winds he turned onto the side street and then the alley. A few yards in, he spotted Sam's car and pulled in behind it. He was reaching for his phone on the passenger seat when he heard a gravel-spitting roar and looked up to see a car fishtailing out of the parking area behind the building. He couldn't see the driver, but the car looked like the one at his uncle's that morning. Probably Terence.

He jumped from the cab, shoving his phone into his jeans pocket and ran to the rear door, passing another car that surely belonged to Howard. The door was locked. He stood back, staring up at the second-floor windows. No sign of life anywhere. He considered dashing around to the front, but hesitated, recalling a security camera there years ago. No sign of police yet, either. Still, he had to do something. About to head for the front, he noticed the door handle rotating.

"DOUBLE THE TROUBLE," said Howard. "Just what I need. Okay. So be it. Terry told me I was on my own with this." He pointed the gun at Sam. "You open the door."

"You can end this right now," said Skye. "Plea bargain, mental breakdown. It could make a big difference to your sentence."

"You must be the agent," he said. "At least I got the right one. And thanks but no thanks. There's too much to lose now. I'm thinking a car accident or something. I'll sort out the details while we're driving."

"You won't get away with it."

"Shut up!" he shouted. "Open the door!" He jerked the gun, and Sam didn't have to be told twice, turning the knob and pushing. Before it was fully opened, he rushed down the steps, grabbed a clump of Skye's hair and pulled her backward against him. She gasped in pain. Sam spun around, trying to grab his arm. He raised the gun, pointed it at Sam and then pressed it into Skye's neck. "Get moving," he ordered.

Sam hesitated.

"Do it," gasped Skye.

Sam stepped out and stopped, blinded by the sunlight. Howard pushed her with his free hand and she stumbled forward. Suddenly a hand grasped her by the forearm and yanked her off to the side. She fell back against the owner of that hand, craning her neck sharply to see.

She opened her mouth to say Chase's name, but was stopped by his finger on her lips. Then Chase moved behind the open door.

Skye burst out followed by Howard. Realizing what was going on, she aimed a hard kick backward at Howard's shin. He shouted in pain, pushing her away from him. Chase lunged forward, knocking the gun from Howard's hand.

Chase's fist landed squarely on his jaw. Howard fell

backward against the hood of his car. He shook his head, then came at Chase. But Skye was ready for him, kicking out her right leg and hitting his knee with enough force for all of them to hear a loud crack. Screaming in pain, Howard crumpled to the ground, facedown. Chase ran to him and placed a steady foot on his back.

"Well done, Skye. That was some kick." He locked eyes with Sam and smiled.

When the first siren wail rang through the alley, he stepped away from Howard, extended an arm and folded Sam into his side, pressing the top of her head into the curve of his neck. She snuggled close, waves of relief and peace flowing through her.

After Howard was taken away and the duct tape snipped from Skye's wrists, Sam and Chase sat in the back of a patrol car while Skye talked to the police.

"I'm sorry…" Sam began to say until Chase leaned over and kissed her on the forehead.

"Not now. I'm hoping we'll have many days—and years—to go over all this. I just want to hold you close." He wrapped his arms around her and Sam gladly sank into them. She was almost asleep when the peal of cell phones jarred her. They looked at each other and dragged their phones out.

"My mom," said Sam.

"The hospital," said Chase.

Sam kissed him once more, knowing the peaceful interlude was over.

A PATROL CAR drove them to the hospital, siren blaring. Every second counted now, in the time left for Emily Benson. When the elevator door opened on the palliative ward, Danny was standing in the hall, Nina a few feet behind. He ran into Chase's arms, burying his face in his father's chest. Nina gestured to Sam, indicating the waiting area at the end of the hall, and left them alone.

Danny led the way into Emily's room, Chase's arm across his shoulders. Sam followed, but stayed in the doorway. An oxygen mask covered the lower part of Emily's face and her eyes were closed. Yet it seemed to Sam that she stirred slightly as Chase and Danny sat in the chairs next to her bed. Danny placed his hand on hers, while Chase wrapped his arm around him.

Except for the whirr of the oxygen machine, silence filled the room. Sam watched, a lump swelling in her throat. She was about to go down the hall to join her mother when Chase glanced up and smiled, cocking his head to the empty chair beside his. She hesitated. Did she really belong in that family grouping?

But when Danny turned and beckoned, Sam tiptoed into the room. Chase extended his free hand, clasping hers, and squeezed gently. The three of them sat silently, a tableau locked together in Chase's embrace, watching Emily.

And Sam knew she did belong.

EPILOGUE

SAM STACKED the last few dessert plates from the dining-room table, gathered up the cloth napkins and started for the kitchen. Then, on impulse, she decided to take a peek into the living room, where Chase was going through some legal papers. The four weeks since Emily's death had been difficult for everyone, especially Danny. But now the healing process had begun and their lives were settling into a kind of normalcy.

Chase was sitting at the end of the couch, a briefcase opened on the floor at his feet and files of papers beside it. He looked up when Sam entered the room and smiled.

"Hi, beautiful," he said.

The familiar and delicious fluttering set off by his voice, his smile, his touch, seeped through every part of her. "Hi, to you, too," she said softly. "How's it going?"

He set the sheaf of papers he'd been reading onto the couch. "It all looks more complex than it really is. Basically, my cousins and Uncle Bryant were pilfering from the company and various agencies for years, as we all suspected. I had an interesting talk earlier with Bill while you and Skye were getting the cake ready."

Bill Carter had offered to look into the sale of Martha Sullivan's shares in Trade Winds on Chase's behalf. He'd joined them for Nina's birthday dinner that night, but had to leave early. "Oh? Did he say anything about your chances of getting the proper sale price?"

"Yep. He said we have a solid case and Mother will have a large sum of money coming to her…well, to Harbor House, for her care. But there's something else no one knew about. It came out when Bryant's lawyers were probating his will."

Chase's uncle had suffered a fatal heart attack less than twenty-four hours after Howard and Terence were arrested. The likely convictions of the pair and the scandal resulting from the newly opened fraud investigation had sent Trade Winds into receivership. Sam had thought there'd be no more surprises.

"What is it?" she asked, intrigued.

"Although my uncle owned the whole business after he swindled my mother out of her shares, he apparently didn't own the building itself."

"What do you mean?"

"I told you before the building was the original Sullivan family home, two generations back. It turns out it was never part of the company's holdings, but privately owned. The oldest son of each generation inherited it."

"So your father…"

"Yep. As the older son, he inherited it from his father and he rented it to the business for a nominal fee. When we had our big fight years ago, he threatened to disinherit me. When he died, I never received any money, but apparently he kept me in his will as the next and rightful owner of the house. Uncle Bryant was the executor and my father's lawyer was also Bryant's. He managed to convince the lawyer that he'd informed me and that I'd agreed to let the company rent the building. Of course, it was all a lie."

"He was a calculating man, wasn't he? But that's wonderful about the building."

"Yeah. I wish I'd known much earlier. I could have turfed them all out of there." His laugh was harsh.

"The property's very valuable. That's good for you and Danny."

"For the three of us," he murmured.

Sam liked the sound of that. *The three of us.* She smiled, her gaze locked with his.

"Are you almost finished in there?" he asked.

"Yes. I'm going to change into my sweats and relieve Skye with the pots and pans."

"Hmm. Can I watch?"

She laughed. "What? Watch me wash dirty pots?"

"I was thinking about the changing part."

Heat rose into her face. Memories of the previous weekend—their first alone together—surfaced. They'd arranged for Danny to spend the time with Nina, and she and Chase had gone into seclusion at Sam's place. "Hold on to that wish," she said. "We're definitely going to have a repeat of last weekend."

"I can hardly wait."

Knowing she'd either have to take the dishes to the kitchen or put them down, Sam reluctantly said, "Same here. See you in a few minutes."

As she turned to go, he said, "I love you, Sam."

She stopped. "I love you, Chase."

She was still glowing when she entered the kitchen.

Skye was loading the dishwasher. "Thought you got lost," she said.

"I did, kind of."

"The telltale heart."

"Hmm?"

"It's written all over you, sis. You're an open book, as they say."

"Maybe I am," Sam murmured.

Skye rolled her eyes. "Oh, God. I think you'd better join me in a run after we finish in here. Cool down."

"I'd like that."

They smiled, thinking back to two days ago, when they'd talked late into the night after Skye had arrived for Emily's memorial and Nina's birthday dinner. They hadn't seen each other since a few days after *That Day,* as everyone had begun calling the day Emily died.

"Chase has some great news."

"He's going to make an honest woman of you?" Skye teased.

"Ha ha." Sam told her about his family-home inheritance.

"That *is* great, Sam. I'm happy for him. He deserves something after what his relatives did to him."

"Yes, he does." Sam handed the dishes to Skye. "I see you helped yourself to my old clothes."

"Fortunately you had a couple of track suits in your drawers. Who'd have thought we'd have a cool snap in mid-June?"

"It's supposed to warm up tomorrow. We're taking Danny back to Kerry Park in the morning. He wants to scatter some of Emily's ashes there."

Skye stood up from loading the dishwasher. "Is he up to that?"

"Chase thought so. He's adjusting very well, according to Mom." Sam looked across the dark patio to the solarium opposite. Danny and Nina were heavily into a chess game.

"Mom's been fabulous," said Skye, coming up beside her.

"No kidding. It was so good of her to forgo a big party and let us have just a family birthday dinner, instead. My appreciation for her has multiplied over these past few weeks."

"Mine, too," said Skye and added, "And for you, sister."

Sam hugged her twin. "I'm glad you could take a few more days to come home for Mom and for Emily. Danny was excited about your visit. Apparently you promised him a tour of the local field office."

"All arranged for tomorrow afternoon."

"Thanks, Skye."

"No problem. He's a great kid. I really like him."

Sam looked across to the solarium again. "Me, too."

"Do you think Emily knew how things were going to work out?"

Sam teared up. "Yes, I do. There was something in her eyes when she realized the three of us were there together."

"She was an awesome woman."

"And a good mother."

"Yeah." Skye looked toward the solarium. "Like ours. I'll finish the pots and pans. You go get changed."

"Are you sure? You've done most of the cleaning up."

"Of course I'm sure. Do what I say. I *am* your big sister."

"And I love you for it."

Skye bent her head, rolling up the sleeves of her sweat-shirt. When she looked up, her eyes were damp. "Sam, I give thanks every single day for what you did for me."

Sam bit her lip. "I do, too, Skye, for having luck on my side."

Skye shook her head. "It wasn't luck, Sam. You were amazing." After a long moment, she said, "Okay, pots and pans and then a nice run around the neighborhood. Sound good?"

"Very good." Sam started to leave, but remembered something. "How has it been for you, Skye? At work?"

Skye sighed. "Things are fine now. Lots of questions about everything." She flashed a sheepish grin. "I've endured a lot of ribbing about the abduction, I can tell you that. But I also got a lot of praise for finding the evidence to reopen the case."

"I'm glad. And…uh…any more news on the romance side of things?"

"I've been seeing someone very different from the others. He's a chef and he loves to cook for me." She chuckled. "That's why I've taken up running again."

Sam laughed. "Be with you in five."

She hurried to her room and was back within the promised time, walking into the kitchen just as Chase was approaching Skye, finishing up the pots at the sink. Sam froze, heart thudding painfully against her ribs.

"Sam?" Chase said.

Skye turned around and before she could utter a word, Chase added, "Oh. Do you know where Sam is, Skye?"

Skye grinned, pointing her index finger at her twin. "Right behind you."

He turned, his face breaking into the wonderful, heartbreaking smile Sam had come to love so much. "Hi, beautiful."

Sam rushed into his open arms, caught her sister's gaze over Chase's shoulder and winked.

* * * * *

Turn the page for a sneak preview of
AFTERSHOCK, *a new anthology*
featuring New York Times *bestselling author*
Sharon Sala.

Available October 2008.

n✹cturne™

Dramatic and sensual tales of paranormal romance.

Chapter 1

October
New York City

Nicole Masters was sitting cross-legged on her sofa while a cold autumn rain peppered the windows of her fourth-floor apartment. She was poking at the ice cream in her bowl and trying not to be in a mood.

Six weeks ago, a simple trip to her neighborhood pharmacy had turned into a nightmare. She'd walked into the middle of a robbery. She never even saw the man who shot her in the head and left her for dead. She'd survived, but some of her senses had not. She was dealing with short-term memory loss and a tendency to stagger. Even though she'd been told the problems were most likely temporary, she waged a daily battle with depression.

Her parents had been killed in a car wreck when she was twenty-one. And except for a few friends—and most recently her boyfriend, Dominic Tucci, who lived in the apartment right above hers, she was alone. Her doctor kept reminding her that she should be grateful to be alive, and on one level she knew he was right. But he wasn't living in her shoes.

If she'd been anywhere else but at that pharmacy when the robbery happened, she wouldn't have died twice on the way to the hospital. Instead of being grateful that she'd survived, she couldn't stop thinking of what she'd lost.

But that wasn't the end of her troubles. On top of everything else, something strange was happening inside her head. She'd begun to hear odd things: sounds, not voices—at least, she didn't think they were voices. It was more like the distant noise of rapids—a rush of wind and water inside her head that, when it came, blocked out everything around her. It didn't happen often, but when it did, it was frightening, and it was driving her crazy.

The blank moments, which is what she called them, even had a rhythm. First there came that sound, then a cold sweat, then panic with no reason. Part of her feared it was ' the beginning of an emotional breakdown. And part of her feared it wasn't—that it was going to turn out to be a permanent souvenir of her resurrection.

Frustrated with herself and the situation as it stood, she upped the sound on the TV remote. But instead of *Wheel of Fortune,* an announcer broke in with a special bulletin.

"This just in. Police are on the scene of a kidnapping that occurred only hours ago at The Dakota. Molly Dane, the six-year-old daughter of one of Hollywood's blockbuster stars, Lyla Dane, was taken by force from the family apartment. At this time they have yet to receive a ransom demand. The housekeeper was seriously injured during the abduction, and is, at the present time, in surgery. Police are hoping to be able to talk to her once she regains consciousness. In the meantime, we are going now to a press conference with Lyla Dane."

Horrified, Nicole stilled as the cameras went live to where the actress was speaking before a bank of microphones. The shock and terror in Lyla Dane's voice were physically painful to watch. But even though Nicole kept upping the volume, the sound continued to fade.

Just when she was beginning to think something was wrong with her set, the broadcast suddenly switched from the Dane press conference to what appeared to be footage of the kidnapping, beginning with footage from inside the apartment.

When the front door suddenly flew back against the wall and four men rushed in, Nicole gasped. Horrified, she quickly realized that this must have been caught on a security camera inside the Dane apartment.

As Nicole continued to watch, a small Asian woman, who she guessed was the maid, rushed forward in an effort to keep them out. When one of the men hit her in the face with his gun, Nicole moaned. The violence was too reminiscent of what she'd lived through. Sick to her stomach, she fisted her hands against her belly, wishing it was over, but unable to tear her gaze away.

When the maid dropped to the carpet, the same man followed with a vicious kick to the little woman's midsection that lifted her off the floor.

"Oh, my God," Nicole said. When blood began to pool beneath the maid's head, she started to cry.

As the tape played on, the four men split up in different directions. The camera caught one running down a long marble hallway, then disappearing into a room. Moments later he reappeared, carrying a little girl, who Nicole assumed was Molly Dane. The child was wearing a pair of red pants and a white turtleneck sweater, and her hair was partially blocking her abductor's face as he carried her down the hall. She was kicking and screaming in his arms, and when he slapped her, it elicited an agonized scream that brought the other three running. Nicole watched in horror as one of them ran up and put his hand over Molly's face. Seconds later, she went limp.

One moment they were in the foyer, then they were gone.

Nicole jumped to her feet, then staggered drunkenly. The bowl of ice cream she'd absentmindedly placed in her lap shattered at her feet, splattering glass and melting ice cream everywhere.

The picture on the screen abruptly switched from the kidnapping to what Nicole assumed was a rerun of Lyla Dane's plea for her daughter's safe return, but she was numb.

Before she could think what to do next, the doorbell rang. Startled by the unexpected sound, she shakily swiped at the tears and took a step forward. She didn't feel the glass shards piercing her feet until she took the second step. At that point, sharp pains shot through her foot. She gasped, then looked down in confusion. Her legs looked as if she'd been running through mud, and she was standing in broken glass and ice cream, while a thin ribbon of blood seeped out from beneath her toes.

"Oh, no," Nicole mumbled, then stifled a second moan of pain.

The doorbell rang again. She shivered, then clutched her head in confusion.

"Just a minute!" she yelled, then tried to sidestep the rest of the debris as she hobbled to the door.

When she looked through the peephole in the door, she didn't know whether to be relieved or regretful.

It was Dominic, and as usual, she was a mess.

Nicole smiled a little self-consciously as she opened the door to let him in. "I just don't know what's happening to me. I think I'm losing my mind."

"Hey, don't talk about my woman like that."

Nicole rode the surge of delight his words brought. "So I'm still your woman?"

Dominic lowered his head.

Their lips met.

The kiss proceeded.

Slowly.

Thoroughly.

* * * * *

Be sure to look for the AFTERSHOCK *anthology next month, as well as other exciting paranormal stories from Silhoette Nocturne.*
Available in October wherever books are sold.

nocturne™

NEW YORK TIMES BESTSELLING AUTHOR

SHARON SALA

JANIS REAMES HUDSON
DEBRA COWAN

AFTERSHOCK

Three women are brought to the brink of death...
only to discover the aftershock of their trauma has
left them with unexpected and unwelcome gifts of
paranormal powers. Now each woman must learn to
accept her newfound abilities while fighting for life,
love and second chances....

Available October wherever books are sold.

www.eHarlequin.com
www.paranormalromanceblog.wordpress.com   SN61796

REQUEST YOUR FREE BOOKS!
2 FREE NOVELS PLUS 2 FREE GIFTS!

HARLEQUIN®

Super Romance®

Exciting, emotional, unexpected!

YES! Please send me 2 FREE Harlequin Superromance® novels and my 2 FREE gifts (gifts are worth about $10). After receiving them, if I don't wish to receive any more books, I can return the shipping statement marked "cancel." If I don't cancel, I will receive 6 brand-new novels every month and be billed just $4.69 per book in the U.S. or $5.24 per book in Canada, plus 25¢ shipping and handling per book and applicable taxes, if any*. That's a savings of close to 15% off the cover price! I understand that accepting the 2 free books and gifts places me under no obligation to buy anything. I can always return a shipment and cancel at any time. Even if I never buy another book from Harlequin, the two free books and gifts are mine to keep forever.

135 HDN EEX7   336 HDN EEYK

Name _____ (PLEASE PRINT) _____

Address _____ Apt. # _____

City _____ State/Prov. _____ Zip/Postal Code _____

Signature (if under 18, a parent or guardian must sign)

Mail to the **Harlequin Reader Service:**
IN U.S.A.: P.O. Box 1867, Buffalo, NY 14240-1867
IN CANADA: P.O. Box 609, Fort Erie, Ontario L2A 5X3

Not valid to current subscribers of Harlequin Superromance books.

Want to try two free books from another line?
Call 1-800-873-8635 or visit www.morefreebooks.com.

* Terms and prices subject to change without notice. N.Y. residents add applicable sales tax. Canadian residents will be charged applicable provincial taxes and GST. Offer not valid in Quebec. This offer is limited to one order per household. All orders subject to approval. Credit or debit balances in a customer's account(s) may be offset by any other outstanding balance owed by or to the customer. Please allow 4 to 6 weeks for delivery. Offer available while quantities last.

Your Privacy: Harlequin is committed to protecting your privacy. Our Privacy Policy is available online at www.eHarlequin.com or upon request from the Reader Service. From time to time we make our lists of customers available to reputable third parties who may have a product or service of interest to you. If you would prefer we not share your name and address, please check here. ☐

HSR08